COCO PINCHARD'S

BiG Fat

TiPSY

Wedding

Robert Bryndza

ALSO BY ROBERT BRYNDZA

KATE MARSHALL CRIME THRILLER SERIES

Nine Elms

ERIKA FOSTER CRIME THRILLER SERIES

The Girl in the Ice

The Night Stalker

Dark Water

Last Breath

Cold Blood

Deadly Secrets

ROMANTIC COMEDIES

The Not So Secret Emails Of Coco Pinchard

Coco Pinchard's Big Fat Tipsy Wedding

Coco Pinchard, The Consequences of Love and Sex

A Very Coco Christmas

Coco Pinchard's Must-Have Toy Story

Miss Wrong and Mr Right

Raven Street Publishing
www.ravenstreetpublishing.com

Ebook ISBN: 978-1-9161539-2-9
Print ISBN: 978-1-9161482-3-9
Large Print ISBN: 978-1-9161482-4-6
ALSO AVAILABLE AS AN AUDIOBOOK

To everyone who loved the first book, thank you for all your wonderful letters, emails and tweets - this is for you.

NOVEMBER 2010

Sunday 14th November 21.56
TO: chris@christophercheshire.com

Dear Chris,

Today was the day. Rosencrantz left home. Of course, my
only son flying the nest happened at the worst time. I'm a
week over the deadline to finish my new novel, *The Duchess
Of York: Secret Agent*. So I spent most of the day holed up in
my little office, having to watch him lug boxes past the door
aided by his father and Adam.

He kept popping in to show me things he'd unearthed
whilst packing, including his first teddy bear, a Christening
present from Meryl and Tony. How has Rosencrantz grown
up so quickly? It was like yesterday I remember the Vicar
asking him what he wanted to name the teddy.

"How about something from your Sunday School class,"
he said, sipping his tea by the buffet table. "Noah? Jacob?
Job?"

The guests watched on, charmed by my cute little boy

dressed in a miniature black suit and furrowing his tiny eyebrows deep in thought.

"I'm going to call her... Bitch!" he squeaked, causing the Vicar to choke into his cup. "Meet my new teddy bear Bitch! Bitch, bitch, bitchy, bitch, BITCH!"

Several guests froze with their fruitcake mid-air, and a lady in a big hat gasped in horror.

"He just loves the word 'Bitch'," I said grinning awkwardly. "Of course, he doesn't know what it means. I've been reading that Jackie Collins novel, *The Bitch*."

"Not as a bedtime story to him, I hope?" said the Vicar irritably, mopping tea off his cassock. Suffice it to say Rosencrantz never went back to Sunday school...

I looked fondly at Bitch, now a bit threadbare and faded, sat beside my computer screen; she came with us on every family holiday and was even admitted to hospital with Rosencrantz when he had his appendix removed.

Just then, the phone on my desk rang. I wiped away a tear and picked it up. It was Angie.

"All right love? You finished the bloody book yet?" she said, exhaling cigarette smoke down the line.

"I'm trying to finish but you keep ringing me to ask if I've finished..."

"I need you to come up with a new title," she said.

"You said *The Duchess Of York: Secret Agent* was perfect?"

"Oh it is," she said. "I love it. The PR people love it. Your editor thinks it's genius."

"Then what's the problem?"

"Well, your publisher thinks it's too long for Twittering purposes."

"I don't understand?"

"Twitter is playing a big part in your book launch next year. A Tweet can only be a hundred and forty characters.

They think using thirty-three of them for the title is a waste."

"We've sat through twelve meetings about the title, where everyone has agreed that they love *The Duchess Of York: Secret Agent*. As my literary agent, can't you put your foot down?"

The low drone of a drill started up. Angie is having the basement of her new house excavated for a swimming pool and hot stone massage room.

"Look, Coco," she shouted above the noise. "When you get a six figure advance — you're in hock to the publishing house. If they say the title has to be shorter, it has to be shorter. You think you can come up with something by tomorrow?"

The drilling moved up an octave. I felt like telling her it was thanks to my six-figure advance she would soon be splashing about in a private swimming pool, but she started shouting at her builders so I put the phone down.

Rosencrantz poked his head round the door.

"That's the last of the boxes, Mum," he said. "All that's left is Bitch, do you want her to stay here?"

"No, she belongs with you."

I gave Bitch a last cuddle and he took her downstairs.

I stared at my screen for a few seconds then switched it off. I went to Rosencrantz's bedroom — all but empty apart from a Dieux Du Stade calendar hanging on the wall. A naked French rugby player smouldered back, glancing over his muscled back and impossibly perfect behind.

From the window, I could see Daniel and Adam down in the driveway, helping Rosencrantz fit his boxes into the boot of Daniel's car. Another tear escaped my eye.

"'Ere love," said Ethel, appearing at my elbow. I jumped. She has real stealth for a decrepit old bag. She pulled a tissue from her sleeve. I took it and blew my nose.

"I knew this day would come, just not this quickly," I said.

"'E's twenty-two love... 'E's gotta spread 'is wings."

"Why does he need to spread them south of the river? It's so rough."

"It'll toughen 'im up, put hairs on his chest. Or at least now 'e's payin' rent 'e'll not be able to afford Veet, so the hairs on his chest'll grow back."

Down in the driveway, Rosencrantz loaded in the last box and Daniel closed the boot. The moment had come. All that stood between now and empty nest syndrome was a warm glass of Asti Spumante.

"Oh lord, you'll be fine love," said Ethel. "You'll do the Shake'n'Vac and move the toy boy in... speak of the devil."

Adam came through the door, all lithe and muscular in a tight t-shirt and jeans.

"Hey come on, what's this?" he said, pulling me into his arms and planting a soft sweet kiss on the top of my head. "He'll only be twenty minutes away by car."

"What about rush hour?" I sobbed. "The journey time across London doubles."

"Let it all out, love," said Ethel, proffering another tissue from her cardigan. "I was the same during the change."

"I am not going through the change!" I snapped, blowing my nose.

"If yer say so," she said, winking at Adam.

"Ethel, I am not going through... *Anything...*"

"What's going on?" said Daniel, coming in with Rosencrantz.

"Just your mother, ill-informed as usual," I sniffed.

"It's just basic science, Coco," said Ethel, lighting up a fag. "The only women 'avin babies at your age are Italian and pumped full of hormones."

"Let's talk about something else. Like when do I next see

my gorgeous son?" I said pulling Rosencrantz into the hug with Adam.

"You mean *our* son," said Daniel.

"We all know who you are," said Rosencrantz, shooting him a look.

"Well, I seem to have been airbrushed out of existence in this house," said Daniel sulkily. "I've just noticed the photo of me from the downstairs toilet has gone."

"We all got sick of you grinning down at us when we took a dump," said Rosencrantz.

"It *was* a creepy photo, Daniel," I said. "You were unshaven and hung over with your arm around Minnie Mouse."

"We had a lot of fun at Euro Disney," said Daniel. "It holds very happy memories for me... When we were a family."

"Yeah, you should have thought about that before you got caught bonking that bird in the bedroom," said Rosencrantz.

"Rosencrantz! Don't talk to your father like that!" I chided.

"Yes, it's all been forgotten, Rosencrantz," said Daniel.

"Hang on, I haven't forgotten about it," I said.

"Well, you're moving him in pretty sharpish," said Daniel, pointing at Adam.

"Adam and I have been together for over a year, and *we've* been divorced for eighteen months, Daniel. What's sharpish about that?" I asked.

The three men in my life were all puffing out their chests and shifting on their feet. Ethel's beady eyes were lit up in anticipation of a fight.

"Look, let's all calm down," I said. "It's all water almost, but not quite, under the bridge. Let's go downstairs for a nice drink."

On the way out Ethel said, "Tha's a cracking backside, oo is 'e?"

We turned and regarded the naked French rugby player on the wall.

"That's Pierre Rabadan, Nan," said Rosencrantz, unhooking the calendar and removing the last thing that showed this was his bedroom.

"Yours ain't bad neither," Ethel said, winking at Adam. "I could balance my mug of Bovril on there. Do yer do keep fit?"

Adam regarded his bottom bashfully saying he'd started doing Jiu-Jitsu a couple of times a week.

"Don't you dare fall for her charm," I hissed at him as we all went downstairs, Daniel moaning that his mother hadn't complimented his bottom. I took a last look back at Rosencrantz's room, now the spare room — and shut the door.

I held onto Rosencrantz for a long time before he got in the car with Daniel and Ethel for his drive across the river, and I kept up my waving and happy smile until they were out of sight.

"Come on now. No crying," said Adam slipping his arm round my waist.

"He'll be all right, won't he?"

"He's got your brains, Daniel's cunning and Ethel's gift of the gab — he'll be fine." We came back inside and I closed the front door.

"It's just me and you now," said Adam. "We have the whole house to ourselves." He tucked a lock of hair behind my ear, and leant in for a kiss.

"I have to finish the book," I said weakly.

"Sorry, the book will have to wait," he said, flashing a devilish grin. "I'm taking you upstairs... now."

I shrieked as he chucked me over his shoulder in a fireman's lift and climbed the stairs as if I weighed nothing.

"Ethel's right," I said, squeezing his impossibly pert behind. "You could balance a mug of Bovril on there."

"It's all yours," he growled, chucking me on the bed.

He made me very late for my deadline... I've only just finished the book and emailed it off to Angie.

Love Coco xxx

PS We must arrange to meet up soon. It's been ages since I saw you and Marika. I feel I've been neglecting my best friends.

Monday 15th November 08.14
TO: rosencrantzpinchard@gmail.com

Rosencrantz,

How was your first night in your new home? Did you go out? Be careful on the streets of South London late at night and please remember to carry the little travel size can of anti-perspirant I got you from Superdrug. It's just as good as mace.

Phone me when you get this.

Love Mum xxx

PS the new title of the book is *Agent Fergie*. I think there is now going to be confusion between Fergie the Duchess Of York, Fergie from the Black Eye Peas and Alex Ferguson the Manchester United Manager. Angie, however, is thrilled we have lopped off twenty-one characters for twittering purposes.

PPS Miss you.

Monday 15th November 23.36
TO: marikarolincova@hotmail.co.uk

Hi Marika,

Adam surprised me after work with a takeaway box of the most beautiful handmade sushi. I went upstairs for a shower and when I returned, he had lit candles, laid it all out on the table, and he presented me with a bunch of pink roses and a glass of chilled champagne.

"Here's to my amazing girlfriend finishing her wonderful new novel. I am so proud of you and I love you," he said, as we clinked glasses.

"I love you too," I said.

As we drank he winked at me, and I pretty much melted there and then. It was our first night alone in the house now Rosencrantz has moved out and as we ate, he asked if he could start moving his things over at the weekend.

"We're really going to do it, and live together?" I said.

"Yep, we're shacking up! Do you want to keep your bed, or I should I bring mine?"

"Let's have yours," I said. "It's the cosiest bed in the world."

"My bed it is then," he grinned, topping up our glasses.

Throughout the meal, there was the thrill and anticipation of drunken champagne sex — and he didn't disappoint.

We did it on the kitchen island! It was a bit cold on the smooth granite and apart from accidentally getting a bit of hot Wasabi in a delicate area, it was incredible. It's just what happened afterwards...

Adam got up to pour us both another glass of champagne. He pulled on his boxers, and as I was admiring his tight abs, he farted. It wasn't accidental, he sort of leant to one side, let rip, then carried on topping up our glasses.

"Whoops," he grinned, placing my glass beside me on the kitchen island. I lay there with my mouth open.

"You've never done that before!" I said, sitting up and retrieving my knickers, which had been flung across the room and landed on the juicer.

"Course I have. We all do it."

"You've never done it in front of me before," I said.

I think I was mortified that that stage in our relationship had suddenly announced itself.

"You don't want me to have gut ache, do you?"

"No, but we just had the most amazing sex and..."

"And what?"

"Well, it was like... movie sex."

"What? Porn?"

"Not porn! It was romantic..."

"Coco, I'm supposed to be moving in. What? We're not going to fart in front of each other?"

"No! I still want the romance to last a bit longer," I said.

"So I'm supposed to hide in the bathroom and run the water, like you do at my place?"

"I do not do that."

"You do," he grinned.

I went red, and fumbled my way into my bra.

"It's okay, Coco... I tell you what, let's get it over with."

"Get what over with?" I said.

"Go on, let rip."

"What? No!"

"You must need to after all the rice and booze."

"It's champagne, not *booze,*" I said, opening the dishwasher and loading in the plates.

Adam was laughing.

"Come on Coco. I love you, you love me, it's perfectly normal. You and Daniel were married for years. What did you do then?"

"Let's talk about something else," I snapped, aware I was maybe being a bit unreasonable. "I'm going to put some washing on."

"Do me a favour and put these through on a hot cycle," he said grabbing his bag and chucking his smelly gym gear at my feet.

I stomped off to the washing machine. As I watched the water fill up through the glass, I felt embarrassment and fear. I wanted to still be thrilled and aroused by Adam. He's been like a fantasy come true. So gorgeous, and funny, and the sex is the best I've ever had. I know I'm being silly, but is this the beginning of a slippery slope to drudgery? I was married to Daniel for twenty years and, at the end, we were just flatulent and irritable with one another. I don't want that to happen to Adam and me.

Tuesday 16th November 10.43
TO: adam.rickard@XYZeventsmanagement.com

Is it a busy day at work? I keep ringing but your phone is going to voicemail. I just spoke to Rosencrantz, he is settling in to his new place. The other two guys he is sharing with are actors who were at drama school with him. I asked if I could pop round later and be introduced.

"Just give me a few days to settle in, then we'll have you and Adam over for a dinner party," he said.

Dinner party! He sounded so grown up.

I'm sorry about last night, if I over-reacted about you farting. I was being an idiot. If it happens, it happens. Real life is all about the good and the bad, and I want a real life with you, forever. I cannot wait for you to move in.

This leads on to my new project. I can help you with moving in here.

I have already added your name to my WI-FI network. It's now called COCO&ADAM, so when we switch on the computer it says, 'COCO&ADAM connecting'. How sweet is that?

I am also going to make a start on some other stuff, changing your addresses so all your bills come here.

Call me when you get this.

Love Coco xxx

Tuesday 16th November 10.52
TO: adam.rickard@XYZeventsmanagement.com

Or I can make the WI-FI read 'ADAM&COCO connecting'. It's not a problem.

Tuesday 16th November 11.12

TO: clivethenewsagent@gmail.com

Morning Clive,

Could you please change Adam Rickard's regular delivery of *Top Gear Magazine* and *Men's Health* to my address. We are moving in together.

Kind regards
Coco Pinchard

Tuesday 16th November 11.34
TO: orders@primrosehillvegboxes.co.uk

Dear Primrose Hill Vegetable Boxes,

I currently have a large fresh vegetable box delivered each week. My partner, Adam Rickard, has your seasonal root vegetable box. Would it be possible to merge his root vegetable into my large box?

My address is:
3 Steeplejack Mews
Marylebone
London
NW1 4RF

With thanks,
Coco Pinchard

Tuesday 16th November 14.43
TO: marikarolincova@hotmail.co.uk

I was clearing out one side of the wardrobe for Adam when the doorbell went. I peered through the peephole to see Angie standing outside smoking a cigarette with the wind whipping her dark hair about.

"What you doing, girl?" she said when I opened the door.

She was dressed in her usual Chanel power suit, her shoulder pads dangerously close to her ears. She ground out her cigarette end with a tiny pointed Jimmy Choo, and eased a fresh one into the corner of her mouth.

"I'm making some space in the wardrobe for Adam. He's moving in."

"You're gonna make him live in the wardrobe? Poor bastard," she said.

"No, he's moving into the house," I grinned.

She rolled her eyes and came in.

"I need to talk to you," she said. "I just had a meeting at the Groucho Club, so I thought I'd swing by on my way back to the office."

We went through to the kitchen and she perched at the breakfast bar as I filled the kettle.

"That's a big detour," I said. "Is everything okay with the manuscript for *Agent Fergie*?"

"Yes, the book's fine, and they've just commissioned a cover designer. I'm here to tell you that you've won a literary award!" she grinned, and exhaled smoke through her teeth.

"Oh my God! The Costa Book Award?"

"No."

"The Orange Prize for Fiction?"

"Nope."

"The Amazon Breakthrough Novel Award?"

"No."

"The Edgar Allen Poe Award!"

"That's for mystery writers, you twerp."

"Then what?"

"The Doris Finkelstein Literary Recognition..."

"The what?"

"It's an American award. It's a big deal in the States, loads of famous authors have previously won it," said Angie.

"Is there a cash prize?"

"Well, that's the thing. There's no cash prize per se. It's so prestigious that the 'prize' is attending a ceremony to sign your name on the wall of the Doris Finkelstein Library."

"Oh..."

"In New York, I hasten to add! Which means they want to fly you and a plus one over for an all-expenses paid weekend."

"A free trip to New York!" I screamed excitedly. "When?"

"You fly out Thursday for the ceremony on Friday."

"That's quick?"

"These things are always last minute."

"I can't wait to tell Adam. We've both been so busy with work we haven't had a holiday in ages..."

Angie looked up from scrolling through her iPhone.

"Won't he be working? It's a Thursday."

"I'm sure they'll let him take time off," I said. "He's the boss of his department."

"Oh," she said, lighting another cigarette. There was an awkward pause.

"Did you want to come with me?" I said.

Angie quickly recovered her composure. She flipped the cover over on her iPhone and gathered her things together.

"Angie, 'plus one' means spouse, doesn't it?"

"Course it does," she said. "No, I'm far too busy. The bloody builders need to be supervised and... it's fine. If you can email me your passport numbers, I'll have my assistant arrange it all."

"Do you still want coffee?"

"No, I'd better go. I'm late for a meeting."

She stubbed out her cigarette and clicked off in her little designer shoes with a slam of the front door.

It's funny how people in your life surprise you. Saying that, Adam still hasn't called back, which is unusual for him.

C x

Tuesday 16th November 23.12
TO: marikarolincova@hotmail.co.uk

Adam didn't answer his work phone for the rest of the day, or his mobile. At 8pm, I pulled on my coat and walked round to his flat. I rang the bell several times before he answered. He looked exhausted, and was still wearing his work clothes, which smelt of stale sweat. When I followed him through to the living room, an Enya CD was blaring out. I noticed he had a bottle of whisky open.

"Since when do you like Enya and Johnny Walker?" I shouted, sitting opposite him.

"Since I need to relax," he shouted back.

"Well, can you turn 'Sail Away' off?" I yelled reaching for the remote.

I flicked it off and the silence descended.

"It's called Orinoco Flow, actually," he snapped.

I noticed sweat was beading on his forehead, even though the flat was chilly.

"Are you all right?" I asked.

"Yes, yes... Just work stuff."

"Are you sure? You seem shaken up."

"I'm fine. Tell me about your day," he said.

"Well, if you'd read any of my messages, you'd know all about it."

"Um... I was busy."

I told him all about the meeting with Angie and the award. He seemed to relax a little, until I said we had been invited to go to New York on Thursday.

"I can't go," he said instantly.

"Why not?"

"I'd love to, but I can't. I can't take time off work."

"You took last Friday off to come to the garden centre with me," I said.

"Exactly."

"What do you mean, 'exactly'? You're the boss of the department, surely you can take a day and half off."

There was a pause.

"No, I can't, I really can't," he said.

I got up, sat beside him, and began to massage his shoulders.

"It's a free weekend in New York. First class flights, five star hotel, big double bed... Stop being silly and get your passport."

"Why do you want my passport?" he said, shaking me off.

"How else can Angie book the flights? She needs the passport numbers."

"Look Coco, why don't you go home and I'll take a shower and come over in an hour or so."

"Are you sure everything is okay?" I said.

"It's just work... they've announced redundancies today."

"Oh my God. Are you...?"

"No! Not me, but I have to make people redundant this week, people with mortgages, families. It's got me in a state. Look, go home and I'll be over in a bit."

I agreed and came home, troubled.

A couple of hours later I was dozing off in front of the television when a hand felt its way under my t-shirt. I almost had kittens.

"Hel-lo," whispered Adam drunkenly in my ear.

He was crouched beside the sofa, stark naked and fumbling with a condom wrapper.

"What are you doing?" I gulped, trying to get my breath back.

"Ravishing you," he grinned, leaning in for a kiss.

He'd showered but his breath still smelt of booze.

"I thought you were a murderer!"

"How about *a rapist*!" he joked, hooking his thumb under my pyjama trousers.

"Not funny!" I said, pushing him away.

"Jeez, Coco. I'm trying to lighten the mood."

"Scaring the hell out of me, then cracking a rape joke?" I said. He was still fumbling with the condom wrapper. "Adam. Do I look like I'm in the mood?"

"Coco, I'm being myself," he slurred.

"No. You're being weird."

"I am a bit weird," he said earnestly. "I am... Do you love me?"

His beautiful caramel eyes searched my face, he looked so, vulnerable.

"Of course I love you," I said.

I pulled a rug over us and he snuggled up with his head on my shoulder, and closed his eyes.

"I need to know you love me for who I am," he said.

"I love you more than you know," I said. "I think this trip to New York could be the perfect antidote to horrible work stuff."

"Jeez, Coco," he said jumping up and pulling on a pair of trackies.

"What now?" I said. "You're sending mixed messages!"

"Am I?" he said pulling on a t-shirt. "Well, here's a message. I'm going home."

He stalked off through the kitchen and out of the back door, locking it behind him. I listened for a long time to the silence, the creaks of the house. He didn't come back.

When I went upstairs to bed, I passed Rosencrantz's empty bedroom. I stopped in the doorway, the moonlight shining a bright oblong on the dark carpet.

What do you think it is with Adam? Is he getting cold feet? He was fine yesterday.

Wednesday 17th November 21.56
TO: marikarolincova@hotmail.co.uk

I didn't call Adam all day. It was his job to call and apologise, or at least explain — but he didn't. Just as *Eastenders* was finishing, the doorbell rang. He was stood outside in the rain. I folded my arms and looked at him.

"Can I come in?" he said.

"Why should I let you?"

"It's pissing down!"

I stood to one side and he dashed in. I took his coat and went upstairs to get him a towel. When I came back, he was sat in the living room. I draped the towel over him and switched off the TV. Silence played through the house, accompanied by rain plinking off the roof.

"Do you want a cup of tea?" I said.

"No. I'm fine."

"Did you eat?"

"I'm not hungry."

It felt awkward, like we were strangers. From outside in the back garden there was a loud creaking sound. We looked up and a stream of dead leaves and water began to hurtle past the window followed by a length of guttering. It crashed onto the table and umbrella set on the terrace. I got up and went to the window.

"Shit!" I said, craning my head up to see the damage. Water was now pouring off the roof and straight down the brickwork. "It's gonna cost a fortune to get that fixed... they're zinc gutter pipes, do you know how much zinc costs?"

Adam just stared. The gutter pipe began to slip off the umbrella and tore through the fabric on its way down to the grass. He jumped up, and grabbed the cord to yank down the blinds. One side shot down but the other refused to yield and got into a tangle.

"Let me do it" I snapped, grabbing the cord. "You don't know how."

"Maybe I should just give you my balls," he said. "You can keep them in your desk drawer along with everything else."

"What does that mean?" I said turning to him. "Is this about me changing your addresses? I'm sorry. I thought you'd be pleased."

Adam carried on staring. He opened his mouth to say something, and then closed it.

"What?" I said. "Spit it out, Adam!"

"I need a drink," he said.

I followed him into the kitchen. He cracked open a beer from the fridge and gulped it down, his eyes watching me over the base of the can.

"I can see you're stressed. Why not come to New York. It'll help you relax. I know you can take the time off."

He finished the can and chucked it in the bin.

"Why are you being like this?" he said. "You just don't give up!"

"Like what? I'm not like anything, Adam."

However, he was gone, slamming the front door and out into the pouring rain. Just then, there was a rumble of thunder and the power went out. I fumbled in the darkness to my jacket and came out of the front door. The wind and rain wheeled round and smacked me in the face. The street-lights were off too. The four-storey terraces closed in from either side of the street, blocking out even the light pollution from the rest of the city. A few cars crept along, illuminating everything from the knees down.

When I reached Marylebone High Street, I sheltered in the doorway of a posh deli. I tried calling him, but got his voicemail. The rain fell harder, splattering on the awning above.

The power cut appeared to stretch across half of London. I hurried past the dark tube station to his flat, and let myself in with my key.

A silhouette of Adam was sitting on the living room floor by the bay window, intermittently lit up by the flashes of lightning outside. I heard a tsk as he opened a can of lager and I sat beside him. I reached up and stroked his wet hair. He tilted my chin up and kissed me urgently.

"You're beautiful, Coco, don't forget that," he whispered hoarsely.

He put his finger to my lips, and then traced it down my throat. I reached down and slid his wet t-shirt up and over his head. The heat of his muscly chest hit me. I fumbled with his belt as we quickly undressed, and made love on the pile of wet clothes as the storm raged outside. All our worries fell away and it was just him and me.

Afterwards he pulled me through to the bedroom. We climbed under the covers shivering, and snuggled up in his cosy bed under the window.

The storm was receding but rain continued to hammer on the roof. We lay there watching the water run in rivulets down the window.

"I love you," I said. "But I am not having secrets between us. If you want secrets, you know where the door is. Well, of course this is your flat, so I know you know where the door is... My point is that it's a metaphorical door and..."

But Adam had already drifted off to sleep. He looked so peaceful and beautiful. I traced my finger along his handsome profile.

"Okay. You sleep," I whispered. "I'll give you the ball breaker speech tomorrow."

I woke up just before seven the next morning with the sun streaming through the window. Adam's side of the bed was empty. After a while, I couldn't hear any noises from the bathroom or kitchen so I got up.

On the kitchen table was a note.

It was one of those moments where you see your life from outside your body. The ground tipped under me as I read what Adam had written. He said he was sorry, but he didn't want to move in, and he didn't want to see me anymore. I quickly dressed and ran home, hoping I would find him in my kitchen grinning with his suitcases, and that this was just a bad practical joke. When I let myself in all the lights were on from last night, but no Adam. I then ran back to his flat. *This isn't happening,* I thought, *this isn't what's meant to happen*. When I reached his front door, I dug in my pockets for his key, but it wasn't there. It had been taken off my key ring! I banged on the door, but nothing. Eventually I walked back home.

I keep calling, but he's not answering. I am supposed to be packing for New York. I can't face myself in the mirror, let alone get on a plane.

Thursday 18th November 06.17
TO: marikarolincova@hotmail.co.uk, chris@christo-phercheshire.com

Angie refused to let me cancel going to New York. She said a lot was riding on me showing up and accepting the award. I asked her what, exactly?

"Well, the Doris Finkelstein Foundation has already booked flights and accommodation," she said. "And a ceremony is arranged. Besides, don't you wanna bask in the glory? Do you remember how hard it was to get this book published?"

"Of course I do."

"And how many people who've just been dumped would kill to be whisked off to foreign climes and recognised for their talent and success?"

"Lots..."

"And the publicity means your American publisher will issue a new print run of *Chasing Diana Spencer* and a new eBook edition with a hefty promo on Amazon and Barnes and Noble. You forget that I earn money from your books too," she said pointedly.

There was a silence.

"Oh crap. What time is the flight?" I said.

"Ten in the morning. I'll pick you up in a taxi at five," and she put the phone down. I presume this meant she was coming too.

Trying to work out what to wear and pack nearly killed me. I couldn't plan. My brain kept going back to the realisation that Adam had dumped me, and a cold horror trickled through me. Then I kept racking my brains if there was anything I needed to do, but I have no pets that need feeding, no plants that need watering, no boyfriend or son at home anymore to chivvy along. I can just drop everything and go to New York. I spent years wishing I could just drop everything and go somewhere at the last minute. It doesn't seem such fun in reality.

The taxi pipped its horn outside just before five, and I left the house in the darkness with my face scrubbed clean of makeup and my wet hair scraped back in a ponytail.

Angie was perched inside the taxi looking stunning in a blood red Chanel suit, full makeup, and a matching red patent leather clutch bag.

"Jesus, Coco," she said as I climbed in beside her.

"What?" I said blearily, doing up my seat belt.

"We're off to New York not the pound shop. At least put some bloody makeup on."

"No."

"I can't talk to you until you put on some lipstick," she said pulling a gold Chanel lipstick out of her clutch.

"Fine, don't talk to me," I said.

"Coco, I'm serious. You look like a pile of shite."

I huffed a bit and applied the dramatic red to my lips.

"And put these on," she said handing over a pair of giant black sunglasses.

"I can't see a thing," I said when I'd slipped them on.

"But I can. Now you look like someone who is trying not to be someone, as opposed to nobody not managing to be anybody."

"I'm taking them off," I said.

"It's either wear them or I pay the taxi driver to hold you down whilst I forcibly apply mascara. Your eyes look like two piss holes in the snow…"

I wouldn't have put it past her, so I kept them on.

"You'll thank me when we get to the First Class lounge," she said.

She was right, of course. Now we're sitting in the British Airways First Class lounge I am blending in with all the rich bitches. Angie hasn't mentioned Adam, which I am thankful for, but she did offer a choice of Xanax or Valium to go with the complimentary champagne. I plumped for Xanax.

"You sure love?" she said. "The Valium is stronger."

"No, I like the sound of Xanax, it's a palindrome — it can be pronounced the same way forwards and backwards."

"Bloody writers," she said popping a Valium on her tongue and jerking her head back to swallow it in a well-practised move.

"I'm sorry," I said. "I should have invited you on this trip. You've always stood by me."

"It's fine," she said. "But I'm warning you, I can't do slushy emotional girl chat, and if you suggest we get cupcakes to cheer us up, you can fuck off to economy."

"It's a deal," I said from behind my shades, downing the pill with a gulp of champagne. Angie reached out and squeezed my hand.

"He's an arsehole and you deserve better," she said.

I didn't say anything, I just squeezed her hand back. The problem is, Adam isn't an arsehole, he's wonderful. That's what makes the situation even more confusing.

It's still dark outside, with just the winking lights of

planes taking off and landing. I think the Xanax is kicking in. I feel much better, and I have a sort of slack smile on my face.

Saturday 20th November 23.14
TO: marikarolincova@hotmail.co.uk, chris@christophercheshire.com

We're staying at the Four Seasons overlooking Central Park! I'm sitting in the grand soaring lobby lit by Tiffany lamps; above me is a backlit onyx ceiling. A sexy vibe pervades the air as the staff glide about, all young and gorgeous, filling their crisp immaculate uniforms with firm, toned bodies. I feel like a grubby Brit, with the teeth God gave me and legs I haven't shaved in a few days. I just want to be at home, in a tracksuit, by the fire.

I have an elegant, cavernous room with a giant four-poster bed and floor to ceiling windows. My view over Central Park and the skyscrapers has been framed by a boiling sky. Torrential rain has streamed down the window since we arrived, and if I look down, I can see it continue falling to the tiny cars and people on the streets far below.

Last night Angie was desperate for me to hit the bars with her.

"I'm not in the mood for what you look like you're in the mood for," I said, through the gap in my door.

She looked amazing in a tiny purple Versace dress, pinched in at the waist, and towering heels. She swept in past me and I closed the door behind her. She rummaged around in her tiny bag.

"Well, you can at least stick these on for me," she said,

pulling out a sheaf of nicotine patches. "This non-smoking city is doing my head in."

"There's not much of you covered up to put them on."

"Stick six of them on my back," she said sliding up her dress. I gingerly peeled the backing off the nicotine patches and stuck them on.

"Come on Coco, come with me to some dive bars," she said, pulling her dress back down. "You're my only single author. Sometimes you have to get under one man to get over another…"

"Well, you can do that on my behalf," I said. "Just make sure no one puts anything in your drink."

"It takes a lot to tranquillize me," she said with a brittle laugh. We hugged and then she was off into the night.

I had a shower then ordered room service. A handsome waiter delivered mouth-watering macaroni and cheese and turned down my bed (he turned down the bedcovers — not any salacious offer I made him). Then I ate Reese's Peanut Buttercups from the mini bar in front of back-to-back episodes of *As Time Goes By*, *Keeping Up Appearances,* and *Are you Being Served?* on the PBS channel.

I met Angie the next morning for breakfast. She didn't look happy.

"Didn't you meet anyone?" I asked.

"A divorced stockbroker who offered to take me home."

"Where was home?"

"Staten Island…"

"Why didn't you bring him back here?"

"You can smoke on Staten Island. I was climbing the wall for a fag."

"What was it like?"

"I never got to his place, I got motion sickness, and his toupee blew off into the water. A passion killer on both counts."

After breakfast, we took a non-smoking cab to the Doris Finkelstein Library. It was colossal with a carved ceiling as high as a cathedral, gothic arched windows and row after row of long tables. At the very end, past the thousands of books lining the walls, were rows of seats facing a raised stage and a giant projector screen. A hundred or so audience members and journalists sat waiting.

"This looks *huge*..." I hissed to Angie as a young chap in a canary yellow suit rushed over. "I thought it would be low key and I was just writing my name on a wall."

"We're in New York," whispered Angie. "They don't do low key."

"Hi, hi hi!" said the guy flashing white teeth through an immaculately trimmed beard. "I'm Darryl, head of media communications and public relations here at the library."

"Who are all these people?" I said.

"Ooh. We have *Vogue*, the *New York Times*, *Elle*, and the *New York Post*... PBS, and some *civilians,* but don't worry, they've paid to be here."

I started to sweat. What if I had to make a speech? Angie had said nothing about making a speech.

"How long have we got before it kicks off?" snapped Angie irritably. "I could murder a fag."

Darryl went pale and took a step back from Angie.

"No, it's okay she means, can she have a cigarette?" I said.

"I'm sorry ma'am. We haven't time. I need you to take a seat."

We moved past everyone with Angie muttering darkly, and took our seats on the front row. I was placed next to Doris Finkelstein herself, who was in her eighties, very elegant with twinkly eyes. She was wearing blazing diamond earrings and a huge fur coat, despite the fact we were indoors. I shook her tiny hand which was as dry as paper.

"I'm so pleased you made it all the way from London, England," she purred sweetly.

I grinned but my mouth was so dry my top lip got stuck above my teeth. A small square of the wall that wasn't covered with books was covered in signatures. A big piece of Perspex, which must usually be in place to protect the signatures, was propped against the wall. I went to ask Doris what happens next when the lights dimmed and the huge video screen lit up.

A gravelly movie-trailer voice-over boomed through the auditorium.

"*Coco Pinchard is unique, she's a one-off...*"

My book publicity photo filled the screen, and we zoomed in on my grin as dramatic music began to play.

"*Readers have fallen in love with her Britishness, her charm, her rapier wit. We are here today at the Doris Finkelstein Library to salute her work.*"

Then there was a montage of photos taken at book signings.

"*Coco's debut novel,* Chasing Diana Spencer, *was a unique work of comic originality which re-imagines a history where Prince Charles fell in love with Camilla, not Diana. It has been described as a stunning debut, a sublime work of comic fiction.*"

Then there were photos of when we staged the musical.

"*Not only was it a bestseller worldwide, but it played internationally in theatres as* Chasing Diana Spencer: the Musical *in Edinburgh, Scotland, London's West End and off-Broadway in the Alice Clayton Theatre.*'

The photos were of Rosencrantz, Chris and me with the cast on the Royal Mile, then at the opening nights in London and New York.

Then there was a montage of the television interviews I have done,

"And fear not, after her exciting debut, she's kept on writing. She has a new novel due to drop in spring 2011. And she still finds time to support numerous charities!"

"What charities do I support?" I hissed at Angie.

"Well, you adopted that hippopotamus in Africa last year; that counts doesn't it?" she hissed back.

One of the final photos was of me and Adam at the Edinburgh Festival, when I got the Fringe Award... He had his arm around me and we looked so happy.

I gulped. Angie squeezed my hand. Finally, the voice-over was saying, *"The Doris Finkelstein Library is proud to honour... Coco Pinchard."*

The audience applauded. Darryl appeared on the stage and held out his hand. I went up and gave a rambling speech about how happy I was. I wasn't really; the Adam photo had been like a drive-by shooting straight to my heart. I thanked everyone. I thanked Angie, who was now grey from lack of nicotine. Then the photographers surged forward and took several shots of me signing my name on the wall. I noticed among the signatures Stephen King, Doris Lessing, John Grisham, Patricia Cornwell, and JK Rowling. I then had some photos taken with Doris who refused requests to take off her fur coat.

"It's my body armour," she said through her smile as the cameras flashed. "Never let 'em see your ass."

I never quite found out the significance of her tip as we were whisked through a hundred goodbyes and out onto the street. The sun had come out and, even though it was cold, New York looked so much more alive.

"Quick," said Angie. She saw an alleyway between the library and an apartment block and dragged me down it.

She lit up a cigarette and the colour returned to her cheeks. "Oh my God," she sighed. "That's better than sex."

She offered me one and I lit up. We smoked in silence for a few minutes.

"I vowed I would never fall so hard for a guy again after Daniel left me, and here I am again," I said.

Angie didn't comment, she just carried on smoking.

"Haven't you got anything to say?"

"I've got plenty," she said. "The question is, do you want to hear it?"

"Maybe."

"Coco, were you in that room just now?"

"That's a stupid question."

"Is it? It's so frustrating. You have this amazing career at your fingertips, yet all you concentrate on is what Adam has done to you. Sure, it's horrible, but get a grip, woman. There's more to life than having a boyfriend."

"You're so opinionated," I said.

"That's what my third mother-in-law says," said Angie through a cloud of smoke.

"You've got three mother-in-laws?"

"No. Four. They all hate me. Bet that makes having Ethel look like a picnic," Angie grinned.

We stubbed out our cigarettes and flagged down a yellow cab.

"Where to?" said the taxi driver.

"How about a walk in Central Park?" I suggested.

We spent the rest of the afternoon exploring. We walked through Central Park and ate cheese, mustard and pastrami subs from a deli straight out of a Woody Allen film. We were toying with the idea of going across to the Statue of Liberty but we both had blisters from our shoes, so we headed back to the Four Seasons and ate dinner looking out across the city that never sleeps, winking and blinking in the dark.

"To Coco," said Angie holding up her glass. "May she open her fucking eyes, because there's a whole world out there for the taking — and I want twenty percent of it."

I rolled my eyes and we toasted.

After dinner, Angie headed up to her room for a conference call and I grabbed my swimsuit and went to check out the pool. I was glad to find it empty. It was beautifully done, all steel and coloured lights, and I spent a happy hour gliding about underwater. I felt weirdly safe, thousands of miles away from all the troubles at home.

Now just as I am starting to enjoy being in New York, we have to leave.

Monday 22nd November 03.36
TO: chris@christophercheshire.com,
marikarolincova@hotmail.co.uk

Just back home to a text from Adam:

PLSE PHONE GAS/WATER/ELECTRIC & COUNCIL TAX 2 HAVE MY NAME TAKEN OFF UR ACCOUNT.

He'd also left a little cardboard box on the doorstep containing some of my CDs a couple of bras and a jumper I'd left at his place.

All positive thinking evaporated and I got mad. Really mad. I wished I had smashed something of his when I had the chance, thrown a pot plant at his sixty-inch flat screen television, or plunged his X-box into a sink full of cold water. I scoured the house for something, anything, that belonged to him but there was nothing to say he'd ever existed here, apart from his red toothbrush.

I snatched the toothbrush out of the cup, strained and cursed as I tried to snap it in half — but it wouldn't budge. What are they made of? I sat down on the edge of the bath with the toothbrush in my hand and cried. I then wiped my eyes and placed it back in the cup. Stupid, huh?

Monday 22nd November 16.43
TO: customerservice@britishenergy.com

Dear British Energy,

I am trying to get the name Adam Rickard removed from my British Energy Gas/Electricity account 2098562039485. I am severely jet lagged and I've spent a futile day on the phone to your helpline in India. I have spoken to various elderly Indian ladies with names like Emma and Jane, even a Donna who seemed to have an encyclopaedic knowledge of *Coronation Street*. They have all stated that I need to send something in writing, on headed notepaper, which can prove Adam Rickard doesn't wish to live at this address.

Adam Rickard did write a letter to me, but he didn't use headed notepaper. Who dumps someone else using headed notepaper? Maybe a member of the aristocracy — but Adam is far from being an aristocrat.

As a last resort to try to get this resolved, I have scanned in the note from Adam Rickard ending our relationship. I hope this is now proof enough and the matter will be dealt with as a matter of priority.

Sincerely,

Coco Pinchard

ATTACHMENT - DUMPED.JPEG

> **Wednesday 17th of November**
>
> Dear Coco,
> Things aren't working between us. Your life is so full and busy – I don't know where I fit in! It's killing me Coco. YOU ARE THE WOMAN. The one who grabbed my heart and pulled it into yours. But I can't take the pressure, I want to call it a day. I'm sorry. I think it would be best if we don't see each other anymore. It would be wrong for me to move in with you, only to then leave.
> I'm sorry,
>
> Adam.
>
> P.S I hope one day you'll forgive me.

Thursday 25th November 17.43
TO: chris@christophercheshire.com

I've been over to see Rosencrantz in his new place in Lewisham. He's sharing a little terraced house just down the road from the Docklands Light Railway Station. The door was opened by a huge chap with fake tan and dressed as a genie.

"Did you rub the lamp?" he boomed theatrically, raising his eyebrows.

"Oh hello," I said. "Have I got the right address? I'm looking for my son, Rosencrantz Pinchard."

"He's not in right now," said the genie coming out of character. "Are you Mrs Pinchard?"

"Yes, hello," I said. "I'm Coco."

"I'm Wayne," said the genie, offering a huge hand covered in gold rings.

A tall lean blond guy with a beautiful face appeared behind him. He was dressed in workout gear: shorts, and a sleeveless t-shirt.

"This is Rosencrantz's fabulous mother!" said Wayne.

"Hi Mrs P," said the other chap, also offering his hand. "I'm Oscar."

"I'm the brains, he's the brawn," grinned Wayne. "He's as thick as two short planks but lovely to look at."

"Call yourself a genie? I'd like to see you try and squeeze into a lamp," grinned Oscar.

"I'm big boned!" said Wayne, winking at me.

They showed me through the hallway and into a small front room. The place was a tip, but homely. Wayne said that an old lady had lived in the house since the fifties, and when she died, they carted her off and rented the place out with all her belongings still in situ.

"Why are you dressed as a genie, Wayne?" I asked.

"I'm doing TIE, for my sins."

"What's TIE?"

"Theatre in Education, a tour of local schools with a clapped out version of Aladdin. Today's school was a bit rough," he said.

"One of the little bastards stole his clothes out of the changing room, so he had to come home on the bus in his costume," grinned Oscar.

"Luckily I keep my wallet and keys in my magic lamp," Wayne said. "Would you like a cuppa tea, Mrs P?"

"Yes, please. Do you know when Rosencrantz will be home?"

"He got a job interview," said Wayne.

"Don't you mean a casting?" I said, pushing a pile of magazines along the sofa and sitting down.

"He's got an interview at Abercrombie and Fitch to work in their Savile Row store over Christmas," said Oscar.

"If you can call it work," said Wayne. "All Oscar seems to do is stand outside with his shirt off flirting with the punters!"

"I fold some jumpers too," grinned Oscar. "I'm just going to grab a shower," he added.

"I'm about to put some dark stuff through on a hot cycle, do you want me to do your workout gear?" offered Wayne.

Without any warning, Oscar stripped off his shorts and t-shirt down to his briefs. I couldn't help admire how beautiful he was. They both went off and Wayne came back ten minutes later with a full tea set, side plates, and a giant chocolate cake. I was in heaven.

"I'm sorry to hear about your feller," said Wayne as he poured. "Rosencrantz said he was the one."

"Did he?"

"Yes. Nice, was he?"

"Yes..." I said awkwardly.

"Knew his way around a woman?"

"Um..."

Luckily at that moment Rosencrantz arrived back home.

"Hi Mum," he said, giving me a huge hug. "I see you've met the guys."

"Yes, they've been very hospitable," I said.

"And I approve of Mrs P," said Wayne to Rosencrantz.

Oscar came down the stairs dressed in a tracksuit with wet hair.

"Hey man, how did the interview go?" he said.

"I got the job!"

Oscar did a high five with Rosencrantz.

"Oh love, that's wonderful," I said proudly.

"Come on Oscar," said Wayne. "Let's give them some peace."

They took their tea and disappeared into the kitchen.

"Shall I show you my room?" said Rosencrantz.

We went upstairs to a little bedroom with a view of the railway sidings behind the house. A train clattered past. I sat on his bed, which was neatly made, with Bitch sitting on the pillow.

"Dad phoned me, fishing for the gossip. So did Nan," he said sitting at a little table, which had his TV and laptop on it.

"What did you tell them?"

"That you and Adam had parted company."

"Well, he dumped me, Rosencrantz."

"I wasn't going to give them the satisfaction of hearing that... What are you going to do now?"

"I don't know," I said. "I haven't got any work on till the book is published next year. I'm off to see Chris' new play tomorrow night, the one he's been directing. Do you want to come?"

"I can't, Mum. I've got staff training in the evening at Abercrombie and Fitch."

"I'm so proud of you, supporting yourself," I said.

"I could move back home? If you're lonely," he said.

"No! I'm fine. It looks like fun here, you should enjoy your freedom. That Wayne seems interesting."

"He's great."

"And Oscar is gorgeous."

"I know... I've already shagged him."

"Rosencrantz! I'm your mother!"

"What? I figured shagging him was the sensible thing to do."

"How is shag... sleeping with him sensible?"

"There's no sexual tension now, we can just be friends. I recommend doing it with all your same-sex friends."

"What, so I should jump into bed with Marika?" I said.

"No! I only recommend it if you're gay. With sex out of the way, me and Oscar can be really good friends."

"What about Wayne?"

"Oh no, we haven't shagged Wayne. We think he's asexual. The only thing that seems to excite him is his Royal teacup collection; he's got the Coronation, and Charles and Diana's wedding."

"Isn't he lonely?"

"We're all lonely, in one way or another," said Rosencrantz looking out of the window. "Course, I'm lucky. I've got a wicked mum."

He leaned over and gave me a long hug.

On the train home I tried to get my head around it all. I thought I understood what life was all about, but I'm now more confused than ever.

Friday 26th November 13.14
TO: marikarolincova@hotmail.co.uk

Meryl Skyped me this morning; she pinged into view with baby Wilfred on her lap, screaming his head off with a face like a little red beef tomato. I thought she might be calling about Adam, but she asked if I would take a look at

Wilfred's bottom. Before I could even say hello, she pantsed the poor kid and held his bare backside up to the webcam. There was a prickly red rash dotted across his skin.

"What do you think it is?" asked Meryl, settling the screaming Wilfred back on her knee.

"It looks like nappy rash," I said. "How long has he had it?"

"A week, ever since we switched him over to pull-ups. How did Rosencrantz get on with pull-ups?"

"Well, we didn't have them when Rosencrantz was little," I said. "I'd take him to the doctor if it doesn't clear up."

"Do you know how hard it is to get an appointment at our surgery?" she said. "Sometimes I wish I was an asylum seeker in this country. I'd be far better off!"

"I don't think so, Meryl, you wouldn't want to have to flee from an oppressive regime."

Tony popped behind Meryl looking as greasy as ever.

"Morning Coco!" he said. "What are we talking about?"

"Nappy rash and oppressive regimes," snapped Meryl. "Both of which our government is doing nothing about."

"Here Coco," said Tony, leaning toward the camera. "So sorry to hear about you and Adam."

"Yes, Coco, we're very sorry," said Meryl shifting Wilfred to her other knee. "He was the first black man we felt like we really got to know, after Lenny Henry of course."

"Ah yes... I felt very sorry for him when I heard about the break-up," said Tony.

"Adam broke up with me," I reminded them.

"Oh yes, yes, no. I meant Lenny Henry and Dawn French... Very sad business. Who do you think was funnier, Coco?"

"Out of Dawn French and Lenny Henry?" I said.

"No, out of you and Adam?" he said.

"What's that got to do with anything?"

"Oh nothing, nothing I was just wondering. I thought Adam was rather witty."

"That reminds me, Tony," said Meryl. "Would you set the Sky box to record *The Vicar Of Dibley* for me?"

"Right-o! Nice to talk to you Coco, chin up!" grinned Tony and off he went.

"You're so lucky, Coco," said Meryl. "All alone now and rattling around like Miss Havisham in your big house. I don't get a minute's peace. I'd give anything to be Miss Havisham right now. Of course, unlike her I'd keep up with my hoovering. Byeee!" and she vanished from the screen.

I don't know how Meryl and Tony manage to seem so concerned and disinterested at the same time.

I'm looking forward to seeing you at Chris' new play later. Shall I meet you outside at seven?

Coco xxx

Saturday 27th November 12.33
TO: angie.langford@thebmxliteraryagency.biz

Thanks for your message asking how I am doing. I went to see Chris' new play last night at The Blue Boar Pub Theatre in Kennington. It was great to see him and Marika after such a long time. When my taxi pulled up, they were already there, smoking under the canopy at the front of the theatre.

"Thank God you're here," said Chris, hugging me. "I need more friendly faces. The bar is packed with journalists and critics."

"That's good, isn't it?" I said.

"I think the play is terrible," confided Chris in a low voice.

"Well, you didn't write it, Shakespeare did," said Marika. "Blame him."

"Oh you Eastern Europeans," said Chris. "I admire your direct thinking, but it's the exact opposite with The Bard. He's wonderful to begin with. As a director you have to live up to his text."

Marika rolled her eyes.

"Let me see you properly, Coco," she said, giving me the once over. "You've lost weight."

"Thank you," I said.

"You don't want to lose it too quickly, you'll lose those amazing boobs of yours."

"I do not have amazing boobs," I said.

"You do," said Marika. "I would kill for big boobs like yours."

"I would kill for your little pert ones," I said.

"Ladies, can we stop the booby-talk, I can't cope with this right now," said Chris.

"So what's *Macbeth* about?" asked Marika.

"You can't name it, Marika!" I cried. "It's bad luck."

"It's okay. It's only bad luck to say it in the theatre," said Chris.

Just then, we saw the *Daily Mail* critic Nicholas De Jong walk inside.

"Oh my God, I'm done for. De Jong is going to hate it," said Chris.

"You don't know that," said Marika. "You're a great director."

"I think I've made the mistake of casting my boyfriend Julian as the lead. He's too pretty. He's more McFly than Macbeth. I let lust get in the way..."

We heard a bell ringing faintly.

"Oh God, that's the fifteen minute call, I'd better go," he said.

We wished him luck and he moved off through the crowds and into the pub.

"Do you want some crisps?" said Marika. "Feed you up a bit?"

"I don't fancy food at all," I said. "I can't sleep... I just keep checking my phone and wishing..."

"The hospital would call to say Adam's been involved in a hideous accident?" said Marika.

"No, just wishing that he'd call..."

"Ah, you're still at the stage where you miss him. Let me know when you get to the wanting to seek revenge stage. That's my specialty!"

I gave her a weak grin.

"Come here you," she said, putting her arm around me. "Let's go watch some Shakespeare and get pissed."

The after show party was held at Cathedral private members' club in Soho. We commandeered a table in a quiet corner and Chris treated us to cocktails all night.

"I did this play to try to kickstart some work for me," said Chris after we had sunk a few rounds. "My momentum has ground to a halt since I directed *Chasing Diana Spencer: the Musical...* I should have taken up the offer to stage the nativity play at my niece's school."

We both laughed.

"I'm serious. Benenden is one of the top private girls' schools in the country. I would have got more exposure directing a bunch of twelve year olds in 'Follow that Star'."

"Well, it's only November," I said. "Can't you change your mind?"

"No. they've given it to a trainee director from the Royal Court Theatre."

"Well, I thought your boyfriend did a good job as Macbeth," I said. "Didn't he, Marika?"

"He was terrible," said Marika. "Nice to look at, but how do you say it in English? He couldn't act his way out of a bag..."

I kicked her under the table, wishing she would just lie for once.

"A paper bag," said Chris. "He couldn't act his way out of a paper bag."

We looked over at Julian on the dance floor; he was drunk and dancing on his own, dry humping one of the pillars in a kind of pole dance.

"He's losing interest in me," said Chris. "I think we're at that stage in the older guy, younger guy gay relationship where the Stockholm Syndrome is wearing off."

We both laughed.

"I'm serious, I seem to land these young guys and then I have to keep hold of them by buying them designer gear and paying their bills."

A dark-haired young guy danced up to Julian and, without much introduction, they began snogging.

"And now I'm single," said Chris. "Someone say something to cheer me up, please?"

"I had a blind date last Friday with a complete moron," said Marika. "I slept with him, then didn't return his calls. Then he turned up on Monday at school as our Head OFSTED Inspector. He's deciding on the future of my job and the school."

Chris and I laughed.

"It's not funny!" she protested.

"It is, a little bit," said Chris.

'You're right... Let's forget about all of this crap, go somewhere else and dance," said Marika.

"Okay. You two grab a cab, I have to go and dump my

boyfriend," said Chris, as if he was popping to the bar for a packet of dry roasted peanuts.

We moved on to a pub in Soho with a late licence. We danced, drank, and almost forgot our worries until the bar started thinning out, and the staff flicked the lights on. When we stumbled out, we were shocked to see it was light; it was almost six in the morning.

We waved goodbye to Marika who got the train home. Chris and I flagged down a taxi on Old Compton Street, which dropped me off at the Tesco Metro in Baker Street.

"Thanks hun," I said. "Will you be ok, after Julian?"

"I've got you and Marika, I'll be fine," he said.

I kissed Chris goodbye and made a dash inside Tesco to grab a pint of milk.

Where I ran into Adam. He was fresh from some kind of exercise, showered, and looking in rude health in a red tracksuit. I was wearing last night's crumpled clothes and had the remnants of last night's eyeliner smudged across my cheek. We stopped for a moment, and stared at each other, then he muttered "Excuse me", leaned across and took a pint of skimmed milk. I watched him walk away and go through the self-checkout. I was in shock. Rooted to the spot. I couldn't move. I stared as he dropped coins in the paying dish, took his receipt and left without looking back.

A thought jolted through my brain. He always drinks full cream milk. Since when does he drink skimmed? Who was he trying to impress? Suddenly, I was convinced he was seeing someone else. I dropped my milk, ran out of Tesco, and tried to find him amongst the crowds, but he had vanished.

I then set off for his flat and rang the buzzer. When no one answered, I hammered on the door. It opened suddenly, and I came face to face with a middle-aged woman.

"Who are you?" I demanded.

"I beg your pardon?" she said, shocked. She was wearing a pink towelling dressing gown, her grey hair was scraped back in a ponytail, and she wore specs on a silver chain.

"It's you. Do you drink skimmed milk?"

"Who are you?"

"Don't play games with me," I said and barged past her and into the flat.

I stopped short in the living room. It was full of boxes, some wicker furniture, books, and an old PC with a tabby cat sleeping on the monitor. I turned to her.

"Where did you put Adam's stuff?" I demanded.

"I've just rented the flat from Adam Rickard, if that's who you mean," she said. She looked scared. "Whoever you are, I need you to leave. Now... Or I'll call the police."

I looked around once more and then ran past her out onto the street. I was cold and tired so I came home and sat in last night's clothes thinking... Adam has moved? What's going on?

Although, I now realise that woman is probably his new tenant, and not his girlfriend.

DECEMBER

Wednesday 1st December 16.02
TO: marikarolincova@hotmail.co.uk, chris@christophercheshire.com

I slept fitfully again last night and dreamt about Adam standing at the top of the stairs in his red tracksuit. I started climbing towards him, but halfway up, the stairs turned into an escalator going the wrong way and, as fast as I ran, I couldn't reach him.

I woke at five bathed in sweat. I couldn't face staying in bed, so I came down to make a cup of tea. I flicked the radio on and heard that this is the coldest start to December in twenty years. As it got light, snow began to fall, swirling around lazily before settling on the ground. It carried on snowing and soon the grey streets were transformed.

At half nine there was a knock at the front door. Through the peephole, I could make out Rosencrantz with Wayne and Oscar, all rugged up with the snow whirling around them. I quickly opened the door and pulled them inside.

"It's like London is shut down. There's no people about, no trains or buses running," said Rosencrantz excitedly.

"How did you get here?" I said.

"A dodgy mini-cab, with a driver who was willing to risk it."

I took them through to the kitchen. They were all grinning oddly.

"It's a nice gaff you've got, Mrs P," said Oscar, unzipping his jacket.

"It's elegant, homely," said Wayne, unwinding his scarf theatrically. "Is the kitchen Ikea? Klöepenklund? Flöngenfart? Skänka?"

"Um, I don't remember," I said. "Rosencrantz picked it out for us when he was thirteen."

"It's a Conran kitchen," said Rosencrantz. "And the grooves on the draining board were cut with a laser."

"That's really cool," said Oscar.

I didn't understand why they'd trekked across London in the snow to admire the kitchen, and Rosencrantz was still wearing his huge winter coat.

"Have you had any breakfast?" I asked.

They all shook their heads, smirking.

"Why not put the kettle on, Mum?" said Rosencrantz knowingly.

I turned to fill the kettle and when I turned back, there was a tiny Maltese puppy sitting on the kitchen island.

"Do you like him, Mum? I had him in my coat," grinned Rosencrantz.

"What are you doing getting a dog?" I said. "Do you know how much work a dog is? And you've just gone and got a job!"

"He's for you," said Rosencrantz. "So you won't be lonely."

The little dog stared up at me with eager little eyes. I

opened my mouth to say, *I can't have a dog, I haven't got time!* But, I have got time. Too much time.

The boys were watching curiously, much like they do when a new animal is introduced into a cage at the zoo. I reached out and the little white pup licked me, and then put his tiny furry paw in my hand. I gently scooped him up. He was so soft and beautiful and he snuggled into the crook of my arm. I started to well up.

"Don't you want him?" said Rosencrantz anxiously.

"Yes, he's perfect," I said. "I'm just... I haven't slept much."

Wayne pulled a lace hanky from his bag and handed it over, and Oscar patted my shoulder.

The puppy stood up in my arms with his front legs on my chest and licked my tears with a tiny pink tongue.

"He's so cute!" said Oscar, ruffling his little mop of silky fur.

"He's a matinee idol!" declared Wayne, clasping his hand to an imaginary décolletage.

"He's a pedigree," said Rosencrantz. "His parents are show dogs... Oscar's mum is a breeder."

"We all chipped in," said Oscar.

"Thank you, boys," I grinned. "I never dreamed I'd get a dog... What should I call him?"

"We thought you could call him Rocco," said Wayne.

"In tribute to Rocco Ritchie," said Oscar.

"Madonna's son," added Rosencrantz.

"Hello Rocco," I said.

Rocco sneezed in approval, gave me another lick and I put him on the floor. I made the boys tea and toast, and we spent a happy hour watching Rocco sniff and explore the kitchen. Then they said they would leave me to bond with him.

"We're going to have a walk through St James's Park and

take some snowy photos," said Wayne, pulling a camera out of his bag. "These two are my models."

"Thanks, boys, for everything," I said tearfully as they left. They waved, then pulled up their hoods and crunched off in the snow.

When they'd gone, I realised I had no food for Rocco, no bed or bowl, lead or coat. The poor little thing was starving, but the cupboards were bare. I scrabbled around the kitchen as he shifted on his little paws, snorting and wuffling impatiently, and finally unearthed some of those little UHT milk creamers you put in coffee. I opened one and knelt down, offering him the tiny pot of milk. He went crazy for it, lapping away hungrily, all the time watching me with his little brown eyes. I opened another and another and soon he had drunk six. He licked my hand happily, then stretched out on the kitchen floor and fell asleep.

I'm just about to brave the snow and stock up on doggy things.

Friday 3rd December 14.56
TO: marikarolincova@hotmail.co.uk

Rocco won't eat! I've made him beef stew, grilled chicken, pork chops, all in his lovely new red bowl, but all of which he's sniffed at dismissively then turned on his little paws and pranced off. Not only that, he's rejected all forms of dog food, from the big butch tins to the little gourmet foil containers.

The only thing he will touch is those little milks. I have to open each one individually and hold it out for him to lap at. Myself and Chris have made frequent trips to the coffee shop in Regent's Park, the only place we can get our hands on the little milks.

With all this snow London is eerily empty, well, at least the bits I've seen. The parked cars are covered in a layer of ice.

Despite his disinterest in food, Rocco seems to be thriving. He showers me with affection, he never leaves my side, he's even taken to toilet training. Every two hours he gives a little bark and I let him out in the back garden. I have dug a little path for him in the snow, and he scampers along it to do his business, then scampers back, and I wrap him up in a towel to keep warm. He even sleeps on the bed curled up beside me!

How are you enjoying your school being closed? I wish you could make it across here. I've got a big fire roaring in the living room.

Monday 6th December 16.14
TO: marikarolincova@hotmail.co.uk

After a weekend of Rocco still not eating, Chris came with me to take him to the vet. The snow is so deep and he is so tiny that I carried him in a little wicker basket. He lay there happily with his head poking out from under a blanket. The vet said that Rocco seems to be growing and is perfectly healthy. She suggested I try and hide cottage cheese or peanut butter in the little milk containers, and then normal food, in the hope he'll start eating properly.

The vet is a beautiful young Irish woman. Her examination room was filled with pictures of her and a dashing dark-haired chap. I don't think she's been in London long. As she put Rocco back in his basket she asked me and Chris how long we'd been together.

"We're both single," I said, which hung desperately in the air and I saw a tinge of pity in her eyes.

"How has *she* got a man?" asked Chris when we were back out on the snowy pavement. "She must spend half of her time with her hand up a cow's backside."

"I doubt that" I said. "She's a central London vet, she makes a fortune immunising handbag dogs. Of course she's a catch!"

We needed cheering up so we went for a coffee at Insomnia Café on Marylebone High Street. It's full of twits on laptops and a latte costs £4.75, but it's the only place apart from Regents Park Café that has a big basket full of those little milks. Whilst I went and ordered, Chris filled up his pockets for me. We found a table in the corner and I put Rocco, who was asleep in his basket, on the chair beside me. Christmas music was playing and some of the baristas were hanging lights and decorating a large tree.

"I've got no work on the horizon," said Chris, staring blankly at a pile of Christmas pannetone. "No plans."

"How did *Macbeth* go?" I said.

"It went by without a blip on the radar. No reviews, no press, nothing..."

"And Julian?"

"He's moved out. I miss seeing our iPods, side by side, on their little docks," he said.

"I've still kept Adam's toothbrush, I can't bring myself to throw it away."

Just then *Lonely This Christmas* began to play in the coffee shop.

"Look, why don't we spend Christmas together?" I suggested. "We always talk about, but we've never done it."

"That's another sad story," he said. "I got drunk the other

night and had a blackout. When I woke up I found an email confirming I'd booked Christmas in an ice hotel in Lapland."

I asked him why he would book an ice hotel, as we both know he loathes the cold.

"I vaguely remember sitting on the remote, and the *Pingu* DVD I have for when my niece comes round started playing."

"So you fancied spending Christmas with a little plasticine penguin?" I said.

"It's not funny. They've already debited six grand out of my bank account."

"Six grand!"

"Of course, me being an idiot, I booked the penthouse."

Rocco woke up and sneezed loudly. I lifted the blanket and he was lying on his back, four paws in the air. He shook himself, rolled over onto his front, and tugged at my sleeve with his teeth.

"He needs feeding," I said and opened a couple of the little milks. "It takes him a few times to latch onto the carton."

"Oh my God," said Chris. "My life is flashing before my eyes. This same café, twenty years ago, you feeding Rosencrantz, although back then the milk was in different packaging."

"I remember," I said wistfully. "Back then I was a natural blonde, Amazon was a rainforest, and google was the noise a baby made..."

"And here you are with another baby, of sorts. You've moved on with your life but I'm just as rudderless as I was then."

"You're not rudderless Chris," I said.

"Sorry Cokes, I'm gonna go," he said. "I told Rosencrantz I'd pop in to see him at Abercrombie and Fitch. He's going to let me use his staff discount to buy my Christmas presents. My mother wants a new baseball cap, for when she goes shooting."

"I'm always here for you Chris," I said. He gave me a hug. "Tell Rosencrantz I'll be in to see him as soon as Rocco is on solid food."

He rolled his eyes and went off into the snow. I sipped my £4.75 latte and caught sight of one of the baristas behind the counter looking at me. He was dark, well built, and rather handsome. He winked. I looked round but saw he was winking at me!

At that moment *Rockin' Around The Christmas Tree* started playing and the lights on the huge Christmas tree switched on. The café looked beautiful with the snow falling softly outside.

I am totally unprepared for Christmas. Do you have a tree yet? Have you bought cards? What about decorations? Clothes to wear? Where are you going for Christmas? And what do you want? I can't think of anything, but I can't ask people for cigarettes again. Chris did bring round an advent calendar this morning, and I had the fleeting pleasure of opening six doors at once.

Tuesday 7th December 09.19
TO: chris@christophercheshire.com

I spent ages last night stuffing empty mini milk cartons with titbits of dog food, meat and peanut butter. They were like doggy canapés when I'd finished, but Rocco saw through my attempts to dupe him and barked for milk. He woke me at four, five, and six this morning. There was none left in the house so I had to put him in his little wicker basket full of towels and make a trip back to Insomnia Café. It was one of the only places with the lights on so early. The handsome barista who winked at me was working and, on closer inspection, I have decided to upgrade his description to *gorgeous*. He smiled with the cutest dimples and asked what I wanted.

"A latte please," I said.

Rocco poked his nose out from under his blanket.

"What kind?" he said, placing a cup under the huge silver coffee machine.

"A latte... It's got lots of milk in it," I said helpfully.

"No, I know what a latte is," he grinned. "What kind is your dog?"

"Oh, he's a Maltese," I said.

The guy had on a tight white t-shirt. On his left pectoral a name tag said, 'Xavier'.

"I've got a large sausage," he said.

My eyes strayed to the bulge in the front of his tight black trousers.

"Sausage dogs are a lovely breed," he added.

"Yes, of course," I said, dragging my eyes back up to his.

Then I couldn't think of anything else to say. The milk bubbled and squawked as he steamed it in a big jug. When he turned to brew the coffee, I grabbed a couple of handfuls of Rocco's little milks and slipped them into the pockets of my winter coat. Xavier finished my latte in a swirly pattern, before pressing on a takeaway lid. He leaned over the counter and pulled up the towel. Rocco rolled over and stuck his four paws in the air, yawning.

"You be a good guard dog on the way home," he said.

Rocco opened one eye, sneezed on Xavier's hand and settled back down to sleep.

Xavier came round from behind the counter and opened the door for me.

"Go carefully," he winked. "I'd hate to see you fall over."

As I shuffled off in the snow, I felt a little thrilled by the encounter.

Back at home Rocco drank and drank until he'd emptied sixteen little milks. He then watched me intently whilst I made him a little bowl of plain rice with some organic wild boar meat puppy food (£7.95 a tin) mixed in, but he sniffed it dismissively, then pranced out to pee in the hallway. So I've found myself with another man I'm cooking for and cleaning up after.

Love, Coco x

P.S. Would you babysit Rocco for a couple of hours? I promised I'd go and see Rosencrantz at work.

Wednesday 8th December 15.37
TO: chris@christophercheshire.com

I've just been to the Abercrombie and Fitch store to see Rosencrantz. It feels more like a nightclub than a clothes shop. It's a huge building on Savile Row with video screens filling the windows and music pumping out. The smell of cologne hits you about five hundred yards before you reach the entrance.

Oscar was standing outside, topless, in a pair of jeans and flip flops greeting customers as they streamed past, ogling him.

"Hey Mrs P!" he said with a big grin.

"Aren't you a bit cold?" I asked.

"I'm allowed to wear a woolly hat," he said.

A group of hysterical Japanese girls appeared and started taking photos.

"Sorry Mrs P, I need to concentrate now," he said seriously, as if he were about to perform a heart bypass. The girls threw themselves at him and he almost toppled over.

Inside the lighting was low, making the artfully laid out tables of folded clothes look even more tempting. The supermodel staff were all dancing unselfconsciously to the music.

I spied Rosencrantz boogying away on the second level and climbed the dark wooden staircase to meet him.

"Hello love," I shouted.

"Hi Mum," he said, carrying on dancing. "Are you on your own?"

I said I was.

"The manager isn't keen on my family visiting."

"Why?"

He told me that Ethel had been in yesterday with her friend Irene, but they hadn't twigged that Abercrombie and Fitch is a clothes shop. Ethel went up to the till and ordered half a cider and a port and lemon.

"Nan was really rude to the guy serving," he said. "When he told her she couldn't have a drink, she accused him of being ageist and then barged behind the till to pour her own."

"What happened?"

"He called the manager and had them escorted off the premises. She's now barred from every Abercrombie and Fitch in the UK."

I started laughing.

"It's not funny, Mum. There's now a CCTV picture of Nan in the staffroom, and underneath it says what to do if you see her."

"What *do* you do if you see her?"

"Trigger the silent alarm and then Security comes."

"I wish I had that for when she pops round to the house," I said.

"How about I meet you in the Starbucks opposite in ten minutes," he said. "I'm due for my lunch..."

He joined me as promised and we had turkey cranberry sandwiches and gingerbread lattes amongst the chaos of Christmas shoppers traipsing in and out, laden with bags.

"They've asked me to work on Christmas Eve and Boxing Day," he said through a bite of sandwich. "It's triple time, so I said yes... It means I won't be able to come with you all to Auntie Meryl's."

"Meryl's?" I said.

"Yeah for Christmas."

He saw my face.

"Aren't you going to Auntie Meryl's?"

"No. I haven't been invited," I said.

"Dad is, so is Nan. I just assumed you would be... Well, I'm definitely not going now."

I spent the rest of lunch being nonchalant and saying it was all fine, but it wasn't. A soon as I said goodbye to Rosencrantz, I dived into a shop doorway further down the road, and called Meryl. She wasn't in and her phone went to voicemail.

"Watson Funerals! We take care of *any* body..."

The pun hurt my ears as much as her voice did. I debated leaving a message, but I didn't want to end up actually being invited for Christmas. I just wanted to make a fuss about why I wasn't.

Wednesday 8th December 20.37
TO: marikarolincova@hotmail.co.uk

Meryl is really rubbing it in now. She's just emailed her round robin Christmas letter. I've attached it below.

ATTACHMENT
FROM: meryl.watson@yahoo.com
TO: cocopinchard27@gmail.com

Dear   Friends,   Family,   Acquaintances,   and Tradespersons,

It barely seems like yesterday that I sat down, pulled up a pouffe and reached for the Basildon Bond to write to you with season's greetings.

Apologies for me emailing this letter, but with more work on than ever at our Undertaker's business (a mass shoot-out at our local kebab shop has been keeping us very busy), I haven't had time to organise my stationery. Not that I am too upset; Royal Mail's Wallace and Gromit Christmas stamps are a classic example of this country's slipping standards. Should Queen Elizabeth the Second really share a stamp with two lumps of modelling clay? What is wrong with a nativity scene at Christmas? Moreover, why are we no longer permitted to lick our stamps? They've all gone pre-adhesive, no doubt due to some ridiculous European law for fear that the old ones were too high in calories or that we may cut our tongues. Saying that, it hasn't fazed Tony as he was never much of a fan of all the licking I made him do!

2010 has been a glorious year. I gave birth to our beloved son. He was very punctual and arrived on time, but thanks to a blunder at our local NHS Trust I couldn't have the water birth I so desired. According to the midwife, someone had stolen the plug for the birthing pool.

It was a long labour — 126 hours — and I am proud to say I survived the whole ordeal on just half a paracetamol. Wilfred Ogilvy Thatcher Watson came into the world at 2.03 in the morning on 14th March weighing 13lb 12oz (ouch)! He is my little angel, a gift I never thought I would get so late in life.

And gosh, he's a very advanced baby! I'm quite positive he has already learnt to read. He always claps his hands in delight when he sees the Waitrose sign as we drive to do the weekly shop.

Watson Funerals had its best month ever in August (twenty-three people died after contracting Legionnaires disease from a mucky Jacuzzi at the leisure centre), so in September I decided to completely redecorate the house. I've had the living room and drawing room remodelled as almost an exact replica of Sandringham House, The Queen's private residence. We have our own version of The White Drawing Room and The Saloon!

This will be Wilfred's first Christmas, so we'll be reconnecting with family, spending the festivities with those we really care for: my brother Daniel, mother Ethel, nephew Rosencrantz and Tony's family. I'll be pulling out all of the stops. As we now share the same decor as The Queen, I've decided we'll have the same Christmas! We'll be having the same food, and following the same programme of events, although I won't be addressing the nation at 3pm. I leave that to Her Majesty!

We wish you a very Merry Christmas and a Happy and Prosperous New Year.

Meryl, Tony and Wilfred Watson

The cheeky cow! To think all the years she came here for Christmas, ate my food, and pulled my crackers! I'm seething.

Thursday 9th December 10.45
TO: chris@christophercheshire.com

Marika phoned me from the staff room at work. I asked her what I should do about Meryl.

"Remind me what the problem is?" she said. "You haven't been invited to spend Christmas with her?"

"That's right."

"Or Ethel, or Tony or your idiot ex-husband..."

"Yep."

"And you've always said it was your dream to spend Christmas on your own?"

"Yes..."

There was a silence.

"Are you still there?" I said.

"Yeah, I'm just waiting to hear what the problem is?"

"It's the principle," I whined.

"People who bang on about 'the principle' never get far in life," she said. "What's Meryl's number? I could phone and remind her of the principle involved and demand you be part of her Sandringham Christmas."

"Don't you dare!" I said.

"Just leave it then, Coco. It's her problem, not yours. Buy her a really shit present, like stretch mark cream."

"Hey, I could get Tony some Viagra off the internet too!"

"Talking of Viagra, what's going on with that hottie at the coffee shop?"

"Who? Xavier? Nothing!" I said.

"How often have you been to the café?"

"Well, lots. I've been going in to get milk for Rocco. He's very sweet and a bit flirty."

"Maybe you should do something. God, woman, you'll regret your timidity when you're a pensioner. You make life far more difficult than it should be..."

I came off the phone and thought maybe I *should* do something. Shake things up a bit.

Monday 13th December 11.36
TO: marikarolincova@hotmail.co.uk

Thank you for your chat the other day. Over the weekend I had a think and you're right, I do make things too complicated. I'm going to stop thinking about Meryl and have the most wonderful, selfish, lazy Christmas, eating sushi and a whole tin of Quality Street under the Christmas tree.

I also did something about Xavier. It did strike me that he might be gay (the hot ones usually are) so I dragged Chris out of bed to Insomnia Café.

"He's straight," announced Chris the second we walked through the big glass door.

Xavier hadn't even turned round; he was bent over re-stocking the fridge.

"How do you know?" I whispered.

Xavier was wearing his tight black barista trousers and smart black shoes.

"It's his underwear. See? He's wearing some grey boxers off the market. Any respecting gay guy with his body would most certainly be wearing designer undies."

Sure enough, Xavier had a big pair of grey briefs bunching up and spilling over his waistband.

"That's great," I grinned.

"For you," he huffed. "I'm going back to bed."

"Don't you want coffee? My treat."

"No, I'll use my machine at home. At least my machine won't reject me like a hot, straight guy," and he stomped off in his snow boots.

Xavier made me a latte as usual, and as he was warming the milk, I took a deep breath and invited him to come as my date to Angie's Christmas party next week. He looked a bit surprised — but he said yes! How impressed are you?

P.S. Can you babysit Rocco whilst I'm at the party?

Monday 13th December 13.12
TO: chris@christophercheshire.com

Marika has just phoned me from the staff room.

"Are you mad?" she cried. "What are you doing inviting some random guy from your local coffee shop to Angie's Christmas party?"

"He's not random. He's Xavier."

"Okay, where does he live? What's his surname? Has he got a wife? An ex-wife? Has he got children?"

"I don't know," I said sheepishly.

"Well, you should find out before the party. All these people you work with are going to ask about your date, and you can't say *I don't know*... They'll think you've hired an escort."

"You said I should do something!"

"I meant flirt back! Look Cokes, that's the lunch bell, I've got to go..."

"What should I do now?"

"I'll tell you what I told my year eights before their SATs."

"What?"

"*Revise,* so get down to Insomnia Café and start revising."

Wednesday 15th December 08.12
TO: marikarolincova@hotmail.co.uk

During my past three visits to Insomnia Café, I've managed to winkle some titbits of information about Xavier. He's studying to be an architect and he works the early morning shift and weekends. He has no children "that he knows of" (his joke). His surname is Michael.

I also went for a full six hours without thinking about Adam yesterday, but then felt weirdly guilty that I'd forgotten him for so long.

Thursday 16th December 09.15
TO: marikarolincova@hotmail.co.uk

Rosencrantz sent me an email from Meryl with the arrangements for her Sandringham Christmas. I shudder to think I was married to her flesh and blood for over twenty years.

ATTACHMENT
FROM: rosencrantzpinchard@gmail.com
TO: cocopinchard27@gmail.com

The Watson's Sandringham Christmas.

At the behest and request of Meryl, Tony and Wilfred Watson, you are cordially invited to spend a truly memorable Sandringham-themed Christmas.

When: 24th - 27th December 2010.

Where: 'Bonvivant', Abacus Blvd, Milton Keynes, MK1 7TY

Please familiarise yourself with the following programme of events.

CHRISTMAS EVE
(Dress code; casual tweed)
Guests will be expected to arrive before 4 p.m. when tea will be taken on my Royal Doulton in The White Drawing Room (small-scale replica of the one at Sandringham House)

4 p.m. Earl Grey tea, sandwiches, scones and muffins will be in abundance. This will be a chance to take the first look at the Christmas tree, freshly dug and delivered from Norfolk.

6 p.m. We will open gifts (following in the German tradition of unwrapping gifts the night before Christmas). All gifts will be laid out on a white-linen-covered table with name tags. (Be prepared to make a short thank-you speech if required.)

7.10 p.m. After gifts, it is off to the Saloon for Dubonnet and gin cocktails.

7.45 p.m. Amply refreshed, we will dress for dinner. Ladies in gowns, gents in black tie.

8 p.m. The gong will sound for dinner (I found a nice gong in John Lewis). The Queen always arrives fashionably late at 8.15 p.m. and as your hostess I will observe the same custom. Dinner will be by candlelight in the dining room with a shrimp appetiser, followed by a main course of game and a dessert of tarte Tatin.

10.15 p.m. Coffee, port and brandy.

Midnight. Bed.

CHRISTMAS DAY

(Dress code smart church outfits, no jeans or crop-tops.)

7 a.m. Breakfast in the dining room. Bacon, sausage, eggs, toast and tea. You will be able to take your pick from the traditional English menu for breakfast.

11 a.m. Christmas service at St Michael's Church led by the Reverend Damian Leviticus. This is walking distance, although dial-a-ride will take my mother and any small children.

12.30 p.m. Turkey lunch with all the trimmings. The Queen has a bird from her Norfolk estate so we have done the next best thing and ordered something from Bernard Matthews.

2.30 p.m. Meryl's Christmas speech. I've decided after all to do my own Christmas speech, just before The Queen. This will either be live in the White Drawing Room, or if Tony can get the video camera going, I'll pre-record it.

3 p.m. The Queen's Speech.

3.15 p.m. The Queen's Speech, (The movie starring Helen Mirren).

5.30 p.m. Charades, Monopoly whatever people want, this will be free and easy. (Fill in the enclosed form with which you'd prefer.)

8 p.m. Turkey leftovers with a fresh lobster salad to start.

10.15 p.m. Coffee, port and brandy.
Midnight. Bed.

BOXING DAY
(Warm smart tweed.)
I'm trying to arrange a pheasant shoot, and hire a few corgis to pick up the dead birds. I will keep you posted!

27th DECEMBER
7.00 a.m. Everyone departs. Filled with happy memories of a truly unique Christmas.

Saturday 18th December 03.37
TO: chris@christophercheshire.com

I went to Angie's Christmas party last night. Rocco was devastated I was leaving him. He howled, yowled, and barked, pacing up and down and pulling at my coat when I went to leave.

"What am I doing, dating?" I said.

"You've left it too late to cancel," said Marika. "Xavier is out there in a taxi."

"I can't go!" I said looking down at his Rocco's pleading face. "Look!" I knelt down and he stood on his back legs and put his fluffy paws against my cheek.

"I'll only be gone for a couple of hours," I said. His little eyes searched my face, but he didn't understand and cried even more. I left quickly, hearing his howls from inside as I crunched down the snow-covered path to Xavier.

"Hello," I said when I climbed in the taxi and sat beside

him. He looked very fashionable and young in a tight red shirt and a black bow tie. He also smelt lovely.

"Hello," he grinned, leaning in and kissing me on the cheek. "You look great."

We didn't say anything else for the rest of the journey to Angie's. I was devoid of conversation, and we passed it in awkward silence with the taxi driver eyeballing us in his rearview mirror.

Angie's house looked beautiful. Her living room with its double height ceiling was decorated to within an inch of its life with acres of fairy lights, and three huge Christmas trees. Her giant fireplace was filled with logs and a fierce fire was blazing. The sash windows were all open, but the room was still sweltering.

"Hi love," she said, squeezing through sweaty people to kiss me. "Who's this?"

"This is Xavier Michael," I said. "He's thirty-eight and training to be an architect."

Angie shook his hand.

"Sorry, I'm not hiring anyone new," she said, "although my builders are making a right royal fuck-up..."

"No, he doesn't work as an architect yet, right now he's a barista."

"You look a bit young to be called to the bar," said Angie, exhaling smoke and squinting at him.

"No, a *barista*... he works in my local coffee shop."

"Oh, I see..." said Angie, nodding with a sly smile. She went off to mingle, and on her way past whispered, "You dirty cow, picking up a tradesperson."

"Is she your sister?" said Xavier, grabbing us drinks from a passing waiter.

I realised Xavier knew nothing much about me either. I went to tell him what I did, but Angie came back with her son, Barry.

"Tell him how good further education is," said Angie to Xavier. "He's just been released from Feltham Young Offenders Institution, he could do with further-educating himself out of the shit."

She then pulled me away to talk to my editor.

More guests flooded in and I lost sight of Barry and Xavier. Several drinks later, after talking to my editor, cover designer, and the Head of Media Strategy at my publishing house (they are planning a huge launch for *Agent Fergie* in the spring), I set off to find Xavier.

Angie's new house is *huge*. I climbed three flights of stairs, searching in bedrooms and bathrooms all tastefully decorated in Molton Brown colours. I came to the top landing and noticed a small door ajar on one wall. I pulled it open and climbed up a narrow little staircase which was very tatty in relation to the rest of the house. The cool air hit me as I came out on a flat piece of roof high above London. Xavier and Barry were standing together. They started laughing.

"Shit, I thought you were my mother," said Barry, collapsing into giggles.

"She's not my mother!" said Xavier, exploding in laughter.

I sniffed the air.

"Is that marijuana I can smell?"

Xavier and Barry looked at each other and laughed again.

"Are you smoking..."

"Don't tell my mum, she'll flip," said Barry taking a joint he'd had behind his back and inhaling.

"What? She'd do a back flip? Is she a gymnast?" laughed Xavier.

"No, she's my agent and my friend!" I said. "And she'd kill you if she found out. Aren't you on probation, Barry?"

"Yeah!" He carried on laughing.

"Barry! It's not funny. I don't know why you insist on breaking your mother's heart. And smoking weed fries your brain and makes everything seem futile. Please don't waste your life!"

Suddenly the little door opened. Barry dropped the joint but it skidded into the middle of us all. Angie appeared.

"What are you all doing?" she said. "I can smell weed."

Angie always looks in control but as she searched Barry's face for an answer, I could see she was scared. She looked so vulnerable.

"I'm smoking a joint," I said suddenly.

"*You're* smoking a joint?" said Angie, incredulously.

"Yes, I am," I said picking it up off the floor. "Sorry, it's my joint."

"I, um, showed her up to the roof, to smoke it," said Barry.

"Why the hell are you smoking weed, Coco?" asked Angie.

"I prefer the term medical marijuana," I bluffed.

Angie carried on staring, showing another emotion I've never seen before: shock. I put the joint to my lips and took a big drag. Behind Angie, Barry was frantically signalling to me, and I realised why. It was super-strength and hit me like a train.

"Why are you on medical marijuana?" said Angie in a low voice.

"Um... menopause..." I muttered.

"Ok... uh, okay," she said, seeing Xavier. "Sorry. Just please don't smoke drugs in front of my son. You know how hard it's been to get him away from this stuff."

"Sorry," I gulped and flicked the rest of the joint over the edge. We watched the ember slowly float down to the street below.

"Now come on, Barry," said Angie. "I've got an author of mine I want you to meet, he lectures at Cambridge. He might be able to swing you a place."

They went off and closed the little door behind them. Xavier grinned at me.

"So you're an author and she's your agent?"

"Yes," I said, feeling the roof begin to spin.

"And you just covered for her bad boy son? You've got a wild side."

Xavier suddenly leant over and kissed me. Without thinking I kissed him back. The joint did something reckless to me. I started to unbutton his shirt and run my hand across his chest which was firm and hot. We kissed harder and I moved my hand across his abs and down. Whatever I had inhaled was messing with my head. I closed my eyes and imagined it was Adam kissing me, it was Adam I was touching.

Suddenly, something very warm and thick landed with a thud in my palm, and carried on along my wrist. I opened my eyes and looked down. He'd unzipped his trousers, presenting me with the most enormous penis I've ever seen (and this was in minus temperatures too)! I screamed and leapt away.

"What? Are you okay?" he said.

"I thought it was a snake!" I shrilled, then started laughing uncontrollably. Xavier hurriedly tucked it back in his trousers. He looked embarrassed and a little betrayed. I realised I was being unfair to him, and that I was rather wasted. I suddenly felt sick. I ran to the railing of the roof and threw up over the side. I threw up again and felt Xavier gently hold my hair back for me. When I'd finished he offered me a tissue.

"I'm sorry," I said.

"Do you want me to take you home? I mean, drop you off at home?"

I nodded.

He helped me down all the flights of stairs, through the party and out onto the street. There was a gaggle of people stood around staring up at the house and Angie was watching a black cab drive away.

"What's going on?" I said.

"A right fuck up, that's what! I invited the head of Harper Collins UK, cos I'm *inches* away from a five-book deal with them, and when he arrives he gets splattered in vomit on the doorstep."

"Oh... how terrible," I said.

Xavier raised his eyebrows and managed to hail a passing cab. We thanked Angie, jumped in and drove back to my house.

"Goodnight," he said, as I climbed out of the cab.

"Goodnight," I said. And he shook my hand.

I scuttled out of the taxi and up the snowy path to the door. I turned to wave but the taxi had gone. When I got in Marika was asleep on the sofa with Rocco curled up beside her, his head on her shoulder. The fire had died down and they looked so cosy, so I came up to bed.

Saturday 18th December 12.53
TO: chris@christophercheshire.com

At six o'clock this morning I was woken by a Skype call coming through. It was Meryl. When her white drawing room came into view, it looked like a crate of Christmas decorations had exploded over everything. A ladder stood by the wall and Wilfred was screaming in the other room. Meryl was sat in front of the computer, hair on end, holding a nappy.

"Coco, does this look normal to you?" she shrilled, holding the contents of the nappy close to the webcam.

"It's six o'clock in the morning," I said, recoiling.

"Wilfred did a green whoopsie!" she said. "Did this ever happen with Rosencrantz?"

Behind her, the half-decorated Christmas tree slowly leaned into shot then fell, scattering baubles and tinsel.

"Oh fiddlesticks!" screamed Meryl, leaping up and kicking the Christmas tree. "I've been decorating this Norwegian Spruce all night! No wonder the bloody Queen has servants! I've still got three days of catering and a grouse shoot to try and organise!"

She gave the tree a final exhausted kick and sat back down.

"Won't a grouse shoot be hard to organise in Milton Keynes?" I said.

"It's all under control," she said through gritted teeth. "Now please Coco, look at this whoopsie!"

I peered at it and confirmed it did look unnaturally green. She jumped up shouting, "Tony! TONY! Get the car ready we need to go to hospital NOW!"

She hurdled the giant Christmas tree and ran through the living room door. I suddenly remembered something,

"Didn't Ethel just buy Wilfred some crayons?" I shouted.

Meryl returned wearing her coat with her car keys in one hand and the nappy in the other.

"Meryl, check where the green crayon is!" I said.

She dropped the nappy in the doorway and rushed out again. I sat looking at the empty room for a minute as Wilfred carried on wailing. Marika shuffled up behind me in her dressing gown. On the screen Tony appeared in the doorway and slipped over on the nappy with a cry. Then Meryl rushed back.

"The green crayon is missing!" she shouted happily. "I repeat, the green crayon is missing!" Then she slid over in the mess on top of Tony.

"Is this YouTube?" asked Marika blearily.

I had to turn the camera off as I was laughing too hard.

Tony phoned back a little while later. I was feeling very bad about laughing. I felt worse when he said that they had discovered bits of the green crayon in the nappy, and that Meryl is frantically trying to get the stain out of the carpet. I could hear the carpet cleaner, Meryl and Wilfred all screaming.

"I think I'm going to make her a cup of tea and pop in some Valium when she's not looking," he said wearily. "She hasn't slept in days you know... This bloody Sandringham Christmas. I just wanted to sit under the tree with Wilfred and watch his face as he opened his prezzies."

I don't usually have much time for Tony, but I felt very sorry for him. He wished me a Merry Christmas and put down the phone.

I joined Marika and Rocco downstairs for egg on toast and little milks. I told her about my antics at Angie's Christmas party.

"Jeez Cokes, I knew you'd gone out dating too soon," she said. "But even a normal person would struggle to create that much drama. Still, every cloud has a silver lining."

'What's that?"

"At least you know Xavier would be good in the bedroom department."

"He's not going to be in any department," I said. I then went on to say I was having second thoughts about spending Christmas alone.

"You've got Rocco," said Marika. The fluff, sat on the floor beside me, gave a little indignant bark.

"I know," I said picking him up. "But what if we get lonely and depressed? The snow has melted, it's just grey old London outside again, and I can't face putting up any decorations."

"You could come with me to Slovakia," said Marika.

"What about Rocco?"

"Bring him too, get him a puppy passport and we can go by road. You've got that new car you never drive, let's use it."

Tuesday 21st December 22.21
TO: chris@christophercheshire.com

I have been running round today sorting out Rocco's puppy passport. This morning I went to Marylebone train station and tried to figure out how I would get him to sit still in the instant photo booth. I screwed the seat round until it was as high as possible, but Rocco is so tiny that only the very fluff atop his head was in the frame. The seat was also too smooth for him, and his furry paws kept sliding off. In the end, I had to twist it to its lowest setting and crouch with Rocco balanced on my head. Try as I might I couldn't keep him still and press the button to take the photo.

Just as I was about to give up, the curtain was pulled open. Xavier looked through the gap.

"Oops sorry," he said and quickly pulled it shut.

After a moment, his voice came through the curtain, "Is that you Coco?"

"Um... yes," I said.

He opened it again, and looked at me with Rocco balanced on my head. His face broke into a grin.

"This is for a puppy passport," I said, going red. "He won't keep still and the stool isn't high enough."

Xavier suggested that he and I squatted down on either side of the stool in the booth, and made a little platform for Rocco with our upturned hands. Xavier then used his nose to press the button. He was so kind and funny and I didn't mind in the least being squashed up against him in the photo booth. Whilst we waited for the pictures to be developed, he had a cuddle with Rocco.

"He likes you," I said, as Rocco licked his hand.

"You managed to get him off the little milks?"

"Not yet, he *refuses* to eat anything else. He clamps his mouth shut."

Xavier rummaged around and pulled some little coffee biscuits out of his jeans.

"Can I try?"

"Sure," I said.

He offered one to Rocco. The little shit gave a woof of excitement, took it obediently and wolfed down another four in quick succession! I was mortified.

"Little dogs are actors, they like to play to the crowd," said Xavier kindly.

"Now you must think I'm this crazy woman who jumps you at parties and tells lies about her dog's diet for attention... both of which aren't true. The thing is, I got dumped a few weeks back and it threw me, and everything has seemed to unravel since."

Xavier went to say something but the photos shot out of the machine into the little slot. They were perfect. Little Rocco was sat almost floating mid-air and looking directly into the camera.

"Thank you," I said. "I couldn't have done it without you."

"Coco," he said, "you don't have to explain yourself to me. You're lovely. *I'm* sorry about the other night, I got carried away, I didn't mean to scare you with my... well..."

"What are you doing for Christmas?" I said.

"Going home to my parents in Portsmouth. I'm renewing my Student Railcard for the trip, hence the photo booth."

"Student Railcard? That makes me feel old," I said.

"Mature student!"

We paused and smiled at each other.

"Look. Maybe we could walk our dogs sometime?" he said. "Just dog walking, no pressure."

He gave me a card with his phone number on.

As he walked off, I admired him; all six foot of him. Rocco barked, bringing me out of my thoughts and reminding me we had more to do.

We got to the vet around four and she didn't stop laughing for a full five minutes. All I needed was a photo of Rocco, any photo, it didn't need to be an official passport photo from a photo booth.

We got the puppy passport on the spot, filled in and stamped. I felt so proud of him with his own passport.

When we got home in the dark, it was snowing again, harder, and the temperature was dropping. I'm so excited about going now, I just hope the weather doesn't spoil it for us. The motorways above London are closed but so far, the South looks okay.

There was a strange slurring message from Meryl on my answer phone, something about a fifty pence coin talking to her. I called back but the phone rang out.

I'm pleased to hear that you're having fun at the Ice Hotel in Lapland and that there is plenty of Schnapps. Have you met anyone noteworthy to share your thermal sleeping bag with?

Wednesday 22nd December 06.11
TO: chris@christophercheshire.com

Tony rang to say that Meryl had to be *sectioned* in the early hours of this morning! He found her outside at 3 a.m. disinfecting the driveway in her dressing gown. When he asked her to come back inside, she tried to suffocate him by stuffing a dishcloth down his throat screaming, "The Queen is coming for Christmas!"

She hasn't slept in four days trying to get everything prepared for the Sandringham Christmas, and the lack of sleep made her hallucinate. She flushed all the money from her purse down the toilet because she thought the Queen's head was talking, criticising her skills as a hostess. She's been sedated in the Psychiatric Unit at Milton Keynes General Hospital and kept under observation. Tony said that his sister and Daniel have already arrived and they are helping with Wilfred. Meryl can't have any visitors for a few days. I asked if there was anything I could do. Tony cleared his throat and then said tentatively, "Well yes, there is something you could do Coco."

"What is it? Anything," I said.

"If you could give Ethel her Christmas lunch I'd be most grateful. What with everything that's happened and the M25 being closed southbound with the snow, I don't think I can get to her."

There was a crashing silence. Alarms were going off in my brain.

"Oh... um..." I said.

Then Daniel came on the line,

"Hi Cokes, I know we haven't spoken in a while, but, please," he begged. "I know Mum drives you crazy but this is a unique situation."

"I know it is," I said.

"All the residents in her sheltered housing have gone to their families for Christmas. There won't be a warden on duty. I don't like the idea of her all alone; it's a very rough area. What if looters break in looking for presents?"

"I'm supposed to be..."

"Supposed to be what?"

"Nothing," I said with a heavy heart. "Tell Ethel she can come here."

"Thank you. Thank you. I owe you big time. Merry Christmas Cokes," he said.

"Yeah. Merry Christmas," I said and put the phone down.

Shit.

Wednesday 22nd December 08.44
TO: chris@christophercheshire.com

I thought about palming Ethel off on Rosencrantz, but he is working, and on Christmas Day has been invited to Oscar's house in the Cotswolds. He sounded excited, so I didn't mention the Ethel situation.

I took a deep breath and phoned Marika.

"Why don't you bring Ethel with us?" she said, without missing a beat.

"I wasn't expecting you to say that!"

"It's no problem. I'll call my mum to make up the camp bed."

"Hang on Marika," I said. "Think carefully about what you're suggesting. That we drag that old bag of bones across Europe for your family Christmas."

There was a silence.

"I think it could be good," she said.

"How? This is Ethel."

"She could be a much-needed distraction."

"From what? Fun?"

"No, a much-needed distraction for my mother. She'll go into entertaining overdrive and she won't question me too much..."

There was another long pause.

"Coco. I just quit my job," she said.

"What? As a teacher?!"

"What other job do I do?"

"What are you going to do?" I said. "You just got a mortgage and the teachers' pension scheme is final salary."

"Okay, you're not helping. I don't know what I'm going to do," she said. "What I do know is I can't be a teacher anymore. More importantly, my mother can't know about it until I work out a solution."

"What happened?" I said.

"It all went wrong when I slept with that OFSTED Inspector."

"Well, to be fair you didn't know he was going to be inspecting your school, he was just a bloke in a bar."

"Exactly, but the headmistress is blaming me for the school getting a bad result. Then on the last day of term, I put a movie on for the students. *Ghost*, with Demi Moore and Patrick Swayze,"

"That's a nice film," I said.

"Yes... During the pottery wheel scene the Headmistress

stormed into the classroom, and turned it off saying it was pornographic. She then accused me, in front of the students, of being depraved with loose morals."

"Don't you teach seventeen year olds?"

"Something inside me snapped. I told her to stick her job up her fat fanny and I stormed out."

"What did the kids do?"

"I heard them clapping and cheering as I walked out of the fire exit. I then got in my car and drove home."

"I'm so sorry, hun," I said.

"I just want a nice Christmas, Coco," she said. "My mother is like a mind reader. Having you and Ethel there will distract her, please."

I paused to think.

"If bringing Ethel will give you a nice Christmas, then fine, but I've warned you."

I am cursing myself for answering Tony's phone call this morning. If I'd just kept my phone off for a few hours, I'd have been away with Marika and home free.

Wednesday 22nd December 15.47
TO: chris@christophercheshire.com

I picked up Marika at ten, then we drove on to The Aspidistra Sheltered Housing in Catford. Ethel was waiting outside in the blizzard. Marika jumped out and helped her in beside me.

"'Ello sweethearts," she said. "And little Rocco too... Thanks Marika love for 'avin me, and you Coco for drivin'."

I exchanged a glance with Marika. Ethel seemed to be on her best behaviour.

"Ooh, I like yer car Coco, what is it?" said Ethel.

"A Land Cruiser," I said.

"Must 'ave set you back a few bob," she said, stroking the leather seat as Marika helped her with the seatbelt. "To think you could buy this from writing *your* books!"

I rolled my eyes; twelve seconds was all it took for the first barbed comment.

"Sorry to hear about Meryl," said Marika, changing the subject.

"Oh, she's overdone it again," said Ethel dismissively. "I used to 'ave to sedate 'er meself when she was little an' she wouldn't stop cleaning 'er doll's house. A little nip of brandy in 'er rice pudding used to do it."

I drove off into the snow.

"Ooh!" said Ethel. "Ooh what was that?"

"I put the heated seat on for you," I said.

"Thank gawd for that. I thought I'd pissed meself!" she cackled. Her laugh was like ragged fingernails being dragged down a blackboard.

We crept along the motorway, which was reduced to a whirling white mass, and got to the Channel Tunnel car train at 3 p.m. We're in a line of traffic waiting to drive up the ramp. Nevertheless, we are all in good spirits and Christmas in another country has an air of excitement about it. Maybe, just maybe, this trip could be fun after all.

Thursday 23rd December 10.44
TO: chris@christophercheshire.com

We're on the outskirts of Bratislava. When we emerged from the Channel Tunnel I took the first leg, driving through France and Belgium. Marika swapped in a lay-by outside Frankfurt, and drove until around seven this morning when we crossed the border into Slovakia. Ethel has been strangely quiet. I think she's a little intimidated by it all. I'm not sure if she's really been abroad much. I know she went to the Isle of Wight in 1973.

We stopped for breakfast in a swanky modern McDonald's in Bratislava.

"Iss my treat girls!" said Ethel. "'Ave whatever you want. Ooh, and see if they've got Tetley," said Ethel.

Marika spoke in Slovak to the girl behind the counter, who shook her head. In a practised move, Ethel pulled a teabag from her handbag and asked Marika to get her some hot water.

"She's clever that Marika," said Ethel. "Can you speak anything foreign?"

"I'm quite good at French," I said.

"When I got evacuated up north we only learned things like how to make flaky pastry."

"Marika can't make flaky pastry," I said.

"But she can buy it pre-made," said Ethel regretfully. "Gawd, I wish I could do it all again."

After we'd demolished our McBreakfasts, Marika went off to the loo and Ethel asked me how much twenty-two euros was in pounds.

"There's not a lot of difference now," I said. "It's about twenty quid."

"Twenty quid? I just spent twenty quid!" she spluttered. "She can't 'alf put it away," she said, poking Marika's Egg McMuffin and hash brown wrappers.

"You said to order whatever we wanted?"

"That was before I knew it was daylight robbery! Twenty quid for breakfast! My mother bought 'er first two-up-two-down in Catford for thirty-five quid, and she still 'ad change left over for a mangle."

"That was in 1924," I said.

But Ethel carried on ranting.

"Bloody foreigners. And I thought that dog of yours only drank UHT milk?" Rocco had polished off three hash browns and a sausage patty with a hungry little bark of excitement.

"Why did you offer to buy us all breakfast then?" I said.

"I thought McDonald's in the Eastern bloc would be reasonable. Didn't that power station blowing up make it a cheap 'oliday destination?"

"That was Chernobyl, in the Ukraine."

"Twenty bloody quid," moaned Ethel.

At that point Marika came back.

"'Ello love," smiled Ethel. "'Ave you 'ad enough to eat? Can I get you anything else?"

"No, thanks," said Marika. "That was great."

"It was a pleasure," grinned Ethel. "Now, you must excuse me, I need to go spend a penny."

"Well, don't spend too many," I said.

Ethel gave me a look and shuffled off to the ladies.

"She's being nice, isn't she?" said Marika.

Me and Rocco just looked at each other.

Thursday 23rd December 17.12
TO: chris@christophercheshire.com

Marika's mother lives in a smart three-bed flat in Nitra.

It's a beautiful town. We drove past a medieval castle high on a hill and there were breathtaking views of a snow-covered mountain called Zobor. As we pulled into the car park, we saw her building was encased in black and white striped plastic. A flurry of wind rippled up inside causing a loud crackling.

"Is that some kind of Slovakian Christmas decoration?" said Ethel, as we unloaded our suitcases.

"No. It's Slovakian builders, they're insulating the building," explained Marika.

We were welcomed so warmly into the flat by Marika's mother Blazena, a huge matronly woman with a halo of curly black hair. I hadn't met Marika's stepfather Fero, who is very short, round, bald and in his sixties. He lumbered out of the bedroom drinking a bottle of beer with his shirt off. Blazena went mad shooing him back inside. Fero backed away muttering and shut the door.

"She's telling him to get dressed properly to meet the fine English ladies," said Marika.

I looked at myself and Ethel in our crumpled clothes. She made it sound like Judi Dench and Maggie Smith had arrived to stay.

Blazena gave us rib-cracking hugs. Then she stared at Marika, narrowing her eyes for a moment. I thought she might guess Marika had quit her job, but she was distracted by Fero, now wearing a shirt but still with the bottle of beer. She grabbed it off him and ushered us all into the living room.

It was warm and beautifully decorated. The tree was covered in an exquisite set of fairy lights. The bulbs were hand painted in pale colours and cast a magical hue against the white walls. I counted seven statues of Jesus; three had tinsel adorning his crown of thorns and the biggest one on top of the television was wearing a Santa hat. Blazena sat us at a long dining table and we were given hot chicken soup, followed by roast duck, potatoes and cabbage; it was delicious. Even little Rocco was given a small bowl of duck liver that he wolfed down and then fell asleep under the Christmas tree.

We ate and ate as Blazena talked and talked, mainly to grill Marika. She asked why hasn't she found a husband? Is she keeping her flat clean? When is her next promotion? Marika went pale and answered as best she could. Every time the wind blew round the block of flats the plastic crackled loudly and Blazena cursed the ceiling with a waggling hand.

Then, when we thought we could eat no more, the doorbell started ringing and a stream of elderly ladies came in bearing Christmas tidings and baked goods. It seemed every time I opened my mouth a cake or pastry was being shoved in it.

When it got dark, and the last of the old ladies left, myself, Marika and Ethel took Rocco for a walk in the communal garden. I looked up and saw that all the balconies outside the flats had been removed for the building work. Several of the neighbours had their balcony doors open, and one lady was sat on the step in a big coat smoking a cigarette with her legs dangling above a five-storey drop.

"Isn't that terribly dangerous, and a health and safety risk?" I said.

"Not in Slovakia," said Marika. "The thought is that if you're stupid enough to not see the huge drop outside your kitchen door, then you're stupid enough to plunge to your death."

Myself, Marika, Ethel and Rocco are all sharing the

guest room. I'm just lying on the bed trying to digest the five thousand calories I've consumed. Then in an hour we're going to have our evening meal of goulash and dumplings. I think I'm going to pop.

Friday 24th December 05.30
TO: chris@christophercheshire.com

I woke in the middle of the night. There was a scratching noise and a ragged whisper saying my name. I sat up in bed. A thin line of moonlight escaped from the bottom of the curtain in the guest room. Beside me (we're sharing a double bed) Marika slept soundly. Rocco was in the gap between us lying on his back, his furry little chest slowly rising and falling. Ethel was an indistinct lump of covers on the camp bed in the corner. I thought I must have been dreaming.

I lay back down and closed my eyes, but I heard my name again, now in a low menacing growl. My blood froze. Why wasn't Rocco waking up? I shook Marika, but she wouldn't wake up either. I sat up again and noticed the room was freezing. My breath streamed out in a mist. The knocking came again, insistent,

"Coco, please, it's so cold," rasped the voice.

Despite my terror, I slowly got out of bed, and came out into the hallway. The living room and bedroom doors leading off it were closed. I jumped as a walking stick hanging on the back of the front door rattled.

"Coco! Open up!" rumbled the voice, knocking harder. "It's so cold."

My heart was in my throat as I edged closer to the door. It was even colder in the hallway, my skin was stinging. *Any moment I'll wake up*, I thought, as I slowly reached out and turned the key.

The front door swung inwards and a terrible figure lurched towards me. It had wide bloodshot eyes and a sunken mouth. It was white from head to foot and dressed in some kind of robes.

"You took your bloody time," it growled.

I screamed, my knees gave way, and then everything went black.

It was bright when I woke up. Coloured lights swam into my vision and I was lying under the Christmas tree. I could hear Rocco barking and Marika's face came into view.

"Coco! Are you all right? I was so worried." She was holding out a glass of brandy. Rocco rushed forward and started to lick my face. I took the glass and slowly sat up. Ethel was on the sofa with a towel round her. Blazena was wiping what looked like plaster dust off her face with a flannel and a bowl of hot water.

"Ethel got up for a cigarette," said Marika. "She forgot that there isn't a balcony and fell into a skip full of polystyrene and plaster dust."

Fero was fiddling with the radiator, trying to warm up the flat. I stared at Ethel.

"Jesus! Are you all right?" I asked.

"I made it back up in the lift, I'm fine," said Ethel, sheepishly. "I survived the blitz, you know."

Blazena took Ethel's grubby hands in hers and started talking, and wiping tears from her eyes.

"Woss she sayin'?" said Ethel.

"She's very upset," said Marika. "She thinks she's a terrible hostess, allowing one of her guests to fall out of the kitchen."

"Iss fine love," said Ethel patting Blazena's hand. "It was like landing on an eiderdown."

"I thought she was a ghost!" I said, taking a big gulp of brandy.

"Yeah, I'm the ghost of Christmas future, love. I predict you'll get stuck into the Quality Street and end up with an arse twice its size!" said Ethel. She let out a cackling laugh which turned into a coughing fit.

Blazena said something to Marika.

"Mum thinks Ethel should go to hospital."

"No, iss just a bit of plaster dust," said Ethel, descending into another coughing fit.

"Maybe she should go," said Marika.

We all piled into my car and drove Ethel to Nitra hospital. It was very modern and clean and she was whisked through a series of scans and blood tests by a nice male doctor who even spoke English.

"This woman is in perfect health!" said the doctor in English, as if Ethel were some kind of medical miracle.

Blazena clasped her chest in delight and gave a prayer of thanks. I kept my mouth shut. How does Ethel keep cheating death when every day perfectly wonderful people die in terrible accidents?

We finally got to bed at five in the morning.

Friday 24th December 22.45
TO: chris@christophercheshire.com

It seems a near death experience hasn't given Ethel much pause for thought. She's still the same moaning old bag she was before she plunged four storeys into a skip. From the moment she woke up this morning, she's moaned. She's moaned about the food, she's moaned about the water being too hard, and her bed being too soft. She's moaned about the television being switched off and that she's missing *Noel's Christmas Presents*. She's even moaned about Blazena and the fact she didn't wash her hands properly before cooking! She's also convinced Marika's family is talking about her behind her back. They're not, of course, they're just concerned after what happened last night.

In Slovakia the Christmas tradition is to fast all day and then eat a meal of fish and potato salad in the evening. At 2 pm, to try and distract Ethel from whining about this, I suggested we Skype Daniel.

"Ooh yeah, I miss my Danny boy," said Ethel.

I put my laptop on the living room table as Daniel pinged into view. He was sat in his flat, in Croydon!

"Hey Mum, Cokes," he said. He was lolling on his sofa in his dressing gown with a can of lager.

"Why aren't you at Meryl's?" I said.

"Oh, she's been discharged from hospital."

"She's better?" I said.

"Yeah. It seems all she needed was a couple of good nights' sleep and some pills."

"What about Wilfred?"

"Tony's brother and sister stayed on. The roads were cleared, so I offered to come home and lighten the load." He opened a tin of Quality Street, put on his glasses, and started reading the little card with all the different chocolate descriptions.

"Didn't anyone think to tell us?" I said.

"Look at that," he said, ignoring me. "They got rid of the Peanut Cracknel and the Chocolate Toffee Cup... ooh, but there's a couple of new ones!"

"I'm bloody missing everything being stuck 'ere!" grumbled Ethel.

Blazena came in with a beautiful little plate of fresh fruit she'd sliced especially for her, but Ethel turned up her nose saying, "Yer lucky getting Christmas on yer own, Danny. This lot eat *fish* for Christmas lunch. FISH! No turkey, or spuds, or sprouts!"

"Ooh fish, that's an idea. Hey, I might get sushi," Daniel grinned. "And eat it under the Christmas tree with my tin of Quality Street. Remember Coco, you always used to say that would be your dream Christmas lunch!"

Something snapped in me, and I pressed *End call.*

"Ere, get Danny back on the blower," said Ethel. "I want to find out what them new Quality Streets are... What yer doing?"

I had logged onto Ryanair's website.

"'Ere, that's today," she said as she saw me click *departure date* on the 24th December.

"Marika," I called out. "Would you please get Ethel's passport from our room."

A moment later she came through with the passport.

"'Ere, very funny Coco," said Ethel.

She watched me booking her a flight leaving from Bratislava Airport in three hours' time.

"Now 'ang on..." she said.

"What are you doing, Cokes?" said Marika.

"Giving Ethel what she wants... Priority boarding YES. Wheelchair assistance YES. Insurance NO. Car hire NO." I hit *confirm purchase* and then *print* for her boarding pass.

"Right Ethel. We're leaving in ten minutes," I said.

"'Why did yer do that?!" she gasped, her mouth flapping in shock.

"You've moaned all day about being here, in front of me

and Marika and Blazena and Fero. Think of it as my Christmas gift to you."

Ethel stared at me open-mouthed. I went to the guest room and began to pack her suitcase. A few minutes later, she came in.

"I don't think I should go," she said.

"Well, you should have thought of that."

Then Marika came in.

"Coco, is Ethel really going back to London?"

"Yes," I said, zipping up her wash bag and putting it in her case.

"What should I tell my mother?"

"Tell her Ethel wants to be at home with family, her daughter is ill... It's the truth."

I've never seen Ethel lost for words and she watched silently as I fastened the suitcase.

A few minutes later Blazena knocked on the door and came in with some food wrapped up. She wiped tears from her eyes and wished Ethel well with her sick daughter.

"Um... Marika, tell yer mum, thanks for 'avin me," she said in a small voice.

We took the lift down in silence. Marika looked between Ethel and me awkwardly. When we were outside I loaded up her case and brusquely cleaned ice off the car.

When we were on the motorway, I dialled Daniel's mobile number and put my phone on loudspeaker. I told him that Ethel would be arriving at Luton Airport at nine thirty this evening, and that he must pick her up. He started shouting, but I hung up.

We made it to Bratislava Airport in just over forty-five minutes and I pulled into the car park. It was quiet with the most beautiful starry sky.

"Ethel," I said turning to her. "Merry Christmas."

She opened her mouth to say something but thought

better of it and got out. Marika followed and helped her with her case into the airport terminal. Half an hour later Marika came back. I was on my fifth cigarette. All the adrenalin was flowing away and guilt was taking over.

"She went through security and they've got her in a wheelchair to take her on the plane," she said awkwardly.

"We should make sure the plane takes off okay," I said.

We sat smoking in silence until the plane rose above the glass terminal and off into the sky, its lights winking in the darkness.

"Shit, Coco. I can't believe you did that. You stood up to Ethel," said Marika.

"Or did I just turn an old woman away at Christmas?" I said, chewing my lip.

"Depends how you look at it," said Marika. "It's not English Christmas Day until tomorrow. It's still Christmas Eve. And you got her priority boarding."

"She has had it coming for SO long," I said, but I didn't sound convinced.

Dinner was being served when we arrived back at the flat, and Marika's sister Adrianna and her husband Stevko were there.

"Coco! It's wonderful to see you again," said Adrianna, giving me a huge hug. She looked as dark and gorgeous as I remembered her.

"You look great," said Stevko, equally dashing.

We took our seats at the table, where a whole fish had been steamed and beautifully garnished, surrounded by bowls of soup and potato salad. We said a short prayer in Slovak, then Blazena turned her attention to me and started speaking earnestly.

"Did Ethel leave because of falling off the balcony?" translated Marika.

"No," I said.

"Does she hate the Slovak people?"

"Not at all!"

"Was it because the flat isn't good enough, or are we not good enough?" translated Marika again.

I felt very awkward. Blazena began to cry. She wiped her face with the back of her hand. I made Marika tell them the truth, which took several minutes. Afterwards they sat in silence.

"I can't believe we missed meeting Ethel," said Adrianna. "Now I'm more intrigued than ever."

Blazena started making the sign of the cross and muttering darkly. Stevko raised his eyebrows at me.

"She says she is praying for Ethel, a child of the Lord, all alone on Christmas Day," translated Marika. "She says even the innkeeper let Mary and Joseph stay in the stable."

"I hope you told it right," I said.

"I tried to spin it as best I could, but the fact is you did chuck out an old woman at Christmas."

"You know Ethel! You're supposed to be on my side!"

"You asked me to tell them the truth so I told them the truth!"

"Well, if you're in the mood to tell the truth, tell them about quitting your job!" I said.

Adrianna and Stevko looked shocked. I'd forgotten they understood English.

"Damn! Sorry Marika!"

"You quit your job?" said Adrianna, and then repeated it in Slovak.

Suddenly all hell broke loose. Blazena slammed her fist down on the table and started shouting at Marika, her face turning purple. Marika started shouting back in Slovak. Blazena then leapt up and lunged at Marika, but being a large woman, didn't account for her girth and as she lunged, she tipped the whole table towards me and Fero. The huge fish slid off the plate and into my lap. Glasses, bowls and plates crashed to the floor, slopping creamy soup and potato salad over everything. Marika screamed and ran out, followed by Blazena. Adrianna and Stevko went after them and I sat in shock with a lap full of fish.

Fero leant over and topped up the glass I still had in my hand.

"Nazdravie!" he grinned and downed his brandy in one.

Two hours have passed and the row, which I can't understand, is still raging. I've shut myself in the bedroom with Rocco, who is terrified.

Rosencrantz just sent a text saying;

MERRY XMAS MUM. LOVE U - UR WONDERFUL - THANX FOR MY KINDLE !

And Daniel has sent a text saying;

PICKED UP MUM AT LUTON. SHE'S VERY UPSET. YOU WENT TOO FAR THIS TIME - DANIEL

Rocco is curled up on my chest with his head tucked under my chin. Thank God dogs don't judge us.

Merry Christmas, Coco x

Wednesday 29th December 20.18
TO: chris@christophercheshire.com

Marika finally came to the bedroom in the early hours of Christmas Day and shook me awake.

"I'm still mad at you but I need you to drive," she hissed. "I'm not staying a moment longer in the same place as my mother."

"It's three in the morning," I said.

"I don't care. We're leaving!"

I quickly gathered my things together. Fero was asleep on an armchair in the living room, which still had the Christmas dinner strewn across the carpet. Blazena had locked herself in the bathroom with her rosary beads. Adrianna and Stevko came down with us in the lift.

"We're leaving too," said Stevko. "I nearly dislocated my shoulder pulling Blazena off Marika."

"What was she doing?" I said.

"Beating me with a Bible," said Marika, without humour.

"I'm sorry," I said. "I ruined your Christmas."

"No you didn't," grinned Adrianna. "Something always sets Mum off... Last year it was because Fero forgot to buy the tartare sauce."

"So she slapped him round the head with the fish," said Stevko.

"I don't think Marika will ever speak to me again," I said, as she stalked off into the car park.

Stevko hugged me and ruffled Rocco's tired little head. Adrianna hugged me too.

"Come back when the weather is nice," she said. "We'll go to the house again."

I drove slowly, in silence, in the pitch black and snow, Marika barking directions at me with Rocco on her lap. When the snow got too thick and driving became terrible, we stopped at a petrol station for coffee.

"I'm sorry," I said. "I'm really, really sorry."

"My mother was bound to find out some time. It just might have been better over the phone," said Marika.

"She certainly went for you," I said.

"She's a crazy bitch, she really got me with that Bible," said Marika, rubbing her head bitterly. "But it's *all* okay, she'll go to confession on Sunday, slip the priest a euro and in the eyes of God everything is forgiven."

"Where are we headed?" I said.

"Somewhere that makes me happy."

We stayed in the petrol station until the sun came up over the hills. A snowplough had been past a few times, so the rest of the journey was smooth.

We entered Bratislava by a motorway bridge over the Danube. There's something about arriving in a city just before the sun comes up. The roads are empty, the day feels new. You feel as if it all belongs to you.

Marika guided us to a large boat moored by the Danube. It had three decks of white railings and a light shone by the entrance.

"What's this?" I said.

"Our hotel."

It was a botel, rather than a hotel. A small pleasure cruiser, now permanently tethered to the bank of the Danube, which whipped past with surprising ferocity. The botel is an old haunt of Marika's; she used to stay there a lot as a teenager when she came clubbing in Bratislava.

The woman at reception looked a little surprised to see us when we staggered in just after six in the morning. She hurriedly swallowed the last of her breakfast and fumbled on a board covered in keys to allocate us a room each. Even Rocco was welcome. I'd thought I might have to smuggle him in, hidden in my handbag.

The last few days have been heaven, wandering through

Bratislava. The old town is full of elegant buildings painted in bright pastel colours, like rows of sumptuous cakes decorated in smooth royal icing.

We've done the same thing every day. Wake up late, eat a huge breakfast and then walk to the main square in the old town and choose a café, where we sit drinking endless cups of coffee and smoking.

Two days passed before I realised we hadn't really said much to one another. We were in Café Mayer, which has the air of a 17th-century French salon film: all pink and decadent with a soaring ceiling.

"Why do we do it?" I said.

"Do what?" said Marika.

"Christmas..."

"Well, we don't really have a choice."

"We do! Yet we spend an inordinate amount of time preparing events for people we wouldn't spend ten minutes with any other day of the year."

We carried on smoking for a bit.

"You know, you can stay with me," I said, "if you need to rent your flat out."

Marika smiled. "Thanks... I don't know what I'm going to do about a job."

"Well, you're not going to panic," I said. "You can stay as long as you need to."

"Maybe I could start a company offering Christmas breaks, like what we're doing now," said Marika.

"'What? The anti-Christmas package deal?" I said.

"Yes, no relations or acquaintances allowed. Just time spent relaxing, with friends."

Rocco barked.

"And pets, of course," said Marika.

"We've done nothing for the last few days and it's been

the best Christmas since... well, since Rosencrantz was little," I said.

We watched the empty square as snow began to fall.

"Come on, let's do a bit more nothing," said Marika. "We've got to get back to the real world soon," and she ordered us more cake and coffee.

Thursday 30th December 14.08
TO: chris@christophercheshire.com

On our last night in Bratislava we got dressed up and went to the UFO. It's a huge circular restaurant which sits high above Bratislava on top of a bridge. The waiter, at first, said we couldn't come in with a dog, but I pretended I was the wife of the British Ambassador and Marika pulled out her Slovak I.D. card and pretended she was the sister of Dara Rolincova (a famous singer in Slovakia who shares her surname).

"Here's to 2011 being the most incredible year," said Marika, when we were sat looking out over a panoramic view of the city.

"Where we move forward successfully, you away from teaching," I said.

"And you away from Adam," said Marika. "You'll have to get over him sometime, Cokes, so better to do it now than waste more of your life."

I took a deep breath and we toasted the future. We're about to start the long drive home. We should be back tomorrow afternoon, will you be back from the Ice Hotel?

Coco x

Friday 31st December 15.43
TO: chris@christophercheshire.com

Me and Marika are home. We're going to have a sleep and then do you want to come over and bring in the New Year?

P.S You'll also need to bring some booze.

JANUARY 2011

Monday 3rd January 08.28
TO: angie.langford@thebmxliteraryagency.biz

Happy New Year! I'm full of beans at the thought of a fresh start, new challenges, and moving forward. I spent New Year's Eve with Chris and Marika, and we agreed to make big changes to our lives.

Chris had a rather spiritual Christmas at the Ice Hotel. He was deeply moved by the Northern Lights, which appeared several times during his stay. On his last night, he saw a vivid image of Judi Dench's face amongst the aurora. He's convinced this means great things are in his future as a theatre director.

On New Year's Eve, we stayed in and watched the movie *In Her Shoes* with Cameron Diaz and Toni Collette. This has inspired Marika to change career direction completely, and become a dog walker. She's moving into my spare room and is out now tramping the streets of Marylebone distributing leaflets.

I am going to channel all my energy into forgetting about

Adam, and concentrate on my career and the launch of *Agent Fergie*. This year is all about moving forward!

Coco x

Monday 3rd January 09.11
TO: chris@christophercheshire.com

I was putting down an old sheet of newspaper for Rocco to pee on, when I noticed this article:

LOCAL MAN CHARGED WITH FRAUD. Metropolitan Police last night arrested and charged an NW1 resident in connection to a £200,000 business fraud. Police questioned Adam Rickard, 38, of Baker Street for several hours before releasing him on bail, pending a court appearance. The fraud pertains to an eleven-month period Mr. Rickard spent working at XYZ Event Management as a Health & Safety Officer.

The article is from *The Marylebone Comet*, dated November 17th last year — the same time Adam ended our relationship.

Monday 3rd January 11.12
TO: chris@christophercheshire.com

I have more news. Rosencrantz popped in on his way to an audition and found me staring at the newspaper article.

"Jeez Mum, this is huge!" he said.

I told him I had been trying Adam's phone number, but it seems to be disconnected.

"You want me to help you find him?" offered Rosencrantz.

"What about your audition?" I said.

"I can be late," he said, taking off his coat and booting up my laptop. "It's only for a corporate video about the dangers of asbestos inhalation..."

It took Rosencrantz a mere thirty-seven minutes to track down Adam's whereabouts. He followed Adam's daughter Holly on Twitter. She's on a gap year in America. (A gap from what? The last I heard she was doing a two-week cake decorating course at Watford College.) Anyway, it seems money talks and when we suggested paying her a hundred pounds via PayPal, she sang like a canary.

I stood over Rosencrantz's shoulder whilst we waited for Holly to direct message the address.

"Is this a good idea, Mum?" he said. "What if Adam is guilty? He dumped you, and he's guilty?"

"I can't imagine Adam would steal two hundred thousand pounds."

"Spoken like a true naive woman."

"I'm not naive!"

"You thought butter wouldn't melt in Dad's mouth, then you caught him in bed with his mouth..."

"Rosencrantz!"

"Just saying..."

"No. I have to go and see him. I need to talk to him, if only to get closure."

"Oh I see," said Rosencrantz. "That's what you're calling

it, *closure*. Well, don't get carried away and let him put his closure in your mouth."

"Rosencrantz! I'm not one of your friends you can talk to that way," I said.

Then there was a little plinking noise as Holly's message came through.

"Hurry, open it!" I said.

Rosencrantz clicked on the message, and the following address popped up:

27 The Street
Rochester
Kent
ME1 6BV

"What? What's he doing in *Rochester*?" I said.

"Where is Rochester?" asked Rosencrantz.

"Couple of hours outside London... Why would he be there?"

"Holly says she would be willing to give you a full breakdown of her father's movements for another two hundred," said Rosencrantz, reading off the screen.

"She's a money-grubbing little minx," I said. "But I'll bear it in mind. First, I'm going to drive to Rochester. Attempt the element of surprise. Can you look after Rocco?"

He was curled up asleep on Rosencrantz's lap.

"Yes, my asbestos inhalation role can wait! And Mum..."

"What?"

"Don't do anything stupid."

Rocco opened one little eye, as if in agreement with Rosencrantz. I just nodded and grabbed the car keys.

By some miracle, I've cracked how to work the built-in GPS screen in the Land Cruiser, but I'm stuck in a long line of traffic on the M25.

Ooh, the traffic is moving, better go...

Tuesday 4th January 10.12
TO: chris@christophercheshire.com

I made it to Rochester by lunchtime. It was a world away from London with a cobbled high street and several antique showrooms. An old man with a twirly moustache doffed his Panama as I passed. How did Adam end up here?

I found the address, a terraced house on a lane running parallel to the high street. Smoke curled from a chimney as I opened the gate. A low shiny black door confronted me at the end of the path. My heart climbed into my throat as I reached out for the huge knocker, but the door opened and there stood Adam.

There was an awkward silence. It went on and on, and we just stared at each other. He was thinner with big bags under his eyes, but my heart skipped along a little faster at the sight of him. I finally blurted out, "So, Rochester. It's quite historical."

"Yeah," said Adam. "I haven't been to the castle yet."

Then I punched him in the face.

"Ahhh!" he yelled, clutching at his face with one wide, shocked eye showing. "What did you do that for?"

"What do you think? For everything. For not telling me!" I shouted. "And now you've busted my hand..."

"Your hand, what about my face? And how did you find me?"

"Holly. I bribed her with a hundred quid."

"Bloody hell! Why would she do that?" he said.

I wanted to say "Because she's a conniving, lazy daughter," but I kept my mouth shut.

"Are you going to invite me in?" I said.

"Are you gonna punch me again?" he said, checking his lip for blood.

"I haven't decided yet..."

He regarded me for a minute, and then led me through a low hallway to a sitting room. It was very frilly and flowery with pictures of cats in teacups and a couple of those Anne Geddes babies dressed up as bumble bees.

"Is this your house?"

"Why would it be my house?" he said.

"I don't know. It seems I don't know anything about you. Is your name really Adam?"

"The house belongs to Serena, my boss from my old job in the Civil Service."

"I thought Serena was a lesbian?" I said.

"She is," he said, clearing some papers off a chintz sofa so I could sit. "Should she have pictures of Ellen and KD Lang?"

"No... Is she here?"

"No, she's on holiday with her girlfriend."

I looked around again and then sat down.

"Adam. What's going on?" I said. "Please."

Over coffee, he told me everything. Last summer his employer, XYZ Event Management, hired an outside company to do a cost effectiveness audit. The company discovered that two hundred thousand pounds was missing. The money had been siphoned off through hundreds of fake taxi invoices.

On November 16th last year, he was called into his boss' office where three police officers from the Fraud Squad were waiting. They told him he was being arrested for fraud.

Adam thought at first that it was a joke. Then the Senior Officer produced bank statements from a savings account in Adam's name. The statements showed that over a period of eleven months, £200,000 had been claimed through fake taxi invoices in Adam's name.

"But that's a huge amount for taxi journeys?" I said.

"It's a huge swanky events company. Every day scores of employees are cruising round London in taxis," he said. "The fake invoices were for a few hundred pounds every day. The money was paid into my savings account, then every day withdrawn from a cash machine."

"How did you not know this was happening to your bank account?" I asked.

"It was an old savings account I never check. I thought it only had a few quid in it. All I can think is that someone at the company stole my identity."

"How? Even I don't know your PIN numbers."

Adam paused.

"What, Adam?"

"Do you remember when I first got the job and I left my wallet at the office over the weekend?"

"Yes, but it was still there on the Monday when you went back to work."

"I never told you, but I had all of my PIN numbers and internet banking codes written on bits of paper in my wallet. This whole fraud thing started shortly after I left my wallet at work."

"So you think another work colleague has done this?"

"It must be."

"Who?"

"I don't know. It's an open plan office with a hundred employees. They forged my name on the invoices. They accessed the bank account online at the office. They even ordered a new cash card in my name."

"What about the cash machine where the money was withdrawn? Don't they have cameras?"

"Whoever it was located an old cash machine without a camera. It also happens to be on my daily route to work."

"What's happening now?" I said.

"I've been charged, and I'm on bail for a court appearance later in February."

"Have you got anyone representing you?"

"Yes."

"And what does he or she say?"

"He keeps saying he's not having much luck..."

"That doesn't sound good enough," I said.

I went to the window. It was already starting to get dark. Adam got up and turned on the light. We both winced at the brightness.

"Why? Why didn't you tell me?" I said.

"I wanted to protect you. You've been building your dream. *Agent Fergie* is coming out soon, and I know it's going to be huge. Daniel almost derailed your career when you split up. I didn't want to do that to you again. You have an amazing future."

"Yeah well, an amazing future isn't much fun without an amazing guy to share it with," I said.

"So I'm amazing enough for you to smack in the gob?" he said.

Under the light, I could see his face was swelling up. I took him through to Serena's kitchen where I found some ice and wrapped it in a tea towel. I pressed it gently on the bruise forming under his eye.

"I have to ask you this," I said. "And I need to hear the truth. Did you do it? Did you steal the money?"

"No," said Adam. "No, I didn't do it."

There was something in his eyes; I knew he was telling the truth. I took a deep breath.

"Okay," I said. "I believe you. Now you need to get your things together. You're coming home."

It was the first time I ever saw Adam cry and I didn't think any less of him for it. I held him for a long time, and then he went to kiss me. I remembered what Rosencrantz said and started packing his suitcase, which was on the floor by the sofa. Then we drove home.

I didn't say much during the journey. Part of me was overjoyed, part in a blind panic thinking, *"What happens now?"*

It was snowing again when we arrived back in London. When we turned the corner to my road, I could see a huge van in the driveway, its back doors open and jutting out onto the pavement. I parked by the kerb as Oscar emerged from the van heaving a giant mattress.

"Hello, Mrs P," he smiled, resting the edge of the mattress to catch his breath.

"What's going on?" I asked, getting out of the car.

"We're helping Marika move her stuff in," he said.

A muffled voice came from the back of the van saying, "Why have you stopped, bitch?"

Wayne appeared round the other side of the mattress lugging a headboard.

"Hello Mrs P!" he said.

Then Adam got out of the car. The boys looked him up and down with a practised glance, like scanning a bar code. I almost heard the beep as they registered that Adam is hot.

"Is this...?" whispered Oscar.

"Yeah, it is. Hi, I'm Adam," said Adam, holding out his hand.

Oscar shook it, his fair complexion turning red.

"Hello," said Wayne proffering his hand. "And here I

was, thinking there was no one around who could work an Allen key."

Poor Adam didn't know how to respond to that. Rosencrantz and Marika emerged from the house, followed by Rocco who came running up, yipping and yapping through the snow. Their faces lit up when they saw me. When they saw Adam, they went quiet.

Rosencrantz stopped for a moment than rushed forward and gave him a big hug. There were tears in his eyes.

"Are you okay?" he said.

Adam nodded. Marika held back.

"I'll need an explanation before I start hugging," she said.

"It's okay," said Adam. "If I can come inside, I'll tell you what's going on."

An hour and a couple of bottles of red wine later, Adam finished telling the story. I had quietly bustled around in the background as he talked, making salad, heating up a couple of frozen pizzas and trying to organise my thoughts about Adam being back in my life.

"Jeez," said Rosencrantz. "I'm so sorry."

He poured Adam more wine.

"Hang on, hang on," said Marika. "Isn't your mortgage around two hundred grand?"

"Marika!" I shrieked, as I used a pizza wheel to divide a deep crust pepperoni.

"What? You've got to think of these things, Coco," she said, regarding Adam warily.

"I promise," said Adam, "I didn't take this money."

"Would you be willing to take a lie detector test?" asked Marika.

"Ooh, this is like the Jeremy Kyle Show," said Wayne.

I put the pizzas down on the middle of the table and gave him a look.

"Sorry Mrs P. I appreciate this is serious."

"It is serious," I said.

"I just think it would eliminate any doubt," said Marika. "It's the doubt that will eat away at you, Coco, if you take him back."

"But he left Mum to protect her," said Rosencrantz.

I could see Adam looking round at everyone's faces.

"But he jumped in the car back here pretty quickly," said Marika.

"I've only just met you, and you seem cool to me," said Oscar.

"And you got to smack him in the gob," said Wayne, indicating the bruise on Adam's face.

"Hey, hey, hey," I said. "I appreciate everyone's opinion but this is my house and I have decided Adam is going to be here with me."

"What does that mean? 'Be here'?" said Marika.

"It means that I'm not asking for anyone's permission. Adam is here. So get used to it."

"And what about me?" said Marika.

"You're welcome here too, for however long you need. That hasn't changed." I reached out and squeezed her hand.

"If I found someone who'd do a lie detector test, would you take it?" said Marika to Adam.

"Yes, I would take it," he said seriously.

There was a very awkward moment of silence.

"Okay," she said.

She held out her glass to Adam. He picked his up and they clinked.

"Can we eat now?" pleaded Rosencrantz.

"Yes, dig in," I said.

"Thank God for that," said Wayne as everyone reached

for the pizza. "I could eat a nun's arse through the convent railings."

After pizza, the boys and Adam helped Marika move the rest of her stuff up to the spare room. I went on a mission for spare blankets, unsure of what the sleeping arrangements would be. I was dying to climb into bed with Adam, but a little faint voice in my head was saying I should play hard to get. I decided to have a bath and hope the voice would get a bit louder. When I came out an hour later, all clean and moisturised in a towel, Adam wasn't in my room. I went and knocked on the spare room door. Marika, Wayne, and Oscar were all trying to put her bed back together.

"Sorry, love. I thought Adam might be in here?" I said.

"We haven't seen him since we emptied the van," said Marika, who was sifting through a pile of screws strewn over the carpet.

"If you see Rosencrantz, can you tell him it's not a Svelvik, it's a Leirvik," said Wayne.

"What?"

"Marika's bed. Rosencrantz is printing off the instructions from the Ikea website," said Oscar.

Marika got up from her sifting and came over.

"Look. I'm sorry, Coco, if I gave Adam a hard time," she said. "You know I like him a lot, but I just can't see you get hurt. Do you really think he's innocent?"

"Yes. I do."

"Okay," she said. "Okay... I'm not going to tell you how to live your life. Look at mine. I just walked out of one of the most stable careers during a recession, and now I'm on your floor with my life and my bed in bits."

"Your bed won't be in bits for long," said Oscar. "It'll be quick work with the Allen key."

"If only you could fix everything in life with an Allen key," said Wayne whimsically.

I kissed Marika goodnight and told the boys where the blankets were if they wanted to sleep on the sofas downstairs.

"Thanks Mrs P," they both trilled.

I ran into Rosencrantz coming out of my office.

"I think it's great you're taking Adam back," he said. "You need each other."

"I haven't taken him back," I said.

"Course you have," he grinned. "Just hold off shagging him for one night."

"I beg your pardon!"

"Come on Mum. He's sex on legs. Everyone in this house has been captivated by him."

"Apart from Marika," I said.

"She'll come round... Night, Mum," he grinned, giving me a hug.

When I came downstairs all the lights were off, but the door to the terrace was ajar. Adam was sitting outside in one of the huge winter coats from the hall. I pulled one on too, and went and joined him.

"Rocco's keeping me warm here," he grinned.

A little pink tongue emerged from the opening of his coat, licking Adam's neck. I sat down beside him and lit a cigarette. It was freezing but very clear and the moonlight sparkled on the snow.

"How come you got a dog?" he said, as Rocco's little head popped out of the coat.

"He was a gift from the boys, because I was so..." I held back from saying, "devastated".

After weeks of being devastated, I was suddenly happy again. Should I be? Am I just ignoring the last two months?

"I never thought I'd come back here," said Adam,

breaking the silence. "It was such a terrible feeling." He put his arm around me. "I can sleep on the sofa, if you're not ready?"

I looked into his eyes. *Willpower, must have willpower...* I thought.

"Both the sofas are occupied," I said. "Unless you want to sleep with Wayne and Oscar. Who I'm sure would be delighted."

"What about the spare room?"

"Well, that's now Marika's room."

"The other spare room?"

"You mean my office? It's not a bedroom."

"So there's only your bed free?"

I nodded.

We came inside, Adam carrying Rocco. I locked the doors and he slung his arm over my shoulder as we came upstairs. He put Rocco down on the bed and the little dog bustled about digging around in the covers until he'd burrowed under. Adam went for a shower and came back wearing just a pair of shorts. He was much thinner but his athletic frame held it well.

"Maybe we could just cuddle tonight?" I said.

"Of course," he said pulling back the covers and climbing in.

I got in on my side, shuffled over to him and lay my head on his chest. Rocco curled up in the crook between us. I flicked off the light and we all lay there in the dark: warm, cosy and softly breathing together.

"I could go to prison, Coco," said Adam, breaking the silence.

"No, you won't," I said. "I'll make sure of it."

I really hoped I was right.

Thursday 6th January 14.52
TO: chris@christophercheshire.com

Adam had to report to Marylebone Police Station today, as per his bail conditions, to say he will now be living here. The policewoman on the front desk was very friendly. He had to fill out some forms, and I had to sign that I would inform them if he decides to abscond and leave the country.

Reading the paperwork and seeing the charges in black and white was horrifying. I cannot imagine what Adam is going through.

On the upside, his mug shot is very flattering, so much so that Rosencrantz asked Adam if he knew the name of the police photographer because he needs some new acting head shots.

Friday 7th January 10.12
TO: chris@christophercheshire.com

I was outside on the front door step, putting out the green recycling bin for the council, when Mr and Mrs Cohen came out of their front door with their recycling bin. I said "Hello" as Mrs Cohen peered over the low wall. I could see a satisfied look on her face that they had outdone me again.

"Morning Mrs Pinchard," said Mr. Cohen.

"Morning," I said.

I went to go back indoors when Mrs Cohen started talking. She's usually mute with a suspicious expression on her beaky face.

"Mrs Pinchard, are you planning on getting that guttering fixed?"

"What guttering?" I said.

"On the back of your house."

"Yes,'" I smiled, and went to go indoors.

"Could you be a bit more specific? Only we're worried about the structural damage on the brickwork."

"Soon," I said, and I went to go back in again.

"It's just your brickwork is connected to our brickwork and we'd hate for it to lower the value of the terrace."

"Are you thinking of moving?" I asked hopefully.

"Oh no," said Mr. Cohen. "It's just one of those things that if it goes unchecked it could lead to bigger problems."

I turned back to face them.

"I'm having it fixed as soon as possible. The value of the terrace will remain intact."

We heard a police siren and all turned to look at the end of the road. Six police cars appeared at high speed, fanning out into Steeplejack Mews. The cars had barely halted, when eighteen police officers all jumped out and congregated at the base of the steps.

"We haven't mixed any of our glass and plastics," said Mrs Cohen.

A tall police officer with steel grey hair said,

"Mrs Pinchard?"

"Yes?"

"We have a warrant to search your house."

The rest of the police officers regarded me from under their helmets. The Cohens looked shocked. In fact, Mrs Cohen looked like a piece of guttering had been shoved somewhere delicate.

"A warrant?"

"Yes, as part of our ongoing criminal investigation into Mr Rickard."

My heart sank.

"Do have any choice in the matter?" I enquired.

"Not with a warrant," said Mr Cohen.

The officer turned to look at the Cohens.

"They're my neighbours — who were just going," I said.

They went back inside goggle-eyed, and I led the police officers indoors.

Myself, Marika and Adam (both of whom were still in their pyjamas) were herded together and asked to wait in the kitchen under the watchful eyes of two junior police officers, a man and a woman.

The remaining officers spread out, pulling on latex gloves to comb through the house.

I have just been told my phone and laptop are being seized, so I'll have to sign off now. Unless they take it too, you can reach me on the landline...

Monday 17th January 14.12
TO: chris@christophercheshire.com

A plain-clothes officer returned my computer and iPhone at six o'clock this morning in a large clear plastic sack. He said that it was "clean". I detected a tinge of disappointment in his voice, just like the police were disappointed after they searched the house. I think they were hoping to find the £200,000 stuffed in a cupboard. As we were up early, we took Rocco for a walk. We were walking back along Marylebone High Street, when we saw posters for *Agent Fergie*. Proper posters in bus shelters of the book cover with my name on! Of course, me being the author, I am the last to know. I stood there, unable to contain my excitement.

"Oh babe, that's amazing," said Adam, putting his arm around me and giving me a big kiss.

I pulled out my phone and made Adam take pictures of me beside it.

"It's going to be out on February the twenty-second," I said, reading the writing on the bottom of the poster.

"That's the day of my first court hearing," said Adam. And we came back to earth with a crash.

I'm thinking we should fire his legal representation. The bloke he's got looks more like a harassed social worker, and seems a very ineffective and negative man.

Can I take you up on the offer to meet with your father's new lawyer? We need some clout.

Tuesday 18th January 17.10
TO: marikarolincova@hotmail.co.uk

We went to meet a lawyer at Spencer & Spencer today. Chris recommended her to us, or I should say Chris recommended us to her. She recently got a friend of his father off on a huge embezzlement charge.

Adam was very nervous in the black cab as we nudged along Charing Cross Road in the rain.

"What if she takes one look at me and says 'no'?" he said.

"She won't," I said.

"Does she know about my case?"

"Yes, and she says she wants a challenge."

"Great Coco, great..."

"I didn't mean it like that," I said. "She's the best of the best."

He ran a finger under the collar of his new shirt. I had rushed out and bought it this morning from Marks & Spencer and I'd got him a size too small.

"Coco! You've left the bloody piece of plastic in this!" he moaned, "and a pin!"

"Sorry," I said. I gently removed the pin and eased out the stiff plastic strip. "It's going to be fine..."

"It's going be expensive," said Natasha Hamilton QC, an attractive yet chilly brunette in her late thirties.

We sat across from her at her huge desk. The overcast day and the dark wood paneling made the large office close in on us. Her eyes had a steely resolve and an eager interest in what we were saying, especially when Adam said how much money he had been accused of stealing. She listened as he outlined what had happened so far, occasionally flicking through the case file that had been sent over by the previous law firm.

There was a silence when Adam finished. She regarded us for a long X-Factor moment.

"With the timeframe given," she said, "I'd have to put a team onto this fast, to go through the forensic evidence."

"Forensic?" I said. "This isn't a murder enquiry."

"What I mean is we'll have to request information from Mr Rickard's previous employer, XYZ Event Management: computer records, invoices, data, etc. Comb our way through it, and build a defence."

"What happens if we lose?" I said.

"The minimum sentence would be four years in prison," she said casually.

"Four years!" I said. "People do far worse and get far less."

"The sentencing guidelines for fraud are primarily based on the amount of money involved," said Natasha. "Anything under seventeen thousand pounds would more likely result in a fine or community service, but this is a substantial amount. The court will also take into account adverse effect. I understand XYZ Event Management's exposure to this loss of money has resulted in four redundancies."

"Adam was fired too," I said. "He didn't get any redundancy money."

"Coco, I told you. I'm screwed," said Adam. "You need to understand this, and stop going on about chicken stew."

"Chicken stew?" said Natasha.

"It's chicken soup," I said. "*Chicken Soup For The Soul*. It's a positive thinking book. I think a lot can be achieved through positive thinking."

Natasha looked alarmed. Positive thinking books seemed be at odds with billable hours.

"Look," said Natasha with a confident smile. "You need strong, robust legal representation, which we can provide. In cases such as these, we often find something in the computer records: an error, a data flaw. A high proportion of these cases are thrown out by the judge."

"The case is going to court on February the twenty-second," I said. "Do you think you have enough time?"

"The first thing I would recommend is filing a motion for an extension. As soon as we receive your retainer I would be able to do this."

"How much is your retainer?"

"Five thousand pounds," she said, without blinking.

After the meeting, we found a crowded Starbucks on The Strand, and squeezed onto two chairs in the window with our lattes. The rain was now hammering down and London scurried past; a blur of red buses and black-clad commuters under umbrellas, many of which were turning in on themselves in the wind. Why do the British always invest in crap umbrellas? It rains constantly and not a day goes by where I see a paper thin little umbrella hopelessly broken and dumped in the bin.

"Five grand just as a retainer!" said Adam. "Let's keep the cheap lawyer and I'll risk doing the time. Maybe I can tell him about this forensic evidence thing, maybe he could find a technical error."

He looked beaten and defeated. The window was fogging up with his resigned breathing.

"Your lawyer doesn't look like he could find his arsehole with both hands," I said. "And what do you mean, 'risk doing the time'?!"

"Four years isn't long."

"Four years isn't long? What about the rest of your life?" I said. "Where will you work with a record?"

"I don't have the money for a big lawyer," he said. "End of."

"But she's brilliant. Chris said his father's friend was as guilty as hell, and she won him the case."

"Oh so you think I'm guilty now?" said Adam.

"No, but I think we should hire Natasha, who will prove your innocence. I've got some savings, and when *Agent Fergie* is published I get the rest of my advance."

"No!" he said. "No, you are not doing that."

"But you're my..."

"NO!"

"OK. What about Legal Aid?" I said.

"I am not scrounging off the state!"

"So you're going to be the proudest prisoner on the block, are you?"

He stared shamefully at the foggy window.

"I'm sorry. I didn't mean that," I said.

"Why don't you just go, Coco? Don't get involved in all this."

"I'm involved whether you like it or not. Don't forget I have to tell them if you leave; your bail conditions depend on you living with me."

"Fuck! I hate this!" shouted Adam.

I grabbed his hand.

"That meeting was incredible. Natasha wants to defend you, can't you see that? She's the key to all this. We just need to work out the finances."

Adam gave a resigned smile.

"You have to phone Angie and tell her you're getting involved with all this," he said.

"Angie can wait a bit longer," I said.

I then suggested going to see a film in Leicester Square to try to cheer us up, but when we got to The Odeon there was only *The Lovely Bones* or *Precious* playing. Neither of which I thought would have us rolling in the aisles, so we came home.

Thursday 20th January 22.13
TO: chris@christophercheshire.com

We've made enquiries about legal aid for Adam's case, and discovered it could help his eligibility if he were claiming unemployment benefits. So, this afternoon we went to the JobCentre Plus office round the corner.

Angie phoned as we were waiting to see an advisor.

"Why haven't you been returning my calls?" she said impatiently.

"I can't talk right now," I whispered. There was an

imposing atmosphere in the huge open plan office and 'NO MOBILE PHONES' was plastered all over the walls.

"I've had the publishing house on the phone three times today. They want to arrange a load of interviews and promotion," she said.

"Look, I've got to go," I said.

"Coco!"

"Sorry, I'll call you back."

I hung up as a fierce little Indian lady called Rajdai was looming over us.

"Why are you just sitting there?" demanded. "Do a job search whilst you're waiting."

She pointed to a touchscreen computer terminal embedded into a steel box screwed to the floor.

"Hello. We're only here to ask some questions," I said.

"Are either of you working right now?" she said.

We looked at each other.

"Um no. Not right now," said Adam. "I need to ask about legal..."

"Do you want to claim benefits?" she said.

"I think so," said Adam.

"If you want to claim benefits you need to be available to work and that means you need to be doing a job search," she said.

"We just want to ask..."

"Job search," she snapped, as if I were stupid.

We trudged over guiltily under her malevolent gaze to the greasy computer screens, which excitedly stated, with pictures of happy smiling job hunters, that we could 'SEARCH FOR ANY JOB!'

I grinned at Rajdai, who was still hawking us, and rebelliously typed in *Lap dancer, London*.

Amazingly six adverts came up, plus one for *Webcam*

Stripper stating that it's '*a job with a difference... a work from home vacancy.*'

The terminal made a buzzing, rattling noise and four slips of paper shot out. Rajdai suddenly appeared from behind a pillar and grabbed them.

"Hang on!" I said, but she ushered us over to her desk.

"Is it a joint claim?" she said.

"I don't know," I said. "We just want to..."

"Are you single, married, cohabiting?" she said impatiently.

"We're co-habiting, but look, I want to ask..." began Adam, but she cut him off again.

"When did you last work?"

"Can you please listen to me?" said Adam.

"No sir, you need to listen to me," she said. "I'm trying to work out how I can help you."

"I haven't worked for several months, but the situations is..."

"Right, I'll need you to meet with one of my colleagues upstairs," she said sternly.

We made one last attempt to ask her about legal aid but she said all our questions would be answered on the sixth floor.

We trudged up six flights, helping a young girl with a buggy on the way, and took a seat in another open plan office identical to the one below. There were huge photographs on the wall of smiling happy job hunters laughing with Job Centre Advisors. It was all very different to when Daniel and myself first graduated from university and we lined up at the grimy Labour Exchange on Aberystwyth seafront. Its windows were smeared with the spray from the sea, and it had a scuffed parquet floor.

The next advisor we saw was a pale fleshy girl with an

only wish you'd told me earlier."

"I'm sorry. I didn't know what to do."

"Please, keep me posted."

"Okay, thanks," I said and she hung up.

Adam was dangerously gloomy when we got home. We ___ drenched from the rain, so he went up to have a ___ ___er. I waited until I could hear the water running then ___ two phone calls. The first to an estate agent, who said ___ subject to a viewing, I could rent it out the house for ___al thousand pounds a month. Then I arranged a ___fer of five grand from my savings account and hired ___ha as Adam's lawyer.

___arika found me staring at the laptop. I took a deep ___ and told her what I'd done. Without blinking, she ___ could all move to her two-bedroom flat and split the ___ge.

___ks like we're moving.

24th January 12.12

@christophercheshire.com

___ called on Skype. I haven't seen her since she was ___ but she looked her old self, apart from a new

___u moving house, Coco?" she trilled excitedly.

___did you know?" I said. "The Estate Agent only ___nty minutes ago."

___ Alerts!" she said. "I've got one set up for almost ___you, Daniel, Rosencrantz, David Essex. Steeple-___ust pinged up and I knew I had to call you."

---

annoying singsong customer service voice, and an irritatingly spelt name: Karliegh.

After taking our slips of paper and tapping in our National Insurance numbers she waddled off to the printer and returned with some forms.

"Right Mr Rickard," she said. "I can see you were a civil servant? And you worked in the private sector."

"Yes," said Adam. "But you've spelt civil servant with an 's'," he said, showing her the form which read, 'sivil servant'."

"That is how you spell it, sir," she said with the devastating confidence of ignorance.

"No, it isn't," said Adam. "It's spelt with a 'c'."

She huffed around and changed it, then set her sights on me.

"I see you, madam, are a... a... lap dancer?"

Her voice trailed off as she looked up, taking in my jeans and jumper, and the glasses on top of my head.

"You may have to widen your job search," she said diplomatically.

I tried to explain that I wasn't really a lap dancer, but she seemed to think I was some middle-aged sex worker in denial, and even opened her drawer and took out a leaflet entitled *Breaking The Cycle: Help For Middle-Aged Sex Workers*.

"Stop! I just want to know about benefits in relation to claiming legal aid!" shouted Adam. "How difficult is it for you people to listen?"

"'*You people*?'" echoed Karliegh. "Are you talking about white people? Because you need to know, we have a zero tolerance racism policy. If you continue to racially abuse me, I may have to terminate the interview."

"I meant you people in this job centre!" he raged, "Are you all bloody morons?"

Quick as a flash a huge security guard was at Adam's shoulder.

"You need to cool it, bro," he said.

"I'm not your bro!" shouted Adam. "This woman is saying I'm a racist and my girlfriend is a lap dancer. I'm not a racist!"

The security guard gave me the once over, a little like a farmer admires a cow with a good milk yield.

"And I'm not a lap dancer!" I said.

"Don't you give her that look," said Adam, jumping out of his seat.

"It's okay," I soothed, pushing Adam back down.

A silence had fallen over the office and I could see scared faces from the advisors and a few looks of excitement from the other claimants. Adam was still glowering at the security guard.

"You need to cool down... *sir*," said the security guard.

Karliegh was now taking a keen interest in our forms.

"I see here you both own property in the area. Do you have a mortgage?" she said icily.

I could see a vein beginning to pulse in Adam's head. I told her that Adam had a mortgage and that I owned my house.

"You own a house on Steeplejack Mews?" she said accusingly.

"Yes," I said.

The security guard whistled and raised his eyebrows provocatively at Adam.

"Then I might suggest you start using your property for income, and perhaps leave claiming benefits for those who really need them," she said.

"She didn't even want to claim anything!" growled Adam.

"Come on, let's leave. Now!" I said.

As we scuttled out of JobCentre Plus, en
was an understatement.

I am not sure why they added the 'plus'. It
same desperate people clinging on to life as
all those years ago in Aberystwyth.

It was pouring with rain when we ca
street. My phone rang again, and I could
We dashed over to a bus shelter. Inside v
poster. We both stared at it as my phone c

"I should answer it," I said softly.

Adam kicked at the bus shelter as A
the line.

"Start giving me dates and times,
got your publishing house reaming m
and not in a good way."

I told her everything: about Adam
thing. When I finished, she was quiet

"Are you still there?" I said.

"Yeah... I just wish what you'd
your next book. It sounds like a bes

"We need a happy ending first
of course, there will be," I added q

Adam was now sat gloomily
shelter

"Okay. Here's what we're gon
"Nothing?"

"Yeah. I'll make sure you
minimum of interviews and v
you act normal. If anything
will more than likely be a fe
on sale. By then it will be a b

"Really?" I said. "Why ar
"I'm not being nice. I'm

"So it's like surveillance?" I said.

"Gosh no! I simply like to know what people are up to," she said.

I explained what was happening with Adam.

"Oh dear, ooh I can see him there. Hello Adam," she waved as he shuffled past the computer in his dressing gown to the bathroom.

"Gosh, that is a pickle, two hundred thousand pounds. I'm sure it will all be fine, Coco. Do wish him the best of luck with everything," she said, as if it was a grade six piano exam Adam was facing and not a Crown Court trial.

"Are you okay?" I said to Adam but he slammed the bathroom door. Since I put the house on the market and paid Natasha's retainer, we've had terrible arguments, and he's been very depressed.

I turned back to the computer screen. I could sense Meryl was itching to talk.

"Coco. I must tell you about my time in the hospital," she said.

"Were you in a padded cell?" I asked.

"No. I was in the newly refurbished low-security suite. It's beautifully decorated. It was opened last year by Ronnie Corbett."

"Was it?"

"Yes, and I met a woman who was convinced she was Carole Middleton. You know, Kate Middleton's mother."

'Did she become a good friend?" I said.

"God no. They whisked her off for electro shock therapy and I never saw her again. She did make me realise why I'd had all those visions of the Queen talking to me."

"Why?" I said.

"To put me back on track, Coco," she said. "I'll never be the Queen, and I'll never be able to truly replicate a traditional Sandringham Christmas. However, I could be the next Carole Middleton."

I noticed Rocco had walked up to the bathroom door and was pushing it with his nose, trying to get in and see Adam. Meryl went on.

"Carole Middleton was just an ordinary air hostess, but through Kate, she's now going to be mother to a future Queen. I could do the same thing as she did. Through Wilfred I could be the mother to the future King!"

Rocco started digging at the bathroom door and whimpering.

"I know you think I'm crackers Coco, but it's all within the realms of reality. If Kate and Wills get married and have a baby girl, she'll be close in age to Wilfred. He just needs to go to the same university as she does, and ask her on a date."

I couldn't hear any sounds coming from the bathroom. Rocco was now frantically digging outside the door.

"I've already hired a life coach and he's taking me through each step to achieve my dream, this being my first."

"What?"

"My Carole Middleton haircut!" she said, smoothing her hair. It didn't look much like Carole Middleton's; it looked more like someone had stuck a mixing bowl on her head and cut round it.

"Look, Meryl, I'd better go and see if Adam is okay," I said and ended the call.

I was suddenly gripped with fear. I ran to the bathroom and banged on the door. There was no answer so I banged again.

"What?" said Adam.

"Is everything all right?"

"Yes."

"What are you doing?"

"What do you think? I'm on the loo..."

annoying singsong customer service voice, and an irritatingly spelt name: Karliegh.

After taking our slips of paper and tapping in our National Insurance numbers she waddled off to the printer and returned with some forms.

"Right Mr Rickard," she said. "I can see you were a civil servant? And you worked in the private sector."

"Yes," said Adam. "But you've spelt civil servant with an 's'," he said, showing her the form which read, 'sivil servant'."

"That is how you spell it, sir," she said with the devastating confidence of ignorance.

"No, it isn't," said Adam. "It's spelt with a 'c'."

She huffed around and changed it, then set her sights on me.

"I see you, madam, are a... a... lap dancer?"

Her voice trailed off as she looked up, taking in my jeans and jumper, and the glasses on top of my head.

"You may have to widen your job search," she said diplomatically.

I tried to explain that I wasn't really a lap dancer, but she seemed to think I was some middle-aged sex worker in denial, and even opened her drawer and took out a leaflet entitled *Breaking The Cycle: Help For Middle-Aged Sex Workers*.

"Stop! I just want to know about benefits in relation to claiming legal aid!" shouted Adam. "How difficult is it for you people to listen?"

"'*You people*?'" echoed Karliegh. "Are you talking about white people? Because you need to know, we have a zero tolerance racism policy. If you continue to racially abuse me, I may have to terminate the interview."

"I meant you people in this job centre!" he raged, "Are you all bloody morons?"

Quick as a flash a huge security guard was at Adam's shoulder.

"You need to cool it, bro," he said.

"I'm not your bro!" shouted Adam. "This woman is saying I'm a racist and my girlfriend is a lap dancer. I'm not a racist!"

The security guard gave me the once over, a little like a farmer admires a cow with a good milk yield.

"And I'm not a lap dancer!" I said.

"Don't you give her that look," said Adam, jumping out of his seat.

"It's okay," I soothed, pushing Adam back down.

A silence had fallen over the office and I could see scared faces from the advisors and a few looks of excitement from the other claimants. Adam was still glowering at the security guard.

"You need to cool down... *sir*," said the security guard.

Karliegh was now taking a keen interest in our forms.

"I see here you both own property in the area. Do you have a mortgage?" she said icily.

I could see a vein beginning to pulse in Adam's head. I told her that Adam had a mortgage and that I owned my house.

"You own a house on Steeplejack Mews?" she said accusingly.

"Yes," I said.

The security guard whistled and raised his eyebrows provocatively at Adam.

"Then I might suggest you start using your property for income, and perhaps leave claiming benefits for those who really need them," she said.

"She didn't even want to claim anything!" growled Adam.

"Come on, let's leave. Now!" I said.

As we scuttled out of JobCentre Plus, embarrassment was an understatement.

I am not sure why they added the 'plus'. It was full of the same desperate people clinging on to life as I remembered all those years ago in Aberystwyth.

It was pouring with rain when we came out onto the street. My phone rang again, and I could see it was Angie. We dashed over to a bus shelter. Inside was an *Agent Fergie* poster. We both stared at it as my phone continued to ring.

"I should answer it," I said softly.

Adam kicked at the bus shelter as Angie's voice came on the line.

"Start giving me dates and times, Coco," she said. "I've got your publishing house reaming my arse about you — and not in a good way."

I told her everything: about Adam, the house raid, everything. When I finished, she was quiet for a long time.

"Are you still there?" I said.

"Yeah... I just wish what you'd told me was the plot for your next book. It sounds like a best-seller."

"We need a happy ending first," I said bleakly. "Which, of course, there will be," I added quickly.

Adam was now sat gloomily on the bench in the bus shelter

"Okay. Here's what we're gonna do," she said. "Nothing."

"Nothing?"

"Yeah. I'll make sure you only have to do the bare minimum of interviews and when we do the book launch, you act normal. If anything does come out about Adam, it will more than likely be a few weeks after *Agent Fergie* goes on sale. By then it will be a best-seller and it won't matter."

"Really?" I said. "Why are you being so nice?"

"I'm not being nice. I'm working out a strategy," she said.

"I only wish you'd told me earlier."

"I'm sorry. I didn't know what to do."

"Please, keep me posted."

"Okay, thanks," I said and she hung up.

Adam was dangerously gloomy when we got home. We were drenched from the rain, so he went up to have a shower. I waited until I could hear the water running then made two phone calls. The first to an estate agent, who said that subject to a viewing, I could rent it out the house for several thousand pounds a month. Then I arranged a transfer of five grand from my savings account and hired Natasha as Adam's lawyer.

Marika found me staring at the laptop. I took a deep breath and told her what I'd done. Without blinking, she said we could all move to her two-bedroom flat and split the mortgage.

Looks like we're moving.

Monday 24th January 12.12
TO: chris@christophercheshire.com

Meryl called on Skype. I haven't seen her since she was sectioned, but she looked her old self, apart from a new haircut.

"Are you moving house, Coco?" she trilled excitedly.

"How did you know?" I said. "The Estate Agent only listed it twenty minutes ago."

"Google Alerts!" she said. "I've got one set up for almost everything: you, Daniel, Rosencrantz, David Essex. Steeple-jack Mews just pinged up and I knew I had to call you."

"Oh, well, please don't lock the door," I said. I waited until he came out. He pushed past me, went back to bed and climbed under the covers.

Wednesday 26th January 12.45
TO: marikarolincova@hotmail.co.uk

I was making coffee this morning when Chris knocked on the door.

"Hey Cokes," he said.

I gave him a hug and he came and sat at the breakfast bar. I told him Adam hasn't showered or shaved in four days, and that he seems to hate me.

"He'll thank you in the future," said Chris.

"How far in the future?" I said.

"You did the right thing. Natasha is a winner, and she's working for Adam. And you're only renting out your house for a year, tops. It's win-win."

I told him there hasn't been any interest in the house, no viewings. The teenage estate agent who came to do the paperwork was convinced it would be snapped up within hours. Also Natasha keeps calling to ask Adam to come to her office and start going over his evidence, but he's refused, saying he's ill.

"Let's change the subject," I said. "What's happening with you?"

"Lots," said Chris excitedly. "It seems seeing Dame Judi in the Northern Lights has brought me luck. I've been chosen to direct the new season of plays for The Rabbit Hutch Theatre, in Devon."

"The Rabbit Hutch Theatre?"

"Well, it's bigger than a Rabbit Hutch, obviously. I know it's not hugely well known to civilians, but it's so prestigious and career building. It's one of the few top-notch repertory theatre companies left in the UK."

"That's great!" I said.

"However, I do have to temporarily relocate to Devon, in two days' time," he said.

"How long are you going for?"

"Three months," he said awkwardly. "I won't go, if you need me," he said grabbing my hand.

"Don't you DARE not go!" I said. "I'll be fine. I'm just going to miss you."

"I'll miss you too," he said. "And if you need anything, I'm only a phone call or one of your *long* emails away..."

I looked indignant.

"I love reading them," he grinned. "But try to keep them shorter for a least a few days, I've got to read a ton of plays before the weekend."

He told me about all the plays he'll be directing. It's quite an eclectic season: *The Cherry Orchard*, *Abigail's Party*, *A Long Day's Journey Into Night* and *Xanadu: The Musical*.

"I'm most excited about directing *Xanadu*," he said. "But don't let anyone else hear that!"

It was so good to see Chris finally excited about something as the last few months have been rough on him.

When he'd gone I went up to Adam, who was now beginning to fester in bed. He was just a lump under the duvet.

"Adam, please get up," I said. "I need to change the sheets."

"Leave me alone," he said.

"No, I need to change the sheets. I have to sleep in there too."

He didn't move. I grabbed the duvet and pulled it off the bed. He was rolled up in a ball. I tried to hug him but he turned his head away.

"Adam," I said.

"Nothing you can say will make me feel better so you can save your breath."

I covered him up with the duvet and came back downstairs. A couple of hours later I had a phone call. It was Ethel.

"'Ello," she said.

I hadn't spoken to her since Christmas.

"Look, if you're ringing to fight, I can't," I said. "I haven't got the energy."

"Listen love," she said. "I don't wanna fight, I want to speak to Adam. I've tried 'is mobile but iss off."

"Why do you want to speak to him?" I said.

"Rosencrantz told me 'e's took to 'is bed."

"Yes."

"Can I talk to 'im?"

"You can try but nothing will raise him," I said.

I took the phone upstairs and left it with Adam.

An hour later Adam came downstairs. He had showered and he brought with him the old bed sheets. I followed him into the utility room where he was stuffing them into the washing machine. I watched as he measured out the powder then switched it on. He turned, and gave me a kiss.

"Thank you," he said. "I love you."

"I love you too. What did Ethel say?"

"A few home truths."

I don't know how she managed to raise Adam from his bed, but he's even arranged to go into Natasha's chambers and practise giving evidence.

FEBRUARY

Tuesday 1st February 12.45
TO: angie.langford@thebmxliteraryagency.biz

Adam had his preliminary hearing this morning at South-wark Crown Court, a huge anonymous brown-brick building which sits with its back to the River Thames. A preliminary hearing is the court appearance before the trial proper. The accused enters their plea, and the details of the case are decided.

This was Adam's second preliminary hearing; he had appeared back in December where he had entered a plea of not guilty.

The judge was a grey, humourless man and seemed irritated to see Adam again. Despite Natasha's best efforts, he only granted us an extra two weeks, agreeing now to hear the case on February the twenty-eighth.

We left the courtroom along a corridor full of pale clammy-faced youths waiting to be tried. A couple raised their eyebrows at Adam in a look of solidarity. I grabbed his hand as we passed, hoping to show he is not a criminal and is loved by someone who shops in the Per Una section in Marks & Spencer. Stupid, I know, but being in the court house reminded me how serious this all is.

It was raining when we came outside. Natasha had a little associate with her, a young chap with a huge umbrella, who opened it for us all as we emerged from the giant flying canopy at the front of Southwark Court House.

"Two weeks isn't much of an extension," I said.

"I think for our defence strategy, it's a very positive outcome," said Natasha.

The little associate holding the umbrella nodded sagely.

"The more we look through the case files, and the police report, the more we see a lack of evidence against Adam," she said. "We have a very strong case. I'm itching to get in the courtroom and win!"

I wanted to hear more but Natasha's car arrived and whisked her away to another appointment. We were thinking of walking back to Marylebone via the Thames Embankment but it really began to pour so we ran to the Tube.

When we got home, Daniel was in my kitchen making a cup of tea! By the breakfast bar stood a young lad in a suit far too big for him.

"Um, what's going on?" I said.

"I'm Lee, from McMahon Lettings," said the young lad.

"You're my estate agent?" I said. He didn't look old enough to buy cigarettes. "I thought the viewing was this afternoon?"

"Yeah, I had to move it," said Lee.

"We found them on the doorstep," said Daniel, pulling a couple of mugs from the kitchen cupboard.

"Who's 'we' and who's 'them'?" I said.

"Me and Mum... We came over to get some of our things, before you move house, and we saw young Lee here with Mr Trattore, the guy who is viewing the house."

"So why are you both in here?" I said.

"Well, Mum said she knew the house better than any of us," said Daniel. "Would anyone else like tea?"

"Ethel's *showing him round?*" I shrilled.

"Yeah," said Daniel.

I dropped my bag and dashed out.

"I thought she'd be good at it, a woman's touch and all that," he shouted as I came upstairs. As I rounded the bannister, I heard Ethel's voice in the bedroom.

"Now in there tha's the en suite. En suite is a French word, it means 'avin a loo in the bedroom."

I went through as Ethel was demonstrating the bidet.

"I'm not sure what it means in English, but you use it to wash yer arse," she said.

A handsome and elegant Italian chap dressed in crisp dark jeans and a striped shirt looked up with a smile on his face. He seemed to be amused by Ethel's tour.

"Oh, this is 'er 'oo I was telling you about," said Ethel.

"Hello Mrs Pinchard," he said, speaking with a rich accent. "I am Salvo Trattore. I think I would like to rent your beautiful home."

"Oh... wonderful, so you like the house?" I said.

"I love it, it's very elegant."

"I thought it would be good to finish with the bidet," said Ethel, signalling me to help her up off it.

We came back downstairs and Salvo shook hands with Adam and said he would have to be going. I took him to the front door where he said, "Does she come with the house?"

"Who?"

"The housekeeper?"

I had to stop from smiling. "Ethel? Um, no, afraid not. I'm taking her with me."

"That's a shame… Good help is hard to find," he said.

He kissed me on both cheeks, and drove off in a smart little Porsche. I came back into the kitchen as Adam was showing Daniel how to work the coffee machine.

"'E looks ever so rich, that Italian," said Ethel. "'E seems like a lovely man. So refined."

"He wanted to know if you came with the house," I said.

"You what?" said Ethel.

"He thought you were my housekeeper."

Adam bit his lip to suppress a grin.

"'E thought I was the char lady? I 'ope you set 'im straight?"

"Yes, of course," I said.

"The cheeky bastard. I'll 'ave you know this dress is from Debenhams, and it weren't cheap!"

Lee, the estate agent, who had been watching all of this said he would sort out the "paperwork and stuff" then slunk off back to his office.

"To think you're paying him five percent and Mum did all the leg work," said Daniel.

He pressed a button on the coffee machine and hot milk squirted out and hit the ceiling.

"So tell me again why you're both here?" I said irritably, grabbing a cloth.

"I came to get me salad spinner," said Ethel accusingly. "You've 'ad it fer years."

"Um… I gave Mum a lift," said Daniel.

I've never seen a piece of salad pass Ethel's lips but I told him to try the attic. Daniel went up whilst Ethel stayed cooing over Adam.

"'Ow are yer bearin' up love?" she said.

Adam told her about the hearing.

"You'll be fine," she said patting his hand. "We 'ad a little pep talk on the phone, din't we? I told you things would get better, 'an they 'ave. Thanks to me, Coco's rented out 'er ridiculously big 'ouse."

"Adam was here when it happened, we don't need your commentary," I said, heaving myself up on the kitchen island and scrubbing milk off the ceiling.

"See, Adam? See 'ow she bites me 'ead orf at every turn…"

Adam didn't know what to say.

"'Course, I'm the one what always mends things between us. Did you 'ear? She dumped me at Christmas, like one of them dogs in a cardboard box…"

"What she doesn't mention is I drove her to the airport and got her priority boarding," I said.

"She should look after 'er own. I know 'er an' Danny are divorced but a mother-in-law ain't just fer Christmas, she's fer life!"

Adam nodded along with her sagely whilst I cleared up the rest of Daniel's mess.

Daniel finally came downstairs with Ethel's manky old salad spinner, then my phone rang. It was Lee, the estate agent.

"Mr. Trattore is going to rent for £4,200 per calendar month," he said. "The price is a little higher than we advertised, because he'd like to move in on the fourth."

"The fourth of March?" I said.

"No, this Friday, the fourth of February," said Lee.

I came off the phone in shock.

"Where you gonna live?" said Ethel.

"We're moving in with Marika," said Adam.

"Ooh, you'll be just down the road from me!" said Ethel. "And Adam, if yer need a salad spinner, you know where I am."

It seems like I will never escape the old bag.

Thursday 3rd February 17.40
TO: chris@christophercheshire.com

I never imagined how I'd pack everything up and move. There are four generations' worth of crap stored in this house. However, that myth was busted with one phone call to Big Yellow. They sent round a team of scarily efficient packers who had everything boxed up and in a giant van within six hours.

All I've kept is some clothes, toiletries, a few books, my laptop, and some paperwork I really can't do without. Everything else will sit in a warehouse in East London for the next year.

Marika has gone ahead in the Land Cruiser with Rocco. It's piled high with our stuff. Adam is in a meeting with one of Natasha's associates, preparing for the court case.

Salvo Trattore is going to bring his own furniture. I'm sat in the living room and it's really odd. I've never seen it empty before. It's so big. I've walked from room to room and only really noticed the space. I don't know how we will cope in Marika's back bedroom. How is Devon treating you?

Friday 4th February 11.03
TO: chris@christophercheshire.com

It was strange waking up in our new home this morning.

Our room isn't small but it's piled high with our suitcases. Me, Adam and Rocco lay in bed for a few minutes, listening to a train click clack past outside the window, and then we crept out to the kitchen. Marika had left a note to say she would be working all morning. Her dog walking enterprise is really taking off and she's making good money.

She had prepared us a welcome breakfast. A big plate of cheese, cold meat, some lovely crusty bread, and a little golden block of butter. There was a selection of Nespresso capsules, laid out next to her Nespresso machine, watched over by the life-size George Clooney cut-out she got by bribing the guy in the Nespresso Store on Regent Street.

We now have our own shelf in the fridge, a space each in the bathroom cabinet, and there is a clipboard by the phone with a sheet of paper for us to write down who we call on the landline.

I was quite enjoying the novelty of sharing a house until I came out to the car to get a bag of shoes I'd left in the footwell of the back seat.

Someone had thrown a brick through the driver's window and stolen them, along with the car radio and my Ray Bans, which were in the glove compartment. I have just moved the car to a spot outside the house and we're waiting for someone to come and replace the window.

Now I miss home.

Friday 4th February 22.27
TO: chris@christophercheshire.com

After the car window was fixed, we went to report to a police station to say Adam had moved. However, we had a problem *finding* a police station. The local one round the corner had a sign outside saying that it's only open on a Friday between 1.45pm and 2.30pm, and that it's only manned by volunteers from the community. It was 2.50pm and two old ladies were outside. One was just locking up, whilst the other was carefully carrying a half-completed jigsaw on a tea tray. I could see there hadn't been much crime fighting going on. They were very sweet though, and suggested we try the nearest police station which was in Sydenham.

When we arrived we discovered Sydenham Police Station has just been converted to a Pizza Express. After a rest, a glass of wine and a plate of dough balls, we drove over to the mega police station in Lewisham.

Prisoners were being ferried in and out at an alarming rate, and we had to wait three hours before someone on the desk could see us.

We got to Marika's at seven, but heard she was occupied in the bedroom. She's started dating a fellow dog walker whom she met at a drinking trough on Hilly Fields common. (Their dogs were the ones doing the drinking.)

In the small flat, we couldn't escape the soundtrack of Marika's bedroom Olympics, so Adam suggested we take Rocco for a walk.

There wasn't much to look at on a cold dark night in February. Adam took my hand and we walked past a long row of terraced houses broken up by corner shops and Chinese take-aways. It was very depressing.

"How much further do you want to go?" I moaned. "We've been on our feet all day."

"I can't go back to Marika shagging some bloke. He's going to come out of her room and want to shake my hand, and I don't want to have to think where it's been."

I laughed and he put his arm round me as we passed a

row of shops. There was a small supermarket called 'Mr Gogi's', a key cutter, a launderette, and a Post Office. We carried on past the train station and came to a set of gates with a path leading up into a wooded area. Once inside we let Rocco off the lead and he scampered excitedly up the path. We followed him up a long set of steps and came to the most beautiful church. It was small with a tall spire and, in the moonlight, the flint walls sparkled. Candles glowed invitingly through the stained glass windows in soft reds, blues and greens.

"Shall we go inside?" I said.

"What about Rocco?" said Adam.

"I'll stick him in my coat."

Inside the church, it was so peaceful. Not that outside was particularly loud, but the everyday hum of traffic ceased when we walked through the door. We made our way down the aisle to sit in one of the wooden pews. It smelt of dust and incense and wasn't overly grand, but simple and beautiful. There was a fresh spray of lilies on the altar, and the stone arches were smooth sandstone, with carvings on the ceiling.

I felt so safe and relaxed. I took Adam's hand and without thinking said, "Wouldn't it be wonderful to get married here?"

He turned to look at me.

"This isn't a proposal," I added quickly. Adam carried on staring. "All I meant is that this church would be nice for a wedding..."

"You'd marry me?" he said incredulously.

"Well, maybe, hypothetically... but you're not asking, are you?"

"No, I'm talking hypothetically too," he said hastily.

We sat awkwardly for a few more minutes listening to the sound of Rocco's snoring coming from inside my coat.

We both went to say something, but then my phone beeped. It was Marika saying the coast was clear.

We jumped up, eager to get out of the church and eager to be warm in bed. We didn't mention the marriage thing again. We did meet Marika's new man, Greg. He used to work in The City, but after burning out, and quitting his job, became a fellow dog walker, like Marika. He seems pleasant, and he's good looking. We just wished he'd been more attentive with how his dressing gown was arranged when he sat on the sofa.

Sunday 6th February 21.13
TO: chris@christophercheshire.com

I quite like the area Marika lives in. There is a beautiful deli, a park and an incredible Indian Restaurant. We went there for a meal last night with Rosencrantz, Marika, and Greg. Afterwards we all walked back to Marika's and saw on the huge electronic billboard above the train station a poster for *Agent Fergie*.

It was very quiet in the dark street as we all stared at it.

"That's wicked, Mum," said Rosencrantz.

Then there was an electronic whirring as the plastic strips moved round and the next advert came up.

"What are we looking at?" slurred Greg.

"It's my Mum's new book," said Rosencrantz.

We waited a minute and the advert whirred round again.

"Oh... Cool beans, can you get me a signed copy?" said Greg.

"I won't get any until next week..." I said.

"She doesn't get many. They'll be in shops on the twenty-second," Adam added pointedly.

Greg had wormed out of paying for dinner by saying he had forgotten his wallet. So, we all had to chip in for him. I wouldn't have minded but he ordered so much food that was wasted and a triple shot of thirty-year-old whisky that he didn't even finish.

There was an awkward moment.

"We'll be sure to buy a copy, won't we?" said Marika.

"You bet!" said Greg.

They then headed home whilst we walked Rosencrantz to the train station.

When we got home, Marika was in the bathroom and Greg was in the kitchen. He was sat at the table eating the carrot cake I had bought.

"Hey guys," he said.

We watched him for a moment but he didn't say anything. It was from our shelf in the fridge. He then went to the sink where he plonked the dirty plate, leaving half the cake uneaten!

"Night guys," he said and sloped off to bed.

I was so annoyed.

"Calm down," said Adam, putting his arms round me. "It's just a bit of cake..."

"I know, *our* cake. How rude is he?"

I really hope Marika isn't going to move him in!

Wednesday 9th February 10.31
TO: chris@christophercheshire.com

Angie is managing my book launch with the utmost

secrecy. I'm not allowed to talk to journalists. She has only permitted email interviews, which she has written herself. I picked up a copy of *The Metro* newspaper today and read an interview with an author where she raved on about how much she loves the royal family, and is obsessed with all things royal. I was thinking what a saddo the author was, until I noticed that it was me! I phoned Angie straight away.

"I don't love the royal family and I don't dream about going to a garden party, or being made a dame," I said when she answered.

"Darlin', what are you talking about?" she said. I heard the click of her lighter and a deep exhale.

"This interview in *The Metro*, about *Agent Fergie*. 'Oh to be Dame Coco Pinchard and meet the Queen,' that's what I said, apparently."

"Oh, that. Coco the public are mad on royal stuff at the moment, what with the wedding of William and that scrawny brunette…"

"Kate."

"Yeah. Princess Kate, who'd have thought? It's hip to be a royalist. That's why I'm using it in this interview."

"But I've always prided myself on being a socialist, that's my belief."

"Ha! You're a champagne socialist at best Coco, and the first rule of promotion is that your beliefs can't be too concrete."

"But…"

"Thanks to me you got a huge advance, and your last book sold like hot cakes, am I right?"

"Yes, but…" she didn't let me finish.

"Did I ever disappoint you? I know what I'm doing. Coco, your books are amazing, but without clever marketing you might as well write one out in longhand and put it on the shelf above your bed."

"Could we at least make me sound like a hip royalist then? People are going to think I'm an old spinster in a flowering apron who invites strangers for tea to look at her royal mug collection."

Angie has suggested I join Twitter as @CocoPinchard. I can do some tweeting about my life and what I like, and my publishing house can do some tweeting too.

"It'll give people an insight to your personality," she said. "But for God's sake don't mention anything about Adam!"

Thursday 10th February 11.44
TO: angie.langford@thebmxliteraryagency.biz

I have a hundred and sixty followers on Twitter! Many of whom have read my books, also Marika and Chris have read my books. I hope you are ashamed of yourself Ms. Langford ;)

I've also been welcomed to Twitter by a journalist from *The Independent* and another from the *Daily Mail*. This is quite fun.

Sunday 13th February 14.43
TO: chris@christophercheshire.com

Greg has stayed at the flat for six nights in a row. He's all but moved in! He's eating the food off our shelf in the fridge. Every morning he nabs the newspaper I'm paying for to be delivered. He's even wearing Adam's pants! Admittedly, that was a mistake, as all our stuff has to dry on the same clothes dryer in the living room.

I don't know how to broach the subject of Greg with Marika, particularly the pants, but she seems so happy with him and I'm being all British and I don't want to rock the boat. On the upside, I have five hundred followers on Twitter!

Tuesday 15th February 12.22
TO: chris@christophercheshire.com

Adam had a meeting with Natasha yesterday about his case. She pretended to be the defence QC and grilled him mercilessly. I met him afterwards on The Strand. I had forgotten it was Valentine's Day yesterday, so when he asked if I fancied McDonald's I said "yes" without protest. We set off up St Martin's Lane towards Leicester Square. The wind was cold and outside the Duke of York's Theatre we were caught up amongst the chattering theatregoers before the show, spilling out onto the street with plastic glasses from the bar. I envied their carefree laughter, and I felt homesick. I wanted to be back living here amongst the fun and buzz of Central London.

Adam pulled us past Cranbourn Street, which leads to the Leicester Square McDonald's, and on towards Cambridge Circus.

"McDonald's is this way," I said.

"I have a surprise for you," he said.

We kept walking until we reached The Ivy. Adam said hello to the doorman as if he knew him, and ushered us into the luxury of the restaurant.

"When did you organise this?" I asked, shocked.

"I got Angie to phone up and bully a table," he said. "It is Valentine's Day."

As we were led to our table, I noticed most of the women, and a good few men, were undressing Adam with their eyes. I suddenly saw how damn hot he looked in his suit, the thin crisp fabric clinging to him in all the right places. He pulled out a chair for me and we sat.

It was a stunning meal, and, for the first time in ages, it felt like we were an exciting young couple again, not bowed down with stress. After dessert, a bottle of champagne appeared in an ice bucket.

"Oh, I think you've got the wrong table," I said, seeing it was Krug.

"No, madam," said the waiter softly.

He wrapped the neck of the bottle in a snow-white napkin and squeezed out the cork with an elegant pop. He filled our glasses then melted away. I was looking at Adam in protest, but he was fumbling in his jacket pockets. Then he pushed back his chair and crouched on the floor.

"Did you drop your wallet?" I said, pushing back my chair and squatting down on the floor with him.

He looked at me, now at eye-level with him. Then I noticed he was on one knee... and he was holding out a little velvet box... and nestling on a little cushion inside was a ring! For a moment I stupidly still didn't get it, and then it fell into place with a whump.

"You're not supposed to be down here with me," he whispered.

I noticed the restaurant had gone quiet and everyone was looking to see which of the squatting pair of us was going to pop the question. I quickly rose and sat in my chair. He took a deep breath as I tried to arrange how to sit and what to do with my face. There was something so deeply moving about him looking up at me with his whiskey-coloured eyes, his long tall frame kneeling submissively on that fine carpet.

"Coco, I know I don't have much to offer you right now. In fact, I have nothing but my love for you. But my love is strong and fierce and tender, and I will protect you for the rest of my life. Will you marry me?" he said quietly.

I quickly did a rewind and fast forward in my head. He is wonderful, funny, and very hot. His speech made me melt and most importantly, I do love him. The answer, it seemed, was 'yes'.

"Yes," I said. "Yes, I will marry you."

He took the ring from the box and slipped it on my finger. It was a simple white gold band and it fitted perfectly. He leaned forward and he kissed me. We both had tears in our eyes and the people in the restaurant actually applauded us.

We stayed until late, drinking our champagne, a little in shock and awe. I kept looking at the ring and feeling this warm buzz of excitement in my stomach. We were almost the last people to leave the restaurant and when we stepped out into the dark street it was almost one in the morning.

"We've missed the last train back," I said. "What should we do?"

"How about, for old times' sake, we get creative?" he said, flashing his devilish grin.

So, at half one in the morning, we crept up to my allotment patch in Marylebone. We haven't been there since the autumn. By the glowing light of my iPhone we looked round furtively then climbed over the gate. The ground sparkled in the moonlight as we crept alongside rows of frozen dug-over soil. I nearly had a heart attack when I stood in a puddle, now brittle with ice, which gave a loud hollow crunching sound.

"Jeez!" I said, catching my breath up against a neighbour's shed.

"Relax, there's no one here," smiled Adam.

He came close, pressing the length of his warm body against me. He took my head in his hands and kissed me. I felt his taut muscles against my chest, his powerful legs, and a rapidly growing hardness.

"Come on," I said, dragging him up towards my shed. "You need to warm me up!"

My hands were so cold when we got to the door I had trouble getting the key in the lock, but it finally twisted open and the door yielded. We burst inside. Adam pulled me in for a warm deep kiss, which made my knees buckle a little. I untucked his shirt and put my hands up on the small of his back. He gave a sharp intake of breath and I undid his trousers, sliding my hand over the curve of his hot rump. We pulled out all the spare blankets and collapsed in a hastily made bed on top of two beanbags. Adam shrugged out of his suit and quickly had my clothes off. I gasped at the cold air, which was replaced by his warm naked body on top of mine.

Afterwards we snuggled up in the blankets, and shared a huge cracked mug of whisky. There was no electricity, my phone had died, and it was almost pitch black apart from a strip of moonlight shining across the opposite side of the shed.

I felt so happy; happier than I had in months. As we drifted off in each other's arms I said, "So we're going to do it? We're going to get married?"

"Yeah. I'm going to give you the best wedding you've ever had," said Adam. "It's going to be a big flat party."

"A flat party?"

"I meant a big fat party."

"Are you a bit tipsy?"

"Yes, and our wedding will be too. Big and fun and tipsy with all our friends…"

"A big fat tipsy wedding?"

"Yes… You're going to be a… beautiful bride…" said Adam, drifting off to sleep.

"I don't know if I can wear white, after what we just did," I said, but Adam was already asleep.

I woke up the next morning to the sound of creaking wood and then an icy breeze. I opened my eyes and Adam was sprawled on top of me, naked. The blankets must have dislodged in the night, and a shaft of sunlight illuminated his perfect behind. I looked up and the sunlight was pouring through the open door. The head of the Allotment Association, Agatha Balfour, was standing there with a youngish looking couple and their two small children. They stared, opened–mouthed, as Adam shifted in his sleep, opening his legs and treating them all to a view of his scrotum, which slid across my bare leg and off to dangle pendulously in the cold breeze. One of the children screamed. I yanked the covers over Adam.

"Mrs Pinchard!" shrilled Agatha, with a look of horror. "Get dressed and then come and SEE ME!"

She slammed the door and I heard them move away. When they were gone, Adam opened his eyes.

"Morning," he grinned.

I told him what had happened.

"Shit," he cried, jumping up and pulling on his underwear.

"What?"

"We should apologise."

"Why?"

"She's in charge of all the allotments," he said.

"So? I've had enough of that old bag, acting as if this is some luxury five-star retirement village when it's a bloody allotment! Do you know what she said? 'See me' as if I'm some school kid..."

When we were dressed, I marched up the hill to Agatha's shed, my heels sinking into the soil, which was now melting in the morning sunshine. Adam hurried along behind, tucking in his shirt and doing up his flies.

I reached the door to Agatha's shed and barged in without knocking.

"I'd like to ask why you brought a load of people to look at my shed!" I said.

Agatha looked up from using a little silver spoon to measure tealeaves into a pot.

"Mrs Pinchard," she said not missing a beat. "The reason I did, is because you no longer have an allotment. They were prospective tenants."

Adam caught up, and sheepishly waved hello. Agatha picked up a piece of paper.

"I take it your new address is 12A Berry Road, Honor Oak Park, London SE23 1BZ?"

"Yes," I said. "I left a message on your answering machine. A message you never bothered to return."

"Mrs Pinchard," she said, removing her glasses. "You are only eligible for an allotment if you live in the NW1 postcode."

"I am. I own a house here," I said.

"But you don't *reside* here, Mrs Pinchard."

"That doesn't sound fair!"

"I don't make the rules, Mrs Pinchard. For example, the Sultan of Brunei owns a very nice house overlooking Regent's Park, but even he couldn't have an allotment because he doesn't *reside* here. Having said that, the Sultan of Brunei would do a much better job of weeding."

"Yeah, he does have an awful lot of wives," said Adam.

I turned and looked at him incredulously.

"I'm just saying," he shrugged.

"Well, don't!"

"You have seven days to vacate, Mrs Pinchard," said Agatha. "Good day."

It seems after a couple of years Agatha finally has her wish. She has forced me out. I no longer have an allotment. We trudged back down the hill, doing the worst walk of shame.

As we waited for a taxi in the freezing wind, I could just make out the roof of my house between the bare branches of a tree in the distance. I had an image of Salvo Trattore sitting by a roaring fire, my roaring fire, all cosy with a slice of pannetone.

"I'm sorry," said Adam, as he followed my gaze.

"You've got nothing to be sorry for," I said.

I clung onto him and I really hoped that love was all I needed.

Wednesday 16th February 13.01
TO: angie.langford@thebmxliteraryagency.biz

I'm writing to tell you I'm engaged. None of my friends seem to be overjoyed at this. Chris was rather cool on the phone with his congratulations and then said he had to get back to his rehearsals. I then tried a different tack with Marika, asking if she wanted to be a bridesmaid. She burst into cackles of laughter and then saw I was serious.

"Are you fucking kidding, Coco?" she said.

"No. We haven't set a date yet..."

"Well, of course you haven't. He's nine days away from a crown court trial."

This stopped me in my tracks.

"What do you mean? He's going to be acquitted. Natasha thinks so and she's the best lawyer there is."

"Oh my God, will you listen to yourself," she said. "Did you ever ask Adam to take that lie detector test?"

"No."

"Exactly. Wake up, woman!"

"Yeah, well. What about Greg?"

"What about Greg?" snapped Marika, her eyes flashing dangerously.

"You've moved him in pretty quickly!"

"It's my flat!"

"We're paying half the mortgage! What's he paying? He barely chips in for milk let alone anything else!"

The door went and Greg came bounding in. Talk about timing, the stupid prat had milk, bread and a newspaper in a plastic bag from the newsagent.

"Hello darling," said Marika. "Oh, look what Greg bought,"

"Yeah, well I thought it about time I chipped in," he said.

"Coco has some news," said Marika.

Greg looked up at me. It's funny how the people you are closest to can hurt you the most. I felt like I was back in the playground. Marika was bearing down on me like Kelly Roffey, a girl who used to bully me.

"I'm engaged," I said in a small voice.

"To, Adam? Oh congrats," said Greg. He moved in for an awkward peck on the cheek. "We should go and celebrate."

"Yes," said Marika and I quickly.

I blinked back tears, scooped up Rocco, and took him for a long walk.

Thursday 17th February 22.22
TO: chris@christophercheshire.com

I tweeted to my seven hundred Twitter followers yesterday that I was engaged; I had more excitement from people I don't know. Then Adam's daughter Holly saw it and tweeted the following:

Congrats 2 my new step-mum @CocoPinchard and 2u dad... When does ur trial for fraud begin?

When I saw it on my iPhone, I panicked and went to send her a message to remove it, but by mistake I retweeted it. I finally got a direct message to her, but it took over an hour for her to pick it up and delete the tweet. I couldn't bear the tension so I took Rocco for a walk. Halfway along Brockley Rise, I had a phone call from Angie to say that the release of *Agent Fergie* is being postponed.

"For how long?" I said.

"Well, until the trial is over and we know what's happening with Adam... Thanks to his moron daughter and her stupid tweet, your publishing house knows what's really going on."

"Is Adam's trial that big a deal?"

"Normally they wouldn't care, but they're in talks for a merger with Tranzplanet Publishing which has to be approved by the government..."

"And they don't want to be seen to support a writer who is dating a criminal?"

"Yep. That's about it. Course you're not just dating him, you're *engaged* to him..."

I told Angie she was being harsh.

"Well, we've been here before," she said. "And I'm fed up. You seem to court disaster and it's tedious for those of us who have to rely on you. You know now the final part of your advance is gonna be delayed. Which means my commission gets delayed too..."

I don't know what I'm going to do now. I think I'll have to sell the car.

Saturday 19th February 16.22
TO: chris@christophercheshire.com

Things are getting very awkward here with Marika. She has been watching Kung-Fu movies all day with Greg. (As you know, Marika hates Kung-Fu movies.)

Adam and myself have spent the day in our room. Not having your own space means we can't argue. So we've been hissing at each other quietly.

He had a big row on the phone yesterday with Holly. I've never heard him shout at her before. He says he doesn't want me to sell the car. But I say we don't have a choice. Besides, I don't use it. It's £45,000 worth of metal just sitting outside the flat. It was broken into again last night. The front windscreen and passenger window were smashed. All that was stolen was a map of Slovakia I bought at Christmas. They left the map for the Czech Republic, which shows whoever took it failed geography at school. You have to drive through the Czech Republic to get to Slovakia.

Chris, could I keep the car in your driveway whilst I try to sell it? I want to move it next week when I clear out my allotment shed.

Adam is now napping, and I've started to read *Wolf Hall* by Hilary Mantel. She's such a brilliant writer. She's much better than me. It's made me very gloomy about *Agent Fergie*.

I wish I could be like Hilary Mantel, captivate the world with literary fiction, and be nominated for all those awards. Although, she is a slightly unusual looking woman. It made me wonder if you can be talented and attractive. I asked Adam the same question and, half asleep, he told me I'm gorgeous, which I didn't want to hear.

How is life treating you in Devon?

C xx

Tuesday 22nd February 14.44
TO: chris@christophercheshire.com

I emptied the allotment shed today. It was very sad packing up everything: the deck chairs and blankets, the little mini bar stored in an old cardboard box. I thought of all the fun we'd had there, drinking in the long summer evenings, pretending to garden whenever Agatha came past.

When I had taken the last of the stuff I stopped by the fruit canes, all cut back, their thin hairy branches wiggling in the wind. The blueberry bushes were skeletons, and the strawberry plants were brown, spidery, and squashed flat. I'll miss seeing them spring to life in the summer, and the heavenly smell of fresh strawberries.

A lone crow landed, all polished beak and feathers, and picked around in the bare soil. It was a very poetic end. The cold wind rounded on me and gusted up my coat as if to say,

"Go on, be off with you," so I took the cardboard box mini-bar, and hung the key on Agatha's door as I passed.

Out on the street I discovered I had been clamped.

I walked round to where it was attached to my front wheel, and saw under the dirt was a phone number. I dialled it and after a few rings, Agatha Balfour answered. I quickly hung up, thinking I had mis-dialled; my fingers were rendered into a little sausage claw by the cold. I dialled again, and again Agatha Balfour answered.

"Who is this?" she said.

"It's Coco Pinchard... Your telephone number seems to be written on a car clamp."

She tersely informed me she would be there "in a mo" and hung up.

She came trudging out of the gate swinging her keys, and without a hello or anything, put her muddy boot on the edge of the clamp, inserted a key, and wiggled it free of the wheel. I stood there waiting for an explanation. When none was offered up I said, "Who the hell are you to clamp my car?"

"You are parked in front of the gate. It's an access point. I am allowed to clamp people who block the access point."

"But that's stupid, surely, since that makes it less of an access point?"

"What would *you* suggest? I slash their tyres? Urinate on the bonnet?"

"Why are you saying that?"

"Mrs Pinchard, just when I think I have heard or seen the worst, you plumb the depths even further."

"I parked here for less than an hour!"

"Parking is the least of it! I'm talking about poor Mr Rickard."

"Adam?"

"Yes, Adam! He was a respected member of this community. A diligent Allotment Association secretary with the finest penmanship I've ever seen. Then he meets *you*, and you encourage him to give up his allotment patch. Then I find him *in flagrante* in your potting shed... And now I hear he's charged with fraud amounting to two hundred thousand pounds!"

"You know nothing about me, Agatha!" I said, close to tears.

"Nor do I wish to. Your life is a cesspit! I won't charge you a release fee. I think of it as a bonus that I never have to see you again."

She turned and walked away, swinging the car clamp as she went. I had to steel myself not to cry on the street.

I drove the car over to your place and your sister let me park it in the garage.

I know this sounds odd but I just want the trial to start now; we need to move forward. The waiting is unbearable.

Monday 28th February 19.27
TO: angie.langford@thebmxliteraryagency.biz

The trial began this morning. I came up to Southwark Crown Court with Adam early. It was still dark and there was a fine drizzle. My throat was tight with fear when I kissed him goodbye. He had to go in earlier for a last bit of preparation with Natasha. I grabbed a coffee from a tiny pop-up coffee shop manned by a guy with dreadlocks, and sat on a bench by the river and watched the sun coming up. I felt physically sick, so I left my coffee and, as a distraction, read the final chapter of *Wolf Hall*. It is a brilliant book.

I was just finishing a cigarette when I looked up to see

the author herself, Hilary Mantel, ordering a coffee over at the pop-up stand! I grabbed my bag and lined up behind her. She shot me a sideways glance as I proffered my copy of *Wolf Hall* with a biro.

"I've just finished reading your book," I said. "Would you sign it for me?"

Her look darkened further and she said, "I didn't write *Wolf Hall*."

"Didn't you?" I said, holding the book up beside her head. "The picture looks a lot like you!"

"I am not Hilary Mantel," she snapped, and taking her coffee, she walked off.

"What a snooty cow, who does she think she is?" I said, a bit too loudly. She stopped and looked round with a penetrating gaze, then turned and walked away.

The dreadlocked guy tutted so I moved off to let him serve the queue forming behind me.

I arrived at Southwark Crown Court at a quarter to nine and joined the queue waiting to get through the metal detectors. I tried to imagine I was passing through an airport and kept thinking positive thoughts. I was then shown into the courtroom. I was sat high up at the back in the visitors' gallery.

The jury filed in and I had my first chance to get a good look at them. Six men and six women, who were a good mix of race and age. No one really stood out. I hope this is a good thing. Adam then came in with Natasha. I gave him a little wave, which came out all wrong, and looked like I had come to see him in a nativity play. A couple of the jurors clocked me and I remembered I must act neutral. Then the prosecution entered; a large, dark-haired woman called Annabel Napier QC. She has slanting eyebrows and feline eyes, and regarded Adam much as a cat would before moving in for the kill.

When we were all in place, we were asked to stand for the judge, Her Ladyship Dame Ruby Haute-Penguin. The doors were flung open and I nearly died when the woman I thought was Hilary Mantel entered in her judge's robes.

Fear shot through me. Did I really call the judge a snooty cow? Natasha had warned me about the role of the judge, and even though they don't have a say in the outcome, they can heavily influence the jury during the summing up of the evidence.

We sat and she regarded the courtroom from under her wig. It was far too theatrical for my liking. It made me want to scream; the wigs, the robes, the jury all po-faced and the prospective legal teams posturing. It seemed as if all the people involved were doing it for personal gain and it was forgotten that my Adam was sitting there with his life in the balance. The one-upmanship seemed heightened in that it was all women involved.

I detected a whiff of camaraderie between the prosecution, Annabel Napier QC, and the judge. They seemed to regard Natasha — younger and prettier Natasha — as a threat, and wiping the floor with her pretty face during this trial was the order of the day.

I am not sure if I can sit through this; it could go on for weeks. I'm driving myself mad with analysing every nuance of voice, and every time I see one of the jurors yawn or appear to switch off I want to throw sweets at their head (I have a supply in my handbag to pass the time).

Opening statements were heard from Natasha and Annabel. Both were persuasive and it feels like they could make the case go either way.

After the day's proceedings, Adam stayed behind with Natasha to go over some of the things the prosecution brought up during the opening statements. I hung around outside the courthouse with another cup of coffee, waiting for the judge. I caught her as she was leaving with her bags.

"I'm so sorry I was rude this morning," I said, scuttling along beside her.

She carried on walking, looking straight ahead.

"I said, I'm sorry. I meant it as a compliment. I would love to be mistaken for a Man Booker prizewinner, even if she is a minger. I mean, not that you're a minger! You're a penguin, I mean you're a Dame, Dame Haute-Penguin..."

"I can't talk to you, Mrs Pinchard," she said. "You should know this."

She quickened her pace and I fell back and let her walk away, watching her halo of golden hair fly about in the breeze.

Shit, I've done it now, I thought. Adam is doomed.

He phoned and said to head home, he would talk later. I walked in a circle along the river to London Bridge then doubled back down Tooley Street and past the big multi-storey car park. I stopped as a large Range Rover pulled in front of me. Cars zoomed past and the Range Rover had to wait for a spot to pull out. After a moment, the tinted window slid down. Judge Haute-Penguin was sat regally on her white leather seats, smoking a long thin Capri cigarette.

"When I read a book, I like a good comedy," she said, to no one in particular, her eyes never leaving the traffic zipping by.

"I couldn't get into *Wolf Hall*... *Chasing Diana Spencer* was rather good..."

A spot opened up, and she pulled out, roaring off into the traffic. I stood watching the Range Rover move out of sight. What did this mean? Did it mean anything? At the very least, I must be forgiven... Maybe she thinks Adam is innocent.

MARCH

Wednesday 2nd March 23.11
TO: chris@christophercheshire.com

The prosecution has spent the last two days laying out its case against Adam. I'm glad I can only see the back of his head. Annabel Napier QC has skilfully painted him in a bad, bad light. I watched the jury carefully throughout the day, and I could see some of their gazes hardening towards him.

Annabel Napier is a formidable woman with real stage presence, highly articulate and one of those immaculate larger ladies. She has beautiful shiny chestnut brown hair tied at the nape of her neck. Her face is feline in shape with emerald green eyes and arched eyebrows. She *really* knows her eye makeup and utilises the autumn shades with devastating effect. Dark shading on the lid combined with an elegant swipe of eyeliner, and in all the hours she's been up there attacking Adam's character, she's never suffered eye gloop.

I got to see her up close during a recess. I was in the

toilets brushing my hair when she emerged from a cubicle and came to wash her hands in the next sink. There was an awkward silence. In another world, I'd love to have struck up a conversation. I would have begun by asking her for tips on eye-shadow. I spent years thinking coral and royal blues were flattering, but my efforts always made me look like a slightly anaemic country and western singer. Then when we'd got chatting, I'd launch into a speech about Adam. Tell her all of the wonderful things about him that will never come out in court. However, I was scared to even smile at her. She finished washing her hands and went to the dryer. Over the low drone, we both pretended the other wasn't there.

I had lunch with Adam and Natasha in one of the offices at the court, and when he nipped off to the loo, I confided in her how worried I was.

"I know it's hard, Coco," said Natasha, through a mouthful of Pret No-Bread sandwich. "But you have to remember, it's my turn next."

She said the words "my turn" with real relish.

"We have several things in our favour. The two hundred thousand pounds is nowhere to be found, which we can spin positively: no money, no crime. Then we have CCTV images of Adam placing him in another area of London on four occasions when the cash withdrawals took place from his bank account."

She reached out and squeezed my hand.

"And most importantly, I always win," she said.

Before I could say anything, Adam returned, straightening his tie.

"Are you talking girlie stuff?" he said.

Natasha looked at me.

"Yeah," I said. He put his arm round me and leant in for

a kiss. Then a knock on the door told us we had to go back for the afternoon session.

The onslaught finished just before four-thirty. Annabel finished by saying, "I assure those members of the jury that over the following days the paper-thin defence of Mr Rickard will be dismantled, brick by measly brick, until a guilty verdict is not only necessary but imperative."

She let her words hang theatrically over the jury before thanking the judge.

We went for dinner to Wagamama afterwards. I invited Natasha, but she said she wanted to go back to her office and prepare for tomorrow.

It was raining again as we crossed Tooley Street and passed The London Dungeon, the torches out front blazing in the dusk. Then we picked our way through Clink Street, past the Clink Prison Museum with more flaming torches and signs offering us two for one on tours of the medieval jail. It seemed we couldn't get away from symbols of foreboding. Well, we could have gone across the bridge to the Wetherspoons, but we love the noodles.

I have found it difficult to discuss the trial with Adam at the best of times, but there was no opportunity most of the evening. When we were seated in Wagamama, we were put on one of those long benches where you sit shoulder to shoulder with strangers, so we slurped our noodles awkwardly amongst the deafening chatter. Then, when we left, the walk back through to the station was crowded and the crowds didn't abate. We had to stand on a cramped train all the way home. Even the walk to the flat was chock-a-block with people pouring out of the station and on to the pavements.

When we got in, the lights were all off and Marika and Greg were sprawled out on the sofa watching *The Green*

Mile; more foreboding. Rocco was a scampering, scurrying little fur ball, canon-balling towards us with excitement. We said "Hello" to Marika and asked when Rocco had last been out for a walk.

"Sorry hun, not since this afternoon," she said, her eyes not leaving the screen. Greg just lifted a hand in greeting whilst the other dove into a bowl of Kettle crisps.

Adam said he would take Rocco out. I had a shower and then scuttled to our bedroom in a towel. A whole pile of suitcases had slid over and scattered all of the clothes I had chosen for us to wear in court. I was trawling through it, still in the towel, when Adam came back. Rocco leapt up on the bed, dancing happily with his wet paws across a white shirt I was laying out.

"Jesus, Adam!" I said, "Dry his bloody feet! We're living in a twelve by twelve box as it is."

There was a horrible wailing sound and I turned to see Adam crying, well, not crying, but sobbing uncontrollably. Rocco looked up at him confused and began to bark. I scooped him up and hugged Adam.

"This time next year we'll look back on all of this and laugh," I said, kissing the top of his head.

"This time next year I'll be on a four-year stretch," he said.

Then he started to cry again.

"I'm scared," he said. "I can't go on, I can't sit in that court room... I see the jury, watching me. Why do they get to decide? They don't know me."

I held on to him tight and was suddenly terrified. My life, our life together, seemed to have shrunk drastically, and we were teetering on the brink of something terrible in a messy, cluttered back bedroom. It took every bit of self-control to gulp back the terror clawing up my throat and not to run screaming out into the night. I'm grateful to

Marika that we are staying with her, but not having any space at this time is horrible. We lay on the bed under the harsh overhead light, with the sound blaring out from the television.

When Adam had calmed down, I got up and flicked off the light, leaving just the yellow glow from the street lamps outside. Then a scream cut through everything; it was the scene from *The Green Mile* when the electrocution of a prisoner goes wrong. I had to make the death screams stop. I wrenched open the bedroom door and ran into the living room.

"Please can you turn it down!" I shouted.

Marika leapt up and pulled Greg's arm out from inside her blouse. She jabbed at the remote and the screams subsided.

"You could have said earlier..." she glared. "It's been at this volume since you came back and now you're flipping out."

I grabbed a couple of glasses from the kitchen cupboard and went back into the bedroom. I gave Adam one of the huge fluffy towels and made him take a hot shower. When he got back, I'd tidied up, trying to make it look like our bedroom at home. I poured us both a healthy slug of whiskey, and made him drink it with some aspirin.

I think crying had done him some good. He fell asleep quickly with Rocco curled up on the pillow beside him. I crept out with the empty glasses to find Marika clearing up. Greg was in the shower.

I told her briefly what had happened, but the atmosphere between us was distant. The flat now feels too full.

I came back to bed and lay in the dark. I had thought this was going to work with Marika, that we would have so much fun living together.

When the court case is over, I am going to find us a little flat to live in.

Thursday 3rd March 23.41
TO: chris@christophercheshire.com

Natasha began with a roar on the opening day of defence arguments; she was fierce, charismatic and beautiful. She really brought out the human element of Adam, talking of his strong, honest character and painting him as the victim of stolen identity. I could see the jury soften their attitudes toward him.

However, in court what people are saying is just as important as what they're not, and the jury watched Annabel and Judge Haute-Penguin just as much as they watched Natasha. They both regarded her with an almost wry amusement. The wry smiles were saying, "Don't take her seriously — she's beautiful."

I am annoyed I am even writing about this, but these things matter. If this were a case argued by men, looks wouldn't have entered anyone's head, apart from the stenographer who seems to lament the lack of men, and gives Adam an appraising stare whilst her fingers move almost independently to her bored face.

Natasha argued that CCTV footage would show Adam could be placed away from the cash machines when withdrawals of the stolen money took place, and that the computer systems at the offices of XYZ Event Management lacked even basic security. She finished by saying, "In the modern world, data whirls about us in invisible streams, with paper transactions taking a back seat, and more and more of our personal data are open to fraudulent use. With Internet banking now the norm we are expected to do the job of bank clerks — with no training. My client may have been foolish in not protecting his data, and in not doing a good enough job of administrating his financial affairs, but he does not deserve to be found guilty for a third party's greed and dishonesty. Mr Rickard simply did not perpetrate this fraud. His background, his personality and clean record point to an upstanding citizen who is a tragic victim of stolen identity."

I felt the day ended on a high, but we trudged home with a sense of dread. Dreading Marika would be at home, something I have never experienced with her before. I feel like we are invading her territory. I would give anything just to be able to go home to Marylebone and curl up by the fire.

We got in just before seven. She wasn't home, but we wolfed down the fish and chips we'd bought, trying to minimise the time we had to spend in the kitchen. Then I walked Rocco, whilst Adam took a shower. When I got back Marika was home. Adam was in bed and Greg was now in the shower.

"Hi," I said awkwardly.

She was unloading her shopping into the fridge.

"Hi Cokes," she said. "Is this your fish?" She held up a piece of haddock I'd covered in cling film.

"Yes," I said.

"Are you going to eat it? It's stinking out the fridge."

"Maybe I won"t," I said. "It is a bit old..."

Marika dumped it in the sink. I took a deep breath.

"I just want to say, Marika, that when the court case is over, me and Adam are going to get a flat..."

She paused and looked over the top of the fridge door.

"That's good timing because I'm going to ask Greg to move in here," she said.

This took me by surprise.

"You've been seeing him how long?" I said. "Five weeks?"

"Four and a half," she said pointedly, closing the fridge door. There was another long pause.

"Great, congratulations," I said.

"Thank you," she said.

She folded her arms and we had another pregnant pause. We had nothing to say. When have we ever had nothing to say to each other?

"I'd better get off to bed then," I said, and came in to find Adam asleep in all his clothes and Rocco licking his face. How was he not waking up? I pulled Rocco off and began to prepare for tomorrow which is when the trial properly swings into action.

Monday 7th March 15.06
TO chris@christophercheshire.com

Friday was spent cross-examining DCI Thomas, the police officer who headed the investigation at Adam's former employer, XYZ Events.

No clear winner emerged between Natasha and Annabel. Much of the case hangs on the fact it was Adam's bank account used for the money transfers. If he'd realised it was being used fraudulently, and reported it, then there wouldn't be much of a case against him. But he didn't.

We passed the weekend in our room watching films neither of us could remember afterwards.

Then today Natasha was due to call our first witness,

Adam's boss Serena, from his old job in the civil service. However, her mother was taken ill and she rushed to see her in hospital. The cross examination was expected to last all day, so Judge Haute-Penguin adjourned the case until tomorrow. So after a weekend of waiting, we have to wait some more. Instead of going home, we've decided to go to the cinema in Leicester Square.

Friday 11th March 23.19
TO: chris@christophercheshire.com

It has been a week of cross-examining witnesses, and I think we might be winning. Serena eventually appeared in the witness box and made Adam look very good, and a forensic banking expert was called, who seemed to come down on the side of Natasha, criticising the computer network in the offices of XYZ.

"You'd be a fool to use one of those computers to access anything *remotely* personal," he said. "Bank accounts being out of the question. I'm surprised the company is still standing. Its IT systems appear to be hacked almost on a daily basis."

We had been expecting Adam to take the stand, but things ran over and there is still a member of staff from XYZ to be called, so he has an agonising wait until next week.

Sunday 13th March 19.27
TO: angie.langford@thebmxliteraryagency.biz

Marika went away for a mini-break with Greg this week-end, so we had some peace.

Rosencrantz came over and brought a coffee and walnut cake made by Wayne, and a bottle of sloe gin sent by Oscar. We ordered pizza, drank gin cocktails, and got some DVDs, trying to pretend that everything is normal. There was a succession of phone calls from Ethel, Chris, Meryl and Tony, Adam's daughter Holly and his ex-wife, all asking how things are going, all sending their love.

The highlight of the day was watching Adam put Rocco in the pizza box and drag him round the living room floor. It was the only time he smiled.

Tuesday 15th March 05.06
TO: chris@christophercheshire.com

Annabel called a witness from XYZ Events yesterday, an employee called Sabrina Jones. Sabrina is in her mid-twenties, a stick-thin blonde with white teeth and very fine wrists.

Annabel began by asking her about her position in the company.

"I manage the staff travel," she said.

Annabel then spent an inordinate amount of time questioning Sabrina about the state of the company since the loss was discovered. With great relish, she described the four redundancies. Annabel then asked about staff morale.

"Objection!" trilled Natasha. "How is the staff morale at XYZ Events relevant?"

"I want the men and women of the jury to understand

how this fraud has adversely affected several innocent parties," said Annabel.

"Objection overruled," said the judge.

Annabel smiled.

"Can I ask you, Miss Jones, what your relationship is to Mr Rickard?"

My ears pricked up. Sabrina licked her lips and sighed.

"We had an affair," she said.

I could see Natasha tense up; this was unexpected. Unfortunately, I didn't have as much control. I gripped the railing of the visitors' gallery.

Annabel went on.

"Can I ask how long the affair lasted?"

"About two months," said Sabrina, leaning into the microphone to ensure we all could hear.

Adam's head snapped round to me, and he shook his head.

"And why did the affair conclude?" said Annabel.

"What?" said Sabrina.

"Why did the affair *end*?" said Annabel.

"Oh, um, Adam became possessive, so I ended it. Then the day after, I caught him in my office, he was going through my handbag. He then took my phone and wanted to see all my messages..."

I had sat open-mouthed as I heard this, but I couldn't take it any longer and I found myself standing.

"She's a lying bitch!" I shouted. "She must be lying."

Heads in the courtroom turned round with varying looks of shock and horror on their faces. The horror was reserved mainly for Natasha. Judge Haute-Penguin banged her gavel.

"Mrs Pinchard, I understand this is distressing but..."

"It's not distressing, she's a fucking liar!" I heard myself shout.

There was a sharp intake of breath from the jury as the judge banged her gavel again.

"Right, I won't tolerate this in my court room. Could Mrs Pinchard please be removed."

A steward in a blue uniform appeared at my elbow and asked me to come with him. I clamped my lips together. I was in shock, desperate to believe that this was a lie and desperate to take back what had flown out of my mouth.

I'd been removed from the courtroom. The jury had seen this.

"I'm afraid I have to take you outside," said the steward apologetically.

"Yes, that's fine," I said in a small voice.

We took the lift down and he escorted me out through the x-ray scanners. With a look of sympathy, he left me under the huge low canopy outside the main entrance. I walked down to the edge and lit a cigarette. My legs were shaking uncontrollably and I had to lean on one of the pillars for support.

A minute later, the doors opened behind me and Natasha came out flanked by Adam and her associates.

"What's going on?" I said.

"We've finished for the day," said Natasha coldly.

"Why?"

"The witness was too distressed to continue."

"The witness! What about me? And what about...?"

Adam looked pained.

"You have to understand. What you just did was bad, it could have consequences," said Natasha. "The case has been adjourned until tomorrow. You won't be permitted in court when the witness resumes her evidence."

"That's not evidence, it's..."

"I have to go," said Natasha. "I need to work out how to move forward, and you two need to talk."

She was whisked away in her car and we were left standing together.

I set off for the station, finding a gap in the traffic on Tooley Street and dashing across. I pushed through the crowds at London Bridge and boarded a train waiting on the platform. I didn't check if Adam was behind me, and squeezed into a spot in the crowded carriage. As the train pulled away I saw Adam moving towards me through the irritable commuters in the packed carriage.

"Coco. It's not true," he said.

"Not here," I hissed.

I watched the landscape of London fly past, the flats all jumbled together, the endless construction work; more boxes for more people.

"Well, where?" he hissed back. "We can't talk in court, we can't talk on the train, and we certainly can't talk at Marika's!"

We ended up in the huge sprawling graveyard behind Honor Oak Park Station.

"I didn't sleep with her, please believe me," he said.

I was perching on a bench next to a mossy gravestone. Adam was pacing up and down.

"And?" I said.

"And what?" said Adam.

"That's it. *I didn't sleep with her, full stop*. What do I say? Okay Adam, let's go home and iron our clothes tomorrow..."

"I don't know what else to say."

"Who is she, this *Sabrina*?"

"Someone I worked with."

"You never mentioned her."

"That's because I barely knew her."

"Then why is she called as a character witness?"

"I don't know."

"Oh come on, don't be such a thick *man,* there must be a reason?"

"I really didn't sleep with her. She worked at the other end of the office."

"Am I stupid?" I said. "I keep making excuses for you, but maybe you did steal the money, maybe you did have the affair. At least tell me where it's hidden, so all this will be worth it!"

"It's Annabel. She called her as a witness to rattle our cages, to smear me and provoke you, which obviously wasn't hard."

"What?"

"Well, thanks to you dropping the F bomb across the courtroom, Natasha is going to have to work even harder..."

"Oh poor Natasha, with her tailored size eight suits and her five hundred pounds an hour."

"So you're jealous of Natasha now?"

"I'm not jealous of her, you idiot!" I shouted. "I'm incredibly upset about everything; this, me, you... My shitty life!"

I yanked off my engagement ring and hurled it into the row of trees edging the graveyard.

"Coco!" shouted Adam, as I walked away. "Coco, why did you do that?"

"Stop asking stupid questions and wake up. Take responsibility!" I shouted over my shoulder.

It was a rare evening where Marika didn't have Greg staying over. I walked Rocco, then had a shower, and watched *Eastenders* with her as she painted her toenails.

"Where's Adam?" she said.

"Had to stay late with our lawyer..."

"How the case going?"

"Good," I said.

I asked her what colour her nail polish was.

"Um, Fuchsia Fever," she said.

"It's nice."

"Thanks..."

We passed the rest of *Eastenders* in silence, and then I excused myself and came to bed. I lay with Rocco, watching the little clock on our cluttered beside table with one mad, teary eye.

I heard the front door go just before eleven. Adam murmured something to Marika, then came into our room and left the light off. Rocco leapt up and rushed over with licks and wuffles. He gave him a cuddle then I felt the bed lurch when he got in. I shuffled away from him, but he wiggled in to spoon me. He took my left hand and slid the engagement ring back on.

"You found it?" I said.

"Eventually..."

I opened my mouth to say something.

"Please Coco," he said. "Please can we just lie here, for one night? I just need you."

I pulled his arm around me and I waited for him to fall asleep. When he and Rocco were both snoring lightly, I gently got out of bed, came to the kitchen and fired up the coffee machine. I'm still here, wide awake and it's five in the morning.

Wednesday 16th March 22.31
TO: chris@christophercheshire.com

Natasha asked that I not be present in court for the remainder of Sabrina Jones' evidence. I'm not officially barred, but she said the focus could be pulled by my presence. She seemed calmer than the previous day and promised she would "question Sabrina robustly" about the alleged affair with Adam.

I still came in on the train with Adam. I was unsure of what else I would do if I didn't.

It was the first real spring day of the year, warm and sunny, so I bought coffee and came and sat by the river. A forsythia beside the bench had exploded in yellow, and the sun was sparkling off the Thames. I spent a pleasant couple of hours smoking and sunbathing, letting my mind wander. A text came through from Adam around eleven to say they were having a short recess, but he didn't mention how it was going.

I suddenly noticed Sabrina Jones. She was a little way down, standing by the railing next to the water. She must have come out for a cigarette. Her mobile rang and she pulled it out of her bag. I don't know if it was heavenly intervention or the wind was right, but as she began talking on the phone, I could hear her voice quite clearly being carried downwind.

"Yeah yerite, like it's a grind," she said to whoever was on the other end. She was wearing a huge parka jacket and her long, stick-thin legs poked out of the bottom. Outside the courtroom, she looked more in control, scrappy, like she could take care of herself. Then she started talking more earnestly.

"Just chill, Simon... No one knows, no one has a fucking clue." She turned her head to check if anyone was around. I quickly ducked down, behind the large forsythia. She went on smugly.

"It's me, the nice white girl against the black dude... Simon... I'm *just* a character witness, I keep telling you."

I strained to hear as the wind changed direction.

"Simon, no one knows who you are... No one can link it back to you. I've been watching the jury, they think it's him. No, keep the bag where it is... We wait, we wait, we don't rush, and then when the time is right we move it. I'm gonna quit my job in a month or so and then, we'll slowly start the move... No, chill out! Who's going to be bugging my phone? It's a Blackberry. They're like the hardest phone to bug."

She abruptly changed the subject and droned on for another five minutes, asking Simon to get a pizza out of the freezer, and then she hung up.

I sat there in shock. She must be talking about the money, I thought. Therefore, she has two hundred thousand quid stuffed in some bag!

I waited until she had gone back toward the courthouse, then I followed. I checked to see she was through security, then I went through and took the lift up to the office Natasha was using. She and Adam were just getting ready to go back in.

"I know who did it! I know who took the money!" I blurted. "It's Sabrina!"

Adam and Natasha looked up.

"She's got the money in her house in a bag!"

Natasha jumped up and closed the door. She asked me to explain further and took out a legal pad to make notes. This was thrilling, I thought, as I relayed everything I had heard. Adam is going to be found not guilty!

I noticed that Natasha had stopped writing and was tapping her pen on the yellow legal pad.

"What?" I said.

"What you've told me is a conversation heard downwind with no witnesses but you."

"Yes! But she admitted it all!"

"No, she didn't," said Natasha. "She talked about moving a bag."

"Of money," I added.

"Did she mention money?"

"Well, no, not exactly, but what else could she be talking about?"

"That's the point, anything. You didn't hear the other side of the conversation, so whoever it was could have changed the subject. They could have been talking about moving house, or a completely unrelated issue. He could be a low level drug dealer..."

"Well, that's great, you question her about her boyfriend. If he's drug dealer her flat can be searched for drugs."

"Coco," said Natasha rubbing her eyes, "I can't use the witness box to ask any old questions or elicit information about alleged crimes unrelated to our case."

"Look, I've come to you with information that could blow this case out of the water..." I said. "Well, at least prove that Adam is innocent."

"It's hearsay; you have no witnesses, no proof. You also called the girl an effing liar when the court was in session."

"Well, someone needs to do something!" I said. "How much are we paying you?"

"Coco, calm down," said Adam, rising from his seat.

"Five hundred quid an hour, plus all the cash for your paralegals!" I said.

"Coco I am doing my... I am doing the best," said Natasha.

"Well, that's reassuring, isn't it!"

There was a knock at the door and they were told to come back in to the court. I came back out to the river and was once again fuming and shaking. I ordered another coffee, sat back in the bench, and lit up another cigarette.

Suddenly a realisation flooded over me. Adam was inno-cent. He didn't take the money, he didn't have an affair. I replayed the phone conversation in my mind. It may not hold up in a court of law, but I KNOW.

I met Adam during the lunch break; I was almost skip-ping with glee.

"Natasha didn't make much of a dent in Sabrina. She came off like a wronged waif of a girl," he said.

I gave him a giant hug.

"What?"

"You didn't do it, did you? Any of it. I know Natasha rubbished what I told you, but I know what I heard."

"The case is going so badly," he said. "And I have to give evidence tomorrow."

I took him to the pub. We sat, and I told him, again, exactly what I had heard.

Thursday 17th March 19.44
TO: chris@christophercheshire.com

I'm sorry I haven't been in contact over the last few days, but the days have blurred into one. We've been up at six every morning and rarely back before eight in the evening.

Adam performed very well when he gave evidence. He was calm, composed, and open, and Annabel failed to goad him into anything. However, this case is as slippery as an eel. So much is inconclusive. I think the charm factor worked with the jury; about half were charmed in to smiling and a couple of the men who also like men seemed to warm to

Adam, so that's two-thirds of the jury who could be on our side.

The summing up was completed quite rapidly, and both Annabel and Natasha gave it their all. Annabel pointed the jury toward the fact that the only person who could have taken the money is Adam. Natasha took the line that anybody could have taken it. (They both spent half a day each saying this.)

Judge Haute-Penguin was fair in her summing up, but warned the jury to concentrate on the evidence before them and not the charms of the dashing Mr Rickard.

"Beauty comes in many forms," she said. "Beauty can be both good and bad, and you need to look past this to find the truth, for without the truth we are nothing."

She informed the jury she would only accept a majority verdict and at four this afternoon, she sent the jury out to consider their verdict.

We hung around in the highly unlikely event they would come to an agreement within the hour, and when that passed, we took the train home. It was still early and I said I wanted to go back to the little church and sit in the quiet for a bit. I've never been so tense and on edge.

"All right, but I'm only coming to avoid Marika and Greg snogging on the sofa," said Adam.

We took a seat in a pew near the front and soaked up the silence. I noticed the days were getting longer. It was after five and the sun was glinting off the huge cross above the altar, casting a gold hue over the church. A few minutes later, the vicar entered quietly and began to light candles for the evening service. He had a very gentle, calming presence. I suddenly had an idea.

"Excuse me," I said, breaking the silence. "Do you do weddings?"

He turned and took a minute to find us with his eyes,
"Ah, hello, of course my dear," he said.

"Can I book a wedding?"

"Why yes," he smiled. "I'll go and get the diary."

He disappeared into the nave, the long hem of his cassock following a moment later.

"What are you doing?" hissed Adam.

"Do you want to marry me?" I whispered.

"Yes," he said.

"Then let's have faith in the future and book a wedding."

"But what if I…"

"No. No 'what ifs' or 'buts'," I said. "You're going to be found innocent, I know it. So, we're booking our wedding. Okay?"

Adam gulped and nodded. The vicar came back holding a big dusty old diary and rested it on the end of our pew.

"Right, when were you looking to get hitched?" he grinned.

"As soon as possible," I said.

"Ooh, as soon as possible…" he winked.

"I'm not up the duff or anything," I said.

"I wasn't suggesting anything of the sort!" he said, with a smile on his lips. He flicked through pages and pages filled in with neat handwriting, and eventually came to August.

"Ah. Here we are. Saturday the nineteenth of August is available. Would that suit you?"

"Yes," I said.

Adam nodded. The vicar took down our details.

"I will need a small deposit of fifty pounds," he said.

Adam rummaged in his pockets and pulled out his wallet.

"Here," he said, handing over the last of his money.

The vicar wrote out a receipt and tore it off. We're getting married on the nineteenth of August!

Friday 18th March 11.34
TO: angie.langford@thebmxliteraryagency.biz

I'm glad to hear that my publishing house is taking an interest in the verdict. I will let you know as soon as we hear anything. We've been sitting here all morning. I've had so much coffee I am buzzing. No news is good news...

Friday 18th March 17.44
TO: angie.langford@thebmxliteraryagency.biz

Jury not close to verdict, so they have been sent to a hotel for the weekend.

Monday 21st March 15.46
TO: angie.langford@thebmxliteraryagency.biz

We are about to go in. The jury has reached their verdict.

Monday 21st March 18.05
TO: angie.langford@thebmxliteraryagency.biz

It was a guilty verdict. The jury returned a guilty verdict. Adam has nothing. He's been taken away from me with nothing. I'm in a little shop at the train station, trying to buy some toiletries for him. Rosencrantz is trying to find a clothes shop which is open. Adam has nothing to wear in bed. His pyjamas are still under the pillow. I don't know what happens next.

Saturday 26th March 03.01
TO: chris@christophercheshire.com

I am still in shock, but my head is a bit clearer. I'd had in my mind a triumphant image of emerging from Southwark Crown Court with Adam. Us stopping at the steps, and holding his arm up in victory.

Right up until a member of the jury stood and read out the verdict, I thought Adam would be cleared.

They ruled 10-2 in favour of a guilty verdict. Adam was sentenced to eight years in prison. Providing he adheres to good behaviour, he will serve only four of his eight years and will be released on licence in March 2015. The look on his face will stay with me forever — a look of fear and disbelief. He was taken from the courtroom so quickly, and he had nothing; he was alone in just the clothes he was standing up in. I wasn't even allowed to send him a message. Everyone evaporated after the verdict — Annabel, Natasha, the judge, the jury, everyone. Then it was just me and Rosencrantz in the visitors' gallery, staring down at the empty courtroom.

We then went shopping for things for Adam, and dropped them at the courthouse to be taken to him. I don't know if they were. Then Rosencrantz took me in a cab back to Marika and Greg's. I can't recall what anyone said, I can only remember us standing in a circle in the tiny kitchen. I do remember telling them that Adam had been taken to Belmarsh Prison, and Greg sucked his teeth in, as if to say how bad it was there.

Since then, I have been phoning the main switchboard at Belmarsh Prison every day to try to find out what's going on. Today I was informed by a pleasant sounding chap that Adam was going through the system, and they will know what he is in a few days.

"What do you mean, you'll know 'what he is in a few days'?" I said.

"He's being sorted into what category he'll be as a prisoner. A, B, C, or D. It shouldn't be much longer and he'll join the other prisoners in his category."

In his chirpy voice he made it sound like Adam had arrived at Hogwarts, and he was waiting to have a talking hat plonked on his head by Maggie Smith.

"Could you give him a message from me?" I said.

"I'm sorry that's not permitted, but you can write him a letter."

He gave me an address, which I scribbled down.

I was bundling a letter into an envelope when Marika returned from a dog walking expedition. She now walks about thirty dogs throughout the week and is making double what she did as a teacher. I haven't seen her much in the last few days, and this troubled me. Rocco came bundling up for a cuddle. He loves going with her and meeting all the other local dogs.

"He's very bossy," said Marika, kneeling down and giving him a treat. "There's a German Shepherd and a Dalmatian who are terrified of him."

Rocco barked loudly.

"Shush, Greg's asleep," she told him.

I stood there waiting for her to ask about Adam but she didn't say anything and filled up the kettle.

"I've just written to Adam," I said.

"Must be odd, writing letters. Do you want a coffee?" she said.

"No."

Marika opened the cupboard above the sink and pulled down a mug.

"Do you have any stamps I could use?"

"Sure," she said.

She pulled open a drawer and passed over a book of stamps. I looked at them; they were second-class.

"Have you got any first-class stamps?"

"Um, hang on," she said.

She rummaged around and chucked a book of first class stamps on the table.

I stuffed the letter into an envelope and started making out the address to:

Prisoner 48723
HMP Belmarsh
London
SE28 0EB

"Can I say something?" I said.

Marika looked up as she was spooning instant coffee into her mug.

"What?"

"This tension is horrible... Just say it. You think Adam was guilty, don't you?"

Marika didn't say anything.

"Oh come on. You're acting like nothing has happened.

He's all alone. He hasn't heard from me, and you're giving me second-class stamps! Why do you think I'd want my letter to reach him later?"

"What if Adam did do it?" said Marika, turning round to face me.

"What?"

"You know I always say it like it is... Coco, you need to face up to things."

"What do you mean?"

"He never took a lie detector test, remember? You don't *know* the truth."

All of a sudden, my hand shot out and I slapped her round the face. Hard. We both stood in shock.

Marika looked at me clutching her face, then walked calmly into her bedroom and slammed the door. I took a few deep breaths and then dashed to my room. I quickly packed up everything. Then I stalked round the rest of the flat grabbing bits and bobs I'd left and stuffing them into bags.

I called a taxi.

"Where you going to, love?" said the driver.

I had to think for a moment. I only had twenty pounds cash as I had stupidly given Marika a month's rent yesterday, thinking I might stay there after all.

"Lewisham," I said, "just off the high street... Oh and can I bring my dog in the taxi? He's a good boy."

"Well, if he's a good boy that's fine," said the driver kindly.

I lugged all of the bags downstairs. l left my set of keys on the hall table. As I was clipping on Rocco's lead the taxi pulled up.

We pulled up at Rosencrantz's house half an hour later

and rang the doorbell. Wayne answered wearing his house-coat and a character turban.

"Oh Mrs P, come in," he said. "Boys! Mrs P is on the doorstep with six suitcases!" Rocco looked up at him and barked. "And her little dog too!"

Oscar emerged from the living room in a pair of boxer shorts and Rosencrantz in his pyjamas with a bowl of cereal.

"Shit! Mum," he said, putting the bowl down and grabbing me in a hug.

"Where's a porter when you need one?" said Wayne looking at my pile of luggage.

He and Oscar started to bring the cases inside. Rosencrantz led me through to the living room as the boys lugged my stuff upstairs, Rocco sniffing about and watching them.

The boys came back downstairs just as Rosencrantz had made tea. They told me how sorry they were about everything, and Wayne said I could stay in his bedroom.

"The sofa is fine, thank you," I said.

"I won't hear of it, Mrs P," said Wayne. "Besides, I have terrible insomnia, I barely sleep in my bed."

His room is cramped but cosy. On one wall is a huge sideboard filled with commemorative mugs. There is one from the Queen's wedding to Prince Phillip, and another for her Coronation in 1953. There's Charles and Diana's wedding, Andrew and Fergie plus many of the minor royals. At the foot of the bed is a giant clothes rail filled with what look like pantomime costumes, and beside it, a small table with a sewing machine and scores of cotton reels in different colours.

The boys say I can stay as long as I like, but I need to get a grip. I'm lying here at three in the morning, clueless what to do next.

APRIL

Friday 1st April 16.33
TO: chris@christophercheshire.com

When I opened my eyes this morning there were blurred figures milling about. Then I heard Ethel's voice saying,

"'Ere, I've found what it is... old Chinese."

The room swam into view and Ethel was fishing leftover crispy chili beef out of the little fireplace near the bed. She handed it to Rosencrantz and Oscar, then shooed them out of the door.

"Afternoon," she said, pulling the curtains open. "The neighbours must wonder what yer up to, with the curtains drawn."

There was a sticky sound as the seal on the window parted then cold air sank down over me. I pulled the covers up to my chin as she eased herself onto the end of the single bed.

"Where's Rocco?" I said sleepily.

"'E's gorn out with that Wayne for a run in the park —

although I can't see 'im running, unless the bakery is about to close."

"Ethel, he's nice, he's been looking after me," I said. "They've all been looking after me."

She picked up the mug of the Queen's Coronation.

"I suppose iss not worth asking if 'e's got a girlfriend," she said. Then she spied a little silver bell on the bedside table. "Woss this?"

"The boys said I should ring it if I need anything."

"Christ! What are you, the Dowager Countess of Lewisham?"

"Ethel. If you've come here to gloat..."

"Oh, I'm not 'ere to gloat love... I'm 'ere to tell you to get off yer arse and up and about."

"I'm happy being down and nowhere," I said, turning over to face the wall.

"You need to listen to me. I bet that Judy Garland would 'ave snapped out of it if she'd 'ad me in 'er ear and not all those bloody poofs telling 'er she was a tragic 'eroine."

"Wayne and Oscar don't see me as a tragic heroine."

"Don't they? They're making things very cushy for yer. Is this what yer gonna do fer four years? Loll about in a back bedroom and 'ave three poofs ferry food up on a tray?"

I pulled the pillow over my head. "It's only four years if he gets early release."

"Now you listen 'ere," said Ethel grabbing the pillow. "It's not you stuck in Belmarsh doin' bird. It's that poor innocent man of yours. You need to be the strong one!"

My eyes began to water.

"Now, no tears!" she said. "Yer gonna get up, 'ave a wash, an' do something with that hair so when Adam sees you 'e 'as something to look forward to when 'e gets out. Right now one look at you and 'e'll be knocking on the governor's door asking for 'is sentence to be extended."

"I don't know when I'm going to see him," I said.

"Woss this then?" she said, holding up a visiting order.

I grabbed it. It said that I could visit Adam in Belmarsh on Monday!

"Oh Ethel! How did you manage to get this?" I said, hugging her for the first time ever, I think.

"It was on the mat when I came in," she said, shrugging me off her. "Now, you need to go see that lawyer, get an appeal going, then you need a place of yer own. You can't make Fatty sleep on the settee for ever."

"You think Adam's innocent?" I said, sitting up.

"Course 'e's innocent!" she said. "You 'eard that Sabrina girl by the Thames, mouthing off about the cash. You just need to prove it was 'er."

"How do I prove it?"

"Well, you won't find out anything lolling in bed."

I was shocked to find Ethel was on my side. It gave me hope.

"Yer family, Coco, whether we like it or not. An' family looks out fer family," she said. "Now, where's yer sponge bag?"

I pointed to a pile of clothes and Ethel fished it out.

"Get across that landing and 'ave a wash, I thought it was that old takeaway that stunk but iss you!"

When I came out of the shower, Ethel had gone, but she'd left the visiting order on my pillow with a first-class stamp. I filled it in carefully, and then sealed the envelope. I found something clean to wear, did my hair and makeup and caught a train over to Charing Cross. I dropped the visiting order into a postbox outside the train station, then walked up to the offices of Spencer & Spencer on The Strand.

I was shown through to Natasha's office straight away,

and even offered coffee. I realised why when she slid her bill across the table. I peeked inside the envelope and saw how much it was. *Forty-six thousand pounds.* I stuffed it into my bag and hoped she didn't see how pale I went.

"I was very disappointed it wasn't the verdict we so desired," she said, in typical lawyer speak.

"Well, you did lose," I said.

Natasha gave me a chilly smile.

"How do you feel about launching an appeal?" she said.

"Launch it as soon as you can," I said. "When do you think we could be back in court?"

Then she dropped a bombshell.

"Coco, I can't file an appeal willy-nilly," she said. "I would need to find new evidence, solid evidence, something overlooked by the police to justify an appeal. Trials cost thousands of pounds."

Yes, they do, I thought, feeling the imaginary weight of her bill in my bag. The buzzer on her desk rang and her secretary said she had another client waiting.

"So you'd like to retain me as Adam's lawyer?" she said.

"Yes. I think the first thing you should look into is this Sabrina girl, the witness," I said. "Sabrina Jones."

"Yes, Coco, of course," she said, already at her computer and on to the next meeting. "I'll be in touch in a fortnight with what we've dug up."

"Just so I have an idea of cost, how many of your associates will be digging?" I said.

"Only one. We won't be billing too heavily in the early stages..."

I came out of her office and went straight over the road to the Wetherspoons. I am sitting amongst the winos with a quid bottle of lager trying to make plans. I need to sell my car, sharpish. I think I need to get a loan too. The bill is due in twenty-eight days.

Has Marika been in touch? I thought she might call. Have you spoken to her? If so, what did she say?

Coco x

Saturday 2nd April 22.14
TO: angie.langford@thebmxliteraryagency.biz

Thanks for your voicemail with the news. So, the release of *Agent Fergie* has been postponed indefinitely. I expected as much. I'm sorry. I know you were looking forward to the last installment of the advance just as much as I was.

I got the bill from Adam's lawyer yesterday then went straight to the pub. After a few drinks, I got mad, very mad, and searched around for someone to blame. I kept coming back to Sabrina Jones. With the cheap lager in my blood, I walked up to Holborn and waited across the road from the offices of XYZ Events. At 6.06pm, Sabrina emerged from the big glass doors and walked right past (she was looking down and concentrating on her iPhone). I was going to dash across and confront her, but instead I crossed the road, fell back a bit and kind of followed her home...

I know it sounds mad, but suddenly the prospect of finding out where she lived was too enticing. I wanted to have power over her; she seems to hold so much over my life.

She boarded Central Line to Bank then walked through to the Docklands Light Railway. I followed close behind and boarded a DLR train that said Woolwich Arsenal on the front. By now she was plugged into her iPod and reading a magazine so it was quite easy to stay further down the train carriage as her shadow.

It was getting dark when we got off at Woolwich Arsenal Station. I hung back as the crowds poured off the train and became bunched together at the ticket barriers. As a practised commuter, she had her Oyster Travel Card inside her wallet, and barely looked up from her iPod as she swiped her way through the barriers. I scrabbled around for mine in the bottom of my bag, hoping I had enough credit. I made it through the barriers and emerged from the station. I noticed her further up the road, passing an area of rundown terraced houses and followed. It must have been rubbish day as I had to pick my way through scores of wheelie bins out on the pavements. Most of the houses had been carved up into flats and bedsits with concreted-over front gardens.

Up ahead Sabrina suddenly turned and vanished from view. The rest of the street was deserted. I crossed the road and hurried on. It was now almost dark. Most of the streetlights were out and I stood across the road in the fine drizzle, trying to work out which house she'd gone into. After a minute, a light came on in a top floor front window, casting a square of yellow over the wet road in front of me. Sabrina came to the window and I ducked down behind a cluster of wheelie bins as she fiddled with a blind. I got a glimpse of her happy face as a guy with a shaved head came and put his arms round her waist. She smiled up at him then the blind shot down the window and I was in darkness again.

I crouched there in the cold angrily. Why does she get to come home from her day at work to a warm flat and a partner? Suddenly I was possessed with rage. I stood up to go and bang on her door and confront her, but I had a dead leg and had to grab a wheelie bin for support and wait for the pain to subside.

As I was wiggling my toes in my shoe, a car approached with dipped headlights and they dazzled me. It was a long Volvo and it pulled to a stop beside me. The window slid down and a face I recognised leaned across the passenger seat. It was Mr Cohen, my next-door neighbour from Marylebone.

"Mrs Pinchard?" he said.

"Oh, hello Mr Cohen," I said.

"This isn't your neck of the woods!"

I didn't know what to say. I rather fluffed around, saying I had been meeting a friend for tea.

"Would you like a lift?" he said. "This isn't the nicest place to be walking around at night. Lots of strange people."

I suddenly realised I'd been stopped from doing something stupid. I said "Yes" and got into his warm car. The back seat and the boot were full of books.

"What are you doing out here?" I asked as he indicated and pulled away.

"I've got a lock-up in Woolwich, for the book shop."

"Book shop?"

"Yes, my book shop. Antiquated books on Marylebone High Street. Woolwich is cheap and safe; no one round there wants to steal books!" he grinned.

"I didn't know you had a book shop," I said.

"Yes, I'm full of mystery," he grinned.

It felt oddly comforting to see my old neighbour. We were speeding towards Central London when I realised.

"Oh, I'm not living in Marylebone anymore," I said.

"You're not?"

"No, I had to rent the house out."

"Oh," he waited for me to elaborate, but when I didn't he said, "Where do you live now?"

"Lewisham... if you go through Blackheath, it's on the way."

He didn't ask anymore until we pulled up outside Rosencrantz's flat.

"Thank you Mr Cohen," I said, unclipping my seatbelt. "I owe you one. You've really gone out of your way."

"A pleasure," he said. "Oh, you *could* do something for me."

"Yes?" I said.

Mr Cohen took a deep breath.

"I really like you Mrs Pinchard, more than you know, and I've always wanted you to do something for me, but I've always been too embarrassed to ask."

He unclipped his seat belt and leaned toward me. I froze in shock. He seemed to be moving in to kiss me. I panicked and came over all British and sort of half puckered my lips. He had, after all, given me a lift... At the last moment, he veered to one side and began feeling around in a box behind my seat.

"Ah! Here it is," he said, and pulled out a first edition hardback copy of *Chasing Diana Spencer*.

"Would you sign this? I'm building up a library of signed first editions, for the shop."

"Yes! Yes, of course," I grinned, relieved.

I found a pen in my bag and signed the book.

"Mrs Pinchard, what did you think I was going to ask you for?" he said, bemused.

"Oh, um... I should go," I said. "Thank you."

As I closed the car door, I could see the look on his face: she's a madwoman.

When I got in, I went straight upstairs and took a long shower, trying to wash away the crazy that clung to me. I came out and I went to Wayne's room and found Rocco asleep on the bed. He opened his eyes and stretched and I pulled him onto my lap.

"I'm not mad, am I?" I said, holding Rocco up. He

regarded me with his little wise eyes as if to say, *you're not far off.*

Please email me if anything happens, work-wise. If they decide to go ahead and publish *Agent Fergie*, or if anything else comes up.

Coco x

Tuesday 5th April 09.41
TO: chris@christophercheshire.com

I went to visit Adam yesterday. Horrible, horrible, horrible. The whole process, the whole situation, and I'm not even the one who has to deal with it.

I took the train to Plumstead Station, and I seemed to be in the prisoners' wives carriage. To be honest, they scared me; even their children scared me, running riot, full of e-numbers. We all got off at the station in the rain and filed along a grey road to the Prison Visitors Centre.

The windows were all steamed up inside, and it stunk of industrial floor cleaner. We had to line up and go through a metal detector, then put our belongings in a locker. You need a pound for the lockers, and many of the women didn't have enough money, so their stuff had to be bagged up and left in an office, which took ages. We were led to a waiting room with a view of a brick wall and lots of leaflets about drug abuse and eating disorders lining the walls.

Finally, we were called through into what looked like a huge gymnasium, with row after row of plastic chairs and tables. The prisoners were all sat facing us as we entered. They were wearing yellow sashes. I later found out this is so they can't blend in with the visitors and walk out at the end of visiting.

I saw Adam at the side by the wall, in his sash, sitting and waiting. I quickened my step across the wooden floor and grabbed him in a bear hug. He felt thin, and had a deep sadness in his eyes, a look of defeat. He was wearing the clothes I had sent for him. We hugged for a long time, and then he pulled me in front of him to look at my face.

"It's so good to see you," he whispered.

"Are you eating?" I said.

"Yes."

"Sleeping?"

"Yes, and no..."

His eyes were bloodshot, he had lots of shaving cuts, and his skin was dry and cracked on his hands and face. He told me they only have hand soap to shower with, and they are given the cheapest disposable razors for shaving, which they have to hand back as soon as they've finished.

"Why?"

"So they can't be used as weapons," he said, matter-of-factly.

I gulped and changed the subject.

"How is the food?"

"Disgusting."

"And your cellmate?"

I couldn't believe we were having this conversation, talking about stuff like this...

"I'm in a cell of my own, thank God," he said. "But we're locked up for twenty-three hours a day."

What seemed like a brief exchange had taken up fifteen minutes of our precious hour. There was so much to say.

"What about my appeal?" he said, his eyes lighting up.

I told him I'd been to see Natasha, and she'd give me an update in a couple of weeks.

"Jeez... Coco, time in prison goes so slowly. It feels like months since I came here."

He said he'd had had a ton of cards and letters; from Chris, Ethel, Rosencrantz and the boys, friends from his old job — even Daniel and Marika. Meryl and Tony had sent a very kind card with, bizarrely, a Waterstones book token, and they had written:

Here's hoping you get into an open prison, we've read in The Daily Mail they let the prisoners out to go shopping! Meryl and Tony xxx

He grinned when he told me this, and for a brief moment, I had my old Adam back. He told me he has been classed as a category D prisoner, which is the lowest category, reserved for prisoners who are trusted to not escape and are eligible for transfer to an open prison.

"That's fantastic," I said.

"I'm on the waiting list for transfer," he said. "It could take months."

"So you're stuck with all the rapists and murderers!"

"Shhhh Coco," he hissed.

I looked around but it seemed as if no one was paying us any attention.

"It's not fair. Even if you had done what you're in here for you should be away from..."

"Let's talk about something else," he said. "How are you doing?"

I told him about the fight with Marika and that I would be looking for a place to live. His face clouded over.

"Why are you standing by me, Coco?" he said. "I've screwed your life up. You should find a decent bloke to take care of you."

"You haven't screwed up my life, and you are a decent

bloke. You're more than decent," I said, grabbing his hand. "I love you and I'm determined to get you out so we can be together. You are innocent. I will marry you and we are going to be together for the rest of our lives."

He took my hand and regarded me for a moment, then he leant across and kissed me. After several seconds, some of the other prisoners started whistling and one of the guards told us to move apart.

"I bet I'm going to be searched even more thoroughly," he said. "But it was worth it."

"Why would you be searched even more?"

"Kissing is a good way to smuggle in drugs," he said.

Then a bell rang which told us our hour was up.

"What a thing to end on," he said. "I love you."

"I love you too," I said.

I clung onto him tight before I had to wrench myself away. I kept looking back at him, all the way to the door, and then he was gone.

I discovered I can visit him twice a month for one hour. I can email him twice a week, however he can't email back. My emails have to be sent to an official address where they will be read by a stranger, then printed off and given to him as if it were a letter. He is issued with a phone card once a week, which will last about twelve minutes. I can write letters to him as many times as I want and he can write back, so long as he has money for stamps.

In the modern world of instant communication, this seems so alien and unfair. It's also magnified by the fact Adam is only seven miles away from Rosencrantz's place in Lewisham. I checked this on the AA Route Planner. He might as well be seven million miles away.

When I left the Prisoners Visitors Centre, I felt a determination after seeing Adam. I am determined we will survive this and that I will get him out of there. I need to do my maths so I can find a place to live and get to grips with the future.

Thursday 7th April 12.12
TO: angie.langford@thebmxliteraryagency.biz

I placed an ad last night on Gumtree advertising my car for sale, and within forty minutes I had someone interested. I emailed the guy back and agreed to meet at Chris' place (where the car is parked) this morning.

Rosencrantz had offered to come with me and when he came downstairs this morning he was dressed in a black suit with his hair slicked back.

"You look a bit smart to flog a second hand car," said Wayne, who was dishing up egg on toast for Oscar and me at the kitchen table.

"I want to look, you know..."

"Smart?" I said.

"Straight," said Rosencrantz, awkwardly.

"Oh please," said Wayne, rounding on him with a fish slice and his frilly apron. "You're here, you're queer, get on with it. I can't be doing with all this pretending what you're not rubbish."

"You can be gay and know about cars," said Oscar. "What do you know about cars?"

"Um..." said Rosencrantz.

"'I'll be there," I said.

"But what do you know about cars, Mrs P?" said Oscar.

"There was one time I had steam coming out of my

bonnet and I knew how to fill up the radiator!" I said proudly.

"I didn't know you wore a bonnet, Mrs P!" grinned Wayne. "I bet you look like a right Bo-Peep with that on and a fag hanging out the corner of your mouth!"

"I'm serious guys, Mum needs this to go well," said Rosencrantz.

"Well, maybe you shouldn't be called Rosencrantz," said Wayne.

"How about you call yourself Dean?" suggested Oscar. "Dean is the name of someone not to be messed with. Someone called Dean would know about cars."

Rosencrantz's eyes lit up. He pulled a comb out of his pocket

"Yeah. I'm Dean, and I'm mean," he said.

Rocco barked as Rosencrantz swaggered round the kitchen.

"I'd get the slow train if I were you, Mrs P," said Wayne. "Give him time to rehearse."

"What?" said Rosencrantz.

"You're a bit Dean the Queen right now," grinned Oscar.

We arrived at Chris' place just before eleven. The sun was out and his house on the edge of Regent's Park looked so idyllic. The thatch roof glowed golden in the sunlight, butterflies floated above the green hedges and the garden was filled with tulips and daffodils. A Rolls Royce was parked a little way down the street and, as we approached, the door opened. A short fat little man in his fifties got out with a terrifyingly tall blonde in her twenties. He was clad in clothes far too young for him and carrying a briefcase. A short sundress barely covered the top of her long legs, and as they walked toward us, we saw his head only came up to her shoulder. The guy was called Nick and his girlfriend was Dahlia.

I left Rosencrantz chatting with them and walked up the path to Chris' garage. I used my key to open the roll top door and reversed the Land Cruiser out onto the driveway. I glanced back wistfully at it; white and sleek, its chrome headlights glinting in the sun.

"It's only about seven months old, and it only has a few thousand miles on the clock," I said.

Nick walked around the car inspecting it. Dahlia followed, peering in the windows. He opened the driver's side and helped her into the seat. She pouted her big lips and grasped the steering wheel.

"What do you think, Princess?" said Nick.

"I wuv it," she pouted in a baby voice. "Can I have it?"

"Sure thing, Princess," he said, as if it were nothing more than a new mascara.

"You got the papers?" he said.

I pulled out the little black plastic book housing the paperwork and I handed it over. He flicked through it.

"You got ID?"

"ID?"

"To show me this is you," he said.

I rummaged in my bag; luckily, I had my passport. He peered at it and handed it back. Dahlia was still in the driver's seat turning the wheel and miming driving.

"So, we said twenty-two grand?"

"Twenty-five," said Rosencrantz.

Nick looked at us.

"Well, for twenty-five, shouldn't we hear it in action? Have you got the key?"

I said there was an ignition button and Dahlia started the car with a roar. She giggled and clapped her hands in delight. Nick placed the briefcase on the bonnet, and flicked it open. Bundles of fifty-pound notes lined the case. He picked up a thick wodge sealed together with a paper band.

"You're giving me cash?" I said.

"What else?" said Nick.

I looked at Rosencrantz. Dahlia switched on the radio and Shakira's *Waka Waka* song started booming out mixed with her revs of the engine.

Ten grand was counted out on the bonnet when I heard the front door behind us slam and a stick insect of a woman with a high forehead emerged. Despite the spring weather, she was dressed in a fur coat. She was brandishing a shotgun.

"Stop whatever it is you're doing, this is private property!" she cried, baring her brown aristocratic teeth.

I realised this was Chris's mother, Lady Edwina.

"Are you drug dealers?" she said, cocking the gun. "Turn that blasted racket orf!"

She pointed the gun at Dahlia who was still bopping away to Shakira. She noticed the gun and screamed.

"It's me, Lady Cheshire," I shouted, above the music. "You remember? We met at the Edinburgh Festival, Chris directed my play... I'm a friend of his."

Dahlia turned down the music and we were all stood with our hands in the air.

"Yes, there isn't much money in the theatre these days," she said. "God knows I've tried to dissuade Christopher, but surely you don't need to deal drugs with lowlifes?"

"Hey!" said Nick. "I own my own construction company!"

Lady Edwina looked even more disgusted.

"Rebecca!" yelled Edwina back at the house. "There's some of those *new money* types in the driveway..."

Chris' sister Rebecca came bustling out. She's quite

pretty in a posh and pudgy way. She was wearing a hound-tooth suit and a padded hairband in her long blonde hair.

"Mummy, that's Coco, you silly sausage, she's selling her car..." she said in her little squeaky posh voice.

Lady Edwina finally lowered the shotgun.

"Why are you selling your car?" she said.

"Legal bills," I said.

For some reason this seemed an acceptable excuse for all parties involved, and Nick resumed counting out the money. Rebecca even brought out a special marker pen she uses for work, which shows if a bank note is real. Luckily they were.

When we were done, we shook hands and Nick went back to his Rolls Royce leaving Dahlia to drive my car. Well, her car.

"How much would you take for that fur coat and the gun?" asked Dahlia, pulling up beside Lady Edwina.

"These are family heirlooms and not for sale!" she huffed.

"Okay, bye Dean," she said, winking at Rosencrantz, and she roared away.

I watched wistfully as the car vanished.

"Why did she call you Dean?" asked Lady Edwina.

"Long story, your ladyship," said Rosencrantz.

She offered to phone Coutts for us and get them to come and collect the cash, but I said I had to go to find a branch of the Halifax, which she didn't understand and she went back into the house muttering.

The rest of the day went quickly. I paid in the money and also took out a bank loan and then watched most of it vanish when I paid Natasha's bill.

I've just done my maths. With loan repayments and putting money aside for an appeal, I have £900 a month to live on, which in London terms is nothing. And then this will only last for six or seven months.

Please keep your eye out for any work opportunities!

Wednesday 13th April 11.14
TO: submit@prisonlink.net

EMAIL FOR HMP BELMARSH PRISONER – 48723 (Adam Rickard)

Dear Adam,

Well, here I am, having a go at emailing you. You should receive this 24 hours after I press 'send'. I have also posted some letters, but they are a little waffly. I hadn't wanted to moan about my living situation, considering what yours is. I managed to find a flat within my budget and I thought I would tell you the story.

I had a few days of drudgery, going round the slimy estate agents in South London (of which there are many). None of them had flats in my budget. There were plenty of scuzzy over-priced bedsits. One guy was letting a room in his flat where the damp had made the plaster crumble under the wallpaper so it bulged out, but he didn't want Rocco in case he damaged the furnishings. Another woman was letting out a large airing cupboard and said I could have Rocco as long as he slept in a kennel in the garden. One room was even advertised as free — in exchange for 'light modelling and photographic work'!

On the third day, I was outside a newsagent in Brockley with Rocco, trying to roll a cigarette (I'm economising) when

I noticed a little old man in the window sliding a hand-written card into one of those clear advertising pouches. The card was advertising a one-bedroom flat, all bills included, for £550!

I spat out my tobacco, and waited until he emerged a few minutes later with a copy of *The Guardian* under his arm. I introduced myself enthusiastically. I was dreading he would tell me to ring a number and book an appointment but he was charming in his tweed jacket and flat cap, with a little grey bristly moustache. He knelt down and tickled Rocco under the chin. Rocco, sensing that this was a make or break moment, turned on the cuteness, stood to attention and panted theatrically. Then I realised he knew I had a dog.

"Look, I'm really in need of a flat to rent, but I want to be honest," I said. "Rocco is a wonderful dog, he never makes a mess, but I can't guarantee he won't pee accidentally."

I held my breath as the old man smiled and squinted in the sun.

"Well, I'll be honest too," he said. "My late sister, whose flat this was, also had a habit of peeing accidentally and the carpets are in need of a good scrub."

I didn't know what to say, but he wasn't saying no, so my heart lifted.

"Would you like to come and see it? It's only round the corner," he said.

The flat was a short walk from the newsagent, on a nice terraced street, and the ground floor flat of a Victorian conversion. I estimated it was around a twenty minute walk from Marika's flat in Honor Oak Park.

He opened the communal entrance, and we walked down a dingy little corridor, and into a rather dated one-bedroom flat. There was evidence of his elderly sister every-where; in fact, it looked pretty much as it would have when she was alive. A pile of Danielle Steele library books were stacked on a coffee table — due back in a week, I noticed — and a blue wool blanket was discarded on the sofa beside them. Next to the books was a glass half filled with water and bottles of pills.

On one wall was a huge bookcase filled with novels, paperwork, spider plants in various states of decay and many ornaments. By the sofa was a floor lamp, and, under a bay window which looked out onto a well-kept garden, was a huge bureau with an old television set. The bottom doors hung open and a video recorder blinked off and on. A load of videocassettes, most of them labeled *Midsomer Murders*, were piled high and stuffed beside the machine.

The carpet was nice, Axminster, if a little stained. The sofa and curtains seemed to be in competition with each other as to who could be the most frilly and flowery. However, to my delight, there were the original sash windows, the paint cracking admittedly, but they look far more elegant than the modern plastic ones.

In the other half of the living room was a kitchen of basic pale Formica; an oven with a breadboard on the hobs, a microwave sat on the end of a tiny counter with a kettle on top of it. Beside the oven, a tall fridge-freezer squealed from the exertion. A tap dripped into a sink filled with dirty dishes.

We moved past the back door, which was on the opposite side to the front door, and down a corridor. To the left was a window looking out over the back gardens of the next-door neighbours. Washing whirled on some old rotary dryers, a faded kids' plastic slide sat amongst an overgrown garden.

On the right was the bathroom. It was a bit smelly with a faded avocado suite and brown cork tiling. Rocco put his furry feet up on the edge of the bath and peered inside. The bottom was dry and full of dust; the toilet was clean but ringed with lime scale.

At the end of the short corridor was the bedroom. This shocked me the most. The bed was unmade and some flowery print dresses were laid over a chair by an old fashioned, high wooden wardrobe. The lady who owned this flat hardly seemed to have left; in fact, she had left a bit of herself behind. Her teeth were in a pint of water on the nightstand!

"Ah. I hadn't expected to show anyone around so quickly," said the old man, breaking the silence. "I know it's not ideal for a modern woman like you Mrs..."

"Pinchard," I said. "But please, call me Coco."

"Hello Coco, I'm Mr Mason, Thomas."

We shook hands politely and he went to the foot of the bed and opened the window to let in some air. It looked out over a little strip of concrete that ran between the side of the flat and the gardens of the other houses. Despite all of the mess, I liked it. Mr Mason asked what I thought.

"It's perfect for me," I said eagerly. "When could I move in?"

"Well, I don't know. Theoretically you could move in today, but as you can see I have to phone up someone to come and get my sister's things and I'll need to, I don't know, pay a cleaner."

"Look Mr Mason..."

"Thomas, please..."

"Thomas," I smiled. "I own a house in Marylebone; I've had to rent it out for a year to, erm, pay some bills. So I have a regular income, I have a contract with my tenant which proves this."

"Jolly good," he said.

"It's just that my budget is five hundred pounds a month... What I thought was if I could move in today, I could be the one to help you pack up everything, for free...

Of course, not for free, but I can give you two months' rent, in cash, today."

He looked at me for a moment. I think I'd made my desperation obvious.

"Are you on the run?"

"NO!" I said, sounding like someone who was totally on the run.

"I'm joking, my dear," he grinned. "I'm sure that's fine. My son has drawn up some paperwork. Shall I meet you back here at, say, five o'clock?"

"Yes," I said. "That would be wonderful."

We shook hands, and then he knelt down to Rocco who also held out his little paw.

"Well I never," he said and shook it.

Rocco barked happily. I didn't tell him that Rosencrantz has taught Rocco to do the shake-my-paw thing, and now he does it with just about everyone. However, his timing was spot on and it sealed the deal.

I dashed back home, home being Rosencrantz's, but no one was in to tell the good news to. I wanted to phone you, which was, of course, out of the question. I then went to phone Marika and tell her I'd be living just down the road from her, but remembered we weren't talking... Then I phoned Chris but his phone went to voicemail.

I set to work tidying up and packing all of my things. I stripped off the bed sheets in Wayne's room and put them in the washing machine. I dusted and hoovered. I thought Rocco would be terrified of the vacuum cleaner but he loved it, going as far as sitting on top of the unit (it's a mini Dyson) and he clung on like a little Olympic tobogganist as I went through the house. Rosencrantz, Wayne and Oscar came back just as I finished lugging the cases downstairs.

"Oh Mrs P, you didn't have to go and rent a flat," said

Wayne, genuinely upset. "You're welcome here as long as you need... isn't that right, boys?"

Rosencrantz and Oscar nodded in agreement.

"Thank you, but I need to stand on my own two feet," I said.

"Can we come and help you, Mum?" said Rosencrantz, when I'd told them about the flat.

"Ooh yes! I could wear my new character turban and housecoat!" said Wayne, clapping his hands excitedly.

I thanked them, but I thought it could be weird and a little inappropriate if I rocked up with a load of strangers to offload all the old lady's gear — and I wouldn't want to offend further if Wayne was interested in a few of her dresses for his costume rack.

"Now I feel like *you're* leaving home," said Rosencrantz, when the taxi pulled up. "Do you want Bitch to keep you company?" He offered me his teddy bear.

"She's yours," I said. "And I'd never forgive Rocco if he chewed her up."

I hugged them all then got into the taxi and on to the next adventure.

Mr Mason was waiting outside the flat with a younger, more severe version of himself whom he introduced as his son, Callum. He didn't help with the cases, leaving Mr Mason and me to lug them into the hallway. Callum shifted in his loafers holding the contract impatiently and, when we were ready, he led us into the living room.

There had already been a smash and grab clearing out spree, and a pile of bin liners was stacked against the wall.

"Callum thought it best that we make a dent in clearing out my sister's things," said Mr Mason apologetically.

I wasn't sure what he was apologising for until Callum handed over the tenancy agreement. It was a standard six-month lease but it had "Rent £650 per calendar month" written on it.

I asked why it was a hundred and fifty pounds more than we agreed on and Callum came alive. Well, his face twisted into a sneer. He said I had taken advantage of his father and that the rent should be higher as it included council tax and water.

"I thought it was all bills included," I said.

"Um, my son says this is very competitive for the area," said Mr Mason, rather embarrassed.

I assured Callum I was not taking advantage, and I managed to negotiate him down to six hundred a month. Let's face it, I was desperate and on the doorstep with all my things. Callum wanted twelve hundred cash up front, so I had to take Rocco round to the newsagent and withdraw another £200 from the cash machine. I also bought him some dog food (of course, he only likes the expensive stuff in the little pouches, the little diva) a new bone, some tea bags, bread, butter, honey, milk, and eggs. I also grabbed some cloths and all-purpose cleaner. I returned to find Callum loading up his car with the bin bags. I handed over the cash (which he counted, twice), we signed the tenancy agreements, and he gave me a receipt.

"Sorry about that," said Mr Mason, handing over the keys at the door.

His son beeped the horn from the car.

"Give me a call if you need anything..."

As they drove off I realised they hadn't given me their phone number.

I took Rocco inside and let him off the lead. He woofed excitedly and set to work, nose to the ground, sniffing every inch of the place. All of the paperwork on the shelf had been removed, leaving gaps amongst the books. The television and video recorder had been taken but they'd left the videocassettes. The microwave and kettle were also gone, as were the pictures, leaving the pale walls with a series of circles and squares. I went through to the bedroom and the wardrobe was now empty, but the bedding was still there. The bedside lamp was gone, but the teeth were still in the glass of water!

Despite all of this, I felt calm and relaxed for the first time in ages. I fed Rocco — I'd been left the glassware, plates, and cutlery. I then tried the side door leading out to the garden; it was locked, but I found the key under the saucer of a dead spider plant. The door opened awkwardly and I came outside with Rocco. There was just a thin, fenced-in strip of concrete. The garden I could see through the window was on the other side of one of the fences, and it belonged to the flat above. I squeezed past an old rusting washing machine and peered through a hole in the fence. A set of steps led down from a balcony to green grass and flowers.

I was gutted. There was a gurgling, whooshing sound, and grey water shot out of a drainpipe and flooded over a little square drain beside the back door. The water ran towards us, steaming in the cold air, and Rocco backed away from it barking.

I hoisted myself up on the washing machine and lit a cigarette. It was heavenly. I smoked two and then came back inside to survey the damage.

I was initially only going to hang up some clothes, but I ended cleaning the whole flat. I found some bleach and scoured every inch of the bathroom. I took an old lampshade down, which was damp and misshapen, and the bare bulb made the room a lot lighter. I threw away piles of mouldy food from the fridge and cleaned it, along with the kitchen. I discovered a very old vacuum cleaner in a cupboard with an electricity meter and boiler (both ancient), and I vacuumed and tidied, then dusted with a pair of socks. I stripped the bed and threw all of the blankets away (there was no duvet). I found a clean set in the cupboard above the boiler and I turned the mattress and changed the bed. I hung all of my things in the wardrobe and arranged my meagre belongings — radio/iPod dock, laptop, phone, computer printer, and folders of paperwork on the coffee table.

There is no shower, just a bath, so I found a jug in the bottom of one of the kitchen cupboards and I had a sort of shower, pouring jugs of water over myself.

Finally, at one in the morning, I was clean. The flat was respectable and I made egg on toast with a giant mug of sweet tea. I sat on the sofa, next to the radio/iPod dock, and ate whilst listening to the shipping forecast. What is it about the shipping forecast? It's so comforting — being warm and thinking of all the ships out at sea in the mist and the dark, all listening and being guided to safety. Then I thought of you. Moving into this strange flat with you would be so much more fun.

I fell asleep on the sofa, and woke up at eleven the next morning with Rocco licking my face. It was sunny outside and I opened the back door. I filled a glass with water, grabbed my fags, and followed Rocco out. I put the glass on the washing machine and lit up. Rocco was rolling around in the sun and I watched him for a minute as he jumped up and chased a butterfly. I reached out and grabbed my glass, it was only when my lips touched the edge that I realised it wasn't my glass, it was the glass with the false teeth! I'd put it outside last night during the cleaning spree. I hadn't wanted to throw it away, I mean, what if they came back for her teeth?

I screamed and wrenched the glass away from me. The teeth flew out and sailed over the fence.

I jumped off the washing machine and tried to see over, but I am too short, even on tiptoes. I squinted through the gap. The teeth were lying in the middle of the lawn, glistening revoltingly in the sun. I looked up at the windows of the flat above. The curtains were all closed. Now this was a dilemma I'd like to see covered in the etiquette books: how to retrieve a set of false teeth from the garden of a neighbour to whom you have not yet been introduced. I went to haul myself over the fence and grab them, but I only had on a long t-shirt with nothing underneath so I came back in to get dressed.

As I came out of the bedroom in a tracksuit, my new doorbell buzzed. Rocco barked like mad, so I picked him up to open the door. There was a tall, tanned skinny guy with shoulder length hair. He must have been in his twenties and he grinned with a set of huge white teeth. He had on flip-flops, shorts, and a woven poncho.

"Huj thiiiir," he said, in a broad Australian accent. "I'm Shane, from upstairs."

"Hello," I said.

"Weird question," he said. "Did you throw Doris's teeth over my fence?"

He pulled them out of his poncho.

"Well... Not on purpose," I said.

"Jeez, you guys! They send a different carer each week... You've gotta treat her better, she's so sick." He gave me a look to show he was deeply disappointed. "Can I come and see her?"

"Oh," I said. "You didn't know? She's... she died."

"Shit. When?"

"I don't know," I said. "I'm the new tenant."

"You mean you're renting this place?"

"Yes, hello, I'm Coco."

I explained how the teeth ended up flying across his garden.

"Shit, Coco, I'm sorry to give you the judgment. The council keeps sending these idiot carers and when I saw her yesterday morning she was real frail."

"You saw her yesterday?" I said.

"Yeah, I knew she didn't have long... She was so nice. Still, it's for the best."

"I moved in yesterday!" I said.

"Yeah, well you can see how fast property gets snapped up on the London rental market," he said.

He pulled out a tissue and put the teeth in.

"Would you return these to the family? I know she'd hate to be buried without her teeth."

I was still standing there in shock. Rocco leant out and sniffed the teeth as he placed them in my hand.

"Welcome to the building, Coco," he said. "Just shout if you need anything."

And he bounded up the stairs two at a time and back to his flat.

I closed the door and looked around my flat with new eyes.

I have been a bit scared since then, but I suppose people die all the time. I opened the windows and doors after Shane had gone. To make sure Doris isn't still floating around. I'm glad I've got Rocco, but every time I've taken a shower I haven't dared close my eyes.

Anyway, it's nothing to moan about. I can't really justify moaning at all. I have a place to live and I can't wait to see you again. I love you and I miss you.

Love you, always

C x

P.S. Aargh! I just tried to send this email and I've discovered the flat has no reception for Internet or mobile phone. I've had to come to a coffee place round the corner to email this to you. I will have to work on being connected. I will also make sure I am out walking Rocco during association when you call me on my mobile.

MAY

Monday 2nd May 11.14
TO: submit@prisonlink.net

EMAIL FOR HMP BELMARSH PRISONER – 48723 (Adam
Rickard)

Dear Adam,

I am back emailing! I bit the bullet and had a landline
and broadband put in, which has blown the budget a little,
but now you can phone the flat and I can get online. I'd love
you to be the first person to phone. My new number is 0207
946 0789.

I thought long and hard about having it put in because I
have quite enjoyed the feeling of being cut off from everything. It's helped feel like I am experiencing a tiny bit of
what you are going through.

I tried to avoid the Royal Wedding last Friday. Shane
from upstairs knocked on the door around eleven in the
morning, just as the service was beginning. He had brought

me some parsley, coriander, and red chilies from his garden. I'd told him I've been attempting to cook.

"Thanks, Shane," I said. "Aren't you celebrating?"

"Nah. I'm a Republican," he said. "I can't see anything to get excited about with this wedding,"

"Well, I heard on the radio that Kate's sister Pippa has a rather scrumptious backside in her bridesmaid's dress," I said with a smile. "You could appreciate that and still be a Republican?"

"Is it on TV?" he said, suddenly more interested.

I told him I don't have a TV. He invited me to come up and watch his, but I said no. I didn't want to have to talk about weddings. I had also said no to a street party that Rosencrantz, Wayne, and Oscar were organising, no to visiting Ethel, and a big no to Meryl. She had a viewing party and used it to re-launch Watson Funerals Ltd. They're now called Funeral Pieces, a play on Carole Middleton's company, Party Pieces.

What's more disturbing is that www.funeralpieces.co.uk got so many hits on its first day that it crashed.

Chris phoned on my mobile when I was out walking Rocco this morning. He sounded odd at first, asking why I hadn't been in contact for a couple of weeks. I said he hadn't been in contact either. There was a silence.

"I've been worried about you, Cokes, but I didn't know what to say... I'm sorry."

"It's fine," I said, and explained about my lack of signal, and that I have moved to a new flat.

"Yes, Rosencrantz tells me it's like a granny flat — but the granny dropped dead and now they're renting it out to you!"

"The bed was still warm, Chris, that was how quickly they rented it out."

He laughed and I realised how much I missed him.

"Hey! Why don't we go out for a drink?" he said. "I really want to take you to the champagne bar at St Pancras. It's got the longest bar in Europe with the hottest bartenders, who, I'm reliably informed have the longest..."

"I can't Chris... Didn't Rosencrantz tell you I only have sixty-nine pounds a week to spend?"

"I've never heard the phrase sixty-nine used in a more depressing sentence... No worries, it'll be my treat."

"No. I want to see you but I've made this vow to stand on my own two feet. You've done so much for me. Why don't you come and see the flat, I could cook something."

"Cook something? What can you cook?" he said.

"I'm teaching myself. It'll be something yummy," I lied. "Come on... I've missed you."

"What about Marika?"

"What about her?"

"Well, she lives just down the road from you..."

"She hasn't phoned me," I shot back.

"She's been asking about you."

"But she hasn't phoned me!"

"Okay... okay. Shall we say, eight?"

It felt weird when I got off the phone, like our dynamic had changed. I racked my brain as to what I could cook. I didn't tell him I've had several disasters, and wrecked several saucepans when food became hopelessly burnt and welded onto the bottom. I also thought the flat could do with a little ambience. I have no lamps — just a single sixty-watt bulb in each room.

I came to the edge of Hilly Fields common where Rocco was having a poo. I pulled a bag out of the new dog-do dispenser the council has installed. The bags are hopeless; they are huge and made of thin white paper, and there's this weird square of cardboard in the bottom. It's like trying to pick up shit with a Chinese paper lantern. Then I realised I had solved the ambience problem in the flat. I grabbed a handful of the dog-do bags. On the way home, we stopped in at the off-licence. I bought two bottles of a £1.49 white wine and a litre of value lemonade (29p). I added a big bag of value crisps (49p) and two avocados, which have been rolling around in a cardboard box under the awning outside for the past week (only slightly black and now reduced to 9p each).

I came home, and mashed them up with some cottage cheese and some of the chilies from Shane. I took my doggy-do bags, dotted them around, and lit a tea light in each.

Just when it was getting dark, Chris rang the bell.

"Oh my God!" he said, coming into the flat. "This place, it's idyllic!"

It's strange how the right lighting can set the mood. The tea lights seemed to add mystique and excitement to my staid surroundings.

"This is breathtaking, Coco," he said, as we moved from the gloaming in the living room to the concrete outside. The tea lights on the ground had a weird effect. It was very dark, so you couldn't see much of the tall fences. You just saw the space they cut out in the sky above, so there was a kind of glowing platform with an oblong of starry sky.

I poured him an ice-cold 29p spritzer and brought out my green 18p guacamole garnished with a couple of Shane's shiny red chilies.

"What's this wine?" he asked.

"It's from a local organic vineyard," I lied.

"It's beautiful!" he said. "And this dip! Wow! It's like a taste of Morocco!"

"Yeah, it's from the local farmer's market..."

Despite my blatant lies, he was right; it all tasted

wonderful. The question is, what have I been spending a fortune on over the years of entertaining? All the thirty quid bottles of wine, and equally expensive Waitrose sharing platters?

I brought out the sofa cushions, and we sat under the stars on the little concrete strip with Rocco sleeping at our feet. We talked rubbish, smoked, and drank. It was lovely. He had a wonderful time directing the plays at The Rabbit Hutch Theatre in Devon. He wants me and Marika to visit Devon, and see at least one of them, but I don't know. I would need to find a dogsitter and some money, and Marika and I aren't speaking.

"Think about it," he said. "It could be the thing that gets you two back together."

He stayed for a few hours, and then took a cab home. He has really cut down a lot on his drinking, and seems so much happier. I hope he gets another job soon to keep it all going.

The next morning something odd happened. I came through to feed Rocco, and there on the carpet in front of the huge bookshelf was a photo of you and me. I hadn't seen it in ages. It was taken in the bar of the Carnegie Theatre at the Edinburgh Festival after the last performance of *Chasing Diana Spencer: The Musical*. I didn't even remember bringing the picture with me when we moved out of Marylebone. I looked at the shelves but I haven't put any of my stuff on them yet, and I have only the one folder of paperwork. And besides, all of my photos of you are in my wallet or on my phone.

I picked up my new landline and called Chris to ask what time he left last night.

"Um, about ten thirty," he said wearily. "Why?"

"Were we that drunk?" I said.

"Not really... I think I only had three drinks, which is unprecedented!"

"Did we look at any photos?"

"No..."

I paused.

"Okay," I said. "Just wanted to make sure you got home safely."

"Okay, love you," he said. "What time is it?"

"A little after nine."

"Ugh. I'm going back to sleep. Oh, one other thing, you must remember to give me the details of that organic vineyard you got the wine from."

I crossed my fingers and promised I would, and then he hung up. I looked at the picture again. I cannot work out how it got there.

I'm sitting up writing to you now with all the lights on. A little bit scared to go to bed and missing you like crazy. *Especially* your hot naked body in my bed.

All my love, Coco xxx

Wednesday 4th May 11.14
TO: chris@christophercheshire.com

Adam phoned last night and said he has been moved to a communal cell. He is now sharing with a category A prisoner who is serving life for triple murder. His cellmate is called Kip. He is twenty and has a long shaggy beard. The only food he will eat is Dairylea cheese triangles.

Kip apparently asks all of the other prisoners on their wing to give him their cheese triangles in return for a cigarette or doing their laundry. Adam has been handing over his from lunch and dinner for the last couple of days in return for use of Kip's radio.

"He just stares at me," said Adam. "Whatever I'm doing, he just stares, chewing his cheese triangles. He saves the foil wrappers in his pocket and when he's finished eating, he goes to his bed and counts them."

"Are you on the top or bottom bunk?" I said.

I don't know if this made any difference. I presumed the top would at least be a bit better.

"Bottom," said Adam.

I did my best to calm him down, but what do I know? I know nothing of what it is like for him. He said he was scared, and then he was cut off. I hope it was because his phone card ran out.

Does your dad know anyone influential who could speed up Adam's transfer?

Coco x

Thursday 5th May 21.23
TO: chris@christophercheshire.com

I just spoke to Adam, and his phone card did run out. He said that this evening, during association, when all the prisoners mingle out of their cells, Kip attacked another prisoner with a knife. He calmly walked up behind a prisoner who was playing snooker, and sunk it into the side of his neck. Luckily the guards intervened quickly. Kip is now in solitary confinement, and the prisoner who was stabbed is stable in the hospital wing. And the knife? It was painstakingly fashioned from thousands of foil wrappers from the Dairylea cheese triangles.

Adam was trying to stay calm but said he spent two nights in the same cell as Kip, and that it could have been him who was stabbed.

"You don't know that," I said.

"I do know that. This guy playing snooker had no beef with Kip. It seems random."

"You're even using prison slang now!" I said, then apologised.

I told him your dad has had a word with the governor of Belmarsh Prison and that, fingers crossed, a transfer should be imminent.

Thank you, Coco x

Monday 9th May 11.12
TO: chris@christophercheshire.com

After a weekend of waiting, I've heard nothing from Adam. I had stupidly Googled prison stories and found one where a prisoner sharpened his toilet brush into a weapon and stabbed his cellmate. I was expecting a call to say that the worst has happened, that Kip had returned...

Then this morning I found a letter on the mat with Belmarsh written on the envelope. It said Adam has been transferred to HMP Cambria Sands, a Category D Prison in Norfolk.

I also received a hastily written letter from Adam to say

he had arrived at Cambria Sands, but hasn't been able to phone. He has to wait to be issued with a phone card.

Apparently, he had a knock on his cell door early on Saturday and was told he was being transferred. Adam said he duly packed away his things in a plastic bag, including the radio belonging to the Dairylea Stabber (his words not mine).

It was a three and a half hour journey in the heat, with no water, to HMP Cambria Sands, which is just up the coast from Cromer. He says the new place is much more relaxed. It's an old converted manor house by the sea. The inmates (of which there are only 149) all have their own cell. There is a gym and the food is better. He is now an additional 130 miles away, but life for him should be a lot better, and for that I am thankful. You are the best, Chris. Can I have your father's phone number to thank him?

Coco xxx

Wednesday 11th May 15.14
TO: submit@prisonlink.net

EMAIL FOR HMP CAMBRIA SANDS PRISONER – AG26754 (Adam Rickard)

I finally got your visitor's order. I am coming to see you on Friday! I have booked the train, and I should be there around eleven.

I phoned Chris's father to say thank you for helping with your transfer.

"Not a problem Coco, my dear," he said. "I've known the governor of Belmarsh for years, old Wedgie Mc Duggan."

"Wedgie?"

"Well, he's Reginald or Reggie... he has a soft 'R' so he was Wedgie when we were at Eton. Poor bugger couldn't get down the corridors without someone giving him a... a..."

"Wedgie?" I said.

"Yes..." he guffawed. "How's that silk of yours doing?" (He was referring to Natasha.)

I told him that she has drawn a blank — an expensive blank.

"Ah, terrible business it all is," he said. "And how is Adam?"

I began to tell him but he said another call was coming through and he would have to go, but first Chris's sister Rebecca wanted to talk to me. I heard some pips as I was being transferred and Rebecca answered.

"Hello Coco," she squeaked. "Christopher saw Mummy and me for lunch yesterday and was telling us all about your snug little bijou!"

I had to rack my brain and then I realised he must have told her about the poo-bag tea lights.

"I've got something here that may interest you," she said. "We just took a stand down that we were running at the Ideal Home Exhibition and we have a string of fairy lights and some other bits and bobs left over. Maybe you want them for your little garden?"

It felt distinctly like charity, but I thought a row of fairy lights would be nice, so I said okay.

"Super Coco, give me your address and I'll get one of the chaps to deliver."

I said that posting the stuff would be fine but she insisted.

That afternoon I was cleaning the bedroom when the door buzzer went. Four guys were stood outside in Cheshire Ltd boiler suits. They introduced themselves and said they were making a delivery. I opened the back door for them and went back to my hoovering. After half an hour, I was wondering why they hadn't said goodbye. I came through to the back door, and stared. The concrete strip had been cleared, and lush and very realistic fake grass had been laid. Above it, a long net canopy of LED fairy lights hung from poles. It was a garden.

"How much will this cost?" I asked, suddenly panicking.

The guys looked up from fastening the last corner down of the fake grass.

"Nothing," said one of them. "This was all meant for landfill. You should see the lovely gear we have to throw away. Do you want some plants?"

They took me out to a lorry that was filled with all of the leftovers from corporate events and private parties. I spent the next half an hour choosing freebies. I came away with some long trays of soil with real bamboo shoots, which were around waist height, four tall yuccas in lovely earthenware pots, and three tiny cherry trees still with pink blossom.

The real coup was the seating! Have you seen those kind of low squishy outdoor chairs that are all the rage? I got two large white ones (they were branded all over with the words MOËT & CHANDON). I also got a matching low table.

When they had carted it all through the house for me, I didn't know what to say. I had little money left from my budget for a decent tip, so I gave them each a bottle of £1.49 wine.

"Oh, is this the stuff from the organic vineyard?" said one of the guys. "The boss is trying to get hold of it."

"Yes," I lied. "Yes, it's very crisp."

I said goodbye and they left, looking thrilled.

I arranged the seats and dotted the bamboo and yuccas against the fences, and when it was dark, I switched on the canopy of fairy lights. It was stunning. It covered up the terraced houses at the edge of my vision and it could almost pass for some tiny exotic rooftop nightspot. I came inside to get my cigarettes and noticed a high whining sound. I followed it to the electricity cupboard and pulled it open to see the meter whirring round like the clappers and the numbers going up and up and up. I quickly turned off the lights outside and settled for my poo bags.

I was sunbathing this morning, when I heard the buzzer go. I picked the barking Rocco up, and opened the door.

It was Marika.

I was a little taken aback to see her after so long. It's been just over six weeks since I slapped her round the chops.

"Hi," she said.

"Hello," I said.

We looked at each other for a moment.

"Can I come in?" she said.

"Sure."

I stood aside to let her pass and closed the door behind her. She put her bag on the kitchen counter and went to shrug off her shoes.

"Don't worry about those," I said. "Have you seen the state of the carpet?"

She knelt down to cuddle Rocco and he rolled over and lay back whilst she scratched his stomach.

"Do you want a coffee?" I said.

She nodded.

"It's nice, Coco," she said as I led her through to my new garden. "But this is, well, it's very like the champagne stand at the Ideal Home Exhibition..."

"I think it *was* the champagne stand at the Ideal Home Exhibition," I said.

We sat down in the champagne seats and took a sip of our coffees. There was then a silence.

"I'm sorry if I suggested that Adam was guilty," she said.

"I'm sorry, really sorry, that I slapped you round the face," I said.

We sat in the sun for another moment.

"Coco, this feels inevitable telling you this," she said. "But me and Greg, we broke up."

"I'm sorry," I said, lighting us each a cigarette and passing one over to her.

"I broke up with him... I suppose it was another 'Marika fling' as you and Chris say."

"I don't say that."

'I've heard you and Chris use that expression before."

"Well, I'm sorry."

"Are you? Really? I feel like you and Chris prefer me single — silly single Marika. You haven't even asked what happened."

"Give me a chance! What happened?"

"He's married with kids."

"How many?"

"Five."

"Five?"

"Yeah. They all live in Forest Hill. Five minutes down the road, for God's sake!

"And you didn't know?"

"Course I didn't, I'm a fool. I wondered why he always kept popping out to check his lottery tickets on Saturday and Sunday, then the mid-week draw."

"How did you find out?" I said.

"We were in Tesco, and he asked me to help him fill out a lottery ticket. He didn't know how. Then it all came out..."

"I'm sorry, really." I said. I reached out and squeezed her hand.

"I've missed you Coco," she said getting teary. "You could have called me."

"Marika... If you remember, I was going through stuff with Adam. It's taken you six weeks to come over."

"You were the one who slapped me! I never laid a finger on you."

"Adam had just been sent to prison! What did you expect? I could have done with you. Really."

"I feel like I'm in this box with you and Chris; 'oh it's only Marika, her life is a mess, she loves to get drunk and then sleep with wildly inappropriate guys who then rip out her heart and smear it down the wall'."

"I've definitely never said that."

"But it's true, I'm always getting my heart broken, and I never learn anything."

"That's not true... At least you know how to fill in a lottery ticket."

She looked at me, and then we both burst out laughing.

"You're a bitch, Coco."

"And you're an even bigger bitch, Marika... Do you want to stay for beans on toast on my Ideal Home Exhibition stand?" I grinned. She grinned back at me.

I had a feeling things were going to be okay between us. We got chatting outside in the warm evening, and we stayed up so late she ended up sleeping over on the sofa.

One weird thing happened though. The next morning, just before she left for her dog walking, she said she'd had vivid dreams all night of an old lady dusting the bookshelves behind the sofa. I told her I've had the same dream.

"Goes to show how exciting our lives have become," she said.

It's true, I have had the same dream three times now... Anyway, I think my mind is wandering too much with all this free time. I can't wait to see you on Friday.

All my love, Coco xxx

Saturday 21st May 17.12
TO: marikarolincova@hotmail.co.uk

I have to tell you about my first visit to see Adam. The London part of the journey was okay — we zipped past the new Olympic Stadium and through Essex. Then, when I had to change trains in Norwich, the world seemed to take on a slower, drawn out pace.

I asked a guard if the train pulling up was the one for Cambria Sands and he looked at me if I'd asked him something mind boggling then said, "Uuuuuuy dunt naaaaaaaaw, that muuuuyyt be."

Luckily it was. The train creaked and groaned its way out of Norwich and soon we were lost in the flat, bleak and misty fens. Alongside us ran rippling grey waterways with brown reeds swaying lethargically in the wind. For some reason the rail wasn't in a straight line and we wound our way through the waterways.

I was the only person who got off the train at Cambria Sands Station. It was misty and cold and the wind was screaming across a flat expanse of bare grass from the sea far in the distance. The station was a concrete platform on stilts.

As the train creaked off into the mist, I pulled out my

phone and called one of the taxi numbers advertised on a rusting sign. Ten minutes later, and completely frozen, I saw on the horizon a taxi speeding toward me. I noticed the only way off the platform was a thick rusty set of steps. I climbed down and got in. The driver cheerily asked, "Where to?" and didn't bat an eyelid when I said the prison.

We drove towards the sea, and after a few minutes, the prison came into view. What shocked me the most was that there were no gates or razor wire, and we pootled up to the house as if we were on a jaunt to a National Trust property.

"This is the right place?" I said.

"An open prison don't have high walls. The prisoners are trusted to stay," said the driver.

I imagined Adam walking out with me, and us going on the run. I think the driver saw the look in my eye.

"Course, if they're caught, they spend the rest of their sentence rotting in a Category A prison," he said.

I thanked him and he dropped me in the full car park.

The process of security checks was similar to Belmarsh, but once through I was shown into a visitor's area, which more resembled a library coffee shop, with comfortable chairs and low tables. Visiting times are in shifts so there were only around fifteen inmates with visitors. Adam looked better than when I last saw him. We hugged long and hard, and we were even able to walk hand in hand to a vending machine where I bought him six Kit-Kats and five cans of Coke.

"Are you sure?" he said, as it all clunked into the tray at the bottom of the machine.

I leant in and gave him a long sweet kiss. We sat back down and he said he had news. I perked up, thinking it was good news.

"I've decided not to appeal," he said.

"What!" The room turned to look at us.

"Now hear me out," he said. "Natasha came to visit me yesterday."

"Nice of her to tell me."

"She's billed nearly four thousand for three paralegals who haven't really found any other evidence. There are a few inaccuracies from the forensic computing analysts..."

"Why isn't she looking into Sabrina Jones! It's her! She's the one who took the money!"

"She said they have checked her. They've run a credit and a background check. She's clean."

"She is not!"

"Coco. Please..."

"Why are you doing this? Why are you lying down and accepting defeat?" I said.

"If I do appeal, I go back to Belmarsh. A new trial could take months, or be put off, and then I would have to go through being re-categorised again and without Chris's dad helping me it could be months."

"So you just want to stay in jail?"

"Yeah, Coco it's so wonderful."

His brow furrowed and he reached out and held my hand.

"I have my own cell here. They don't even call it a cell, it's called my room... I can go for walks, see the sea. I'm working in the admin office. In a few months I will be enhanced and have even more freedom, and then next spring I'll be able to go out. We can go on visits. I can even come and see you in your flat."

"But it's four years!" I shrilled.

"Coco. Please," he said, his voice low. "If I'm going to get through this without killing myself then this is the only way."

This pulled me up short. I took his other hand.

"What? Have you thought about..."

"Yes, but only once. You being there for me is the only thing keeping me going."

I looked into his eyes at all the pain and the hurt.

"Okay," I said. "Okay. No appeal."

"And you're not going to stalk that girl, Sabrina," he added. "I heard all about you going to her house."

"From who?"

"Ethel. She writes to me every week."

"She does?"

"Yes, she's not all bad."

And that's how we had to end the conversation as the bell rang. I held him for as long as I could, pressing my face into his warm chest. He put his face in my neck, and then he had to go.

It was only when I went to get my coat that I realised the top of my jumper was wet with his tears.

The journey home was a slow horrible reverse. Luckily it's now light and I didn't have to wait on the windy platform in the dark. I got home just before ten; Rocco was so pleased to see me.

Thursday 26th May 18.11
TO: marikarolincova@hotmail.co.uk

Rosencrantz came over this afternoon and we had a glass of wine in the garden. He said that he had been on a mission for Adam.

"What do you mean?" I said, lighting us both a cigarette.

He pulled a bag from his rucksack and handed it over.

"What's this?"

"Well, open it Mum, obviously," he said.

Inside was a copy of Adele's *21* album and a digital watch.

"It's not my birthday for a few more weeks," I said.

"There's a note too," said Rosencrantz.

He had Rocco on his lap who was straining to see inside the bag. I pulled out this note. I was so touched I thought I should attach it.

ATTACHMENT ADAM1

HMP CAMBRIA SANDS
23.05.2011

Dear Coco,

I found this old typewriter when I was cleaning out the admin office where I work. The guy in charge said I could keep it. Having something of my own is a real thrill.

So many things drive me bonkers about prison life, as well as the obvious things we can't do together ;) I just miss being with you, working on the allotment or listening to music together.

As you know, I have a radio CD player (thanks to the Dairylea Stabber) and I thought what if we made a time where we could to listen to music together?

One of the inmates lent me 21, Adele's new album. I loved it so much that I wanted to talk to you about it, and listen to it with you. So I got Rosencrantz to buy a couple of copies! You have one of them in your hand.

You also have a digital watch which gives the precise time, set by radio signal in Greenwich. My watch is the same. So, at 8.30pm precisely (after my roll-call) on Saturday 28th May will you press play on the first track? I will do the same and we will be listening together.

I love you with all my heart and I miss you with all my heart, and other bits too...

All my love, Adam xxx

"Adam also says to say sorry. He can't call you until next week as arranging this burned out his phone card," said Rosencrantz.

I nodded gratefully.

"And make sure you listen at exactly the right time," he said, putting the watch on my wrist.

"I will," I said, wiping my eyes.

I have a date on Saturday night!

Monday 30th May 16.37
TO: rosencrantzpinchard@gmail.com

Thank you again for sorting out the Adele CD. I listened at exactly 8.30pm and I really did feel close to Adam. I also loved *21*, no wonder everyone is talking about it. It's wonderful.

I just met your Nan for a cup of tea at The Brockley Mess café. It was warm and sunny so we sat out on the pavement. She had been to put flowers on Grandad Wilf's grave. He passed away forty-one years ago.

I was expecting her to be quite melancholy but she stomped up to the table and slammed down her best gloves and handbag.

"I'm fuming!" she said. "Bloody Wilf."

"Did someone vandalise his grave?"

"No, iss covered in pigeon shit, and I broke me emery board trying to scrape the damn stuff orf."

She pulled out two halves of her nail file and held them up.

"It's not Wilf's fault," I said.

"Isn't it?" she said. "You know 'e was a pigeon fancier? That 'ead stone attracts scores of the little buggers and they shit all over it. Even from beyond the grave 'e's still winding me up."

After we ordered some tea, I told her about Adam and the Adele *21* album listening thing.

"Oh that Adam, 'e's good as gold, such a shame 'e's in the slammer," said Ethel. "I love Adele, all us old girls at the 'ome ave got 21. She can't 'alf sing."

"I love 'Rolling In The Deep', and 'Someone Like You' breaks my heart," I said.

"My favourite is 'Set Fire To Lorraine'," said Ethel sipping her tea.

"No, it's 'Set Fire To The Rain'," I said.

"No Coco, it's 'Set Fire To Lorraine'," she said.

"No it's not..."

"It is!"

"No!"

"Coco, love, you've only just got the bloody album. I've 'ad it on a loop since Pancake Tuesday, and I'm tellin' ya, it's 'Set Fire To Lorraine'."

"It's not!" I said. "It's a metaphor, setting fire to the rain."

"Listen, love. If you'd read up on it, and iss been in the papers a lot, you'd know Adele writ the album about a painful breakup, and this song is about 'ow much she 'ates the other woman, hence 'Set Fire To Lorraine'."

"So Adele is singing about wanting to burn another woman to death?" I said.

"Yeah, ask anyone... Gawd Coco, I never thought I'd be more hip than you."

"Adele is more elegant than that!" I said. "A woman would never sing about setting fire to another woman."

"Wouldn't she? I bet you'd love to dump a jug full of unleaded on that Sabrina and set a match to it!"

The argument went on, and in the end I tried phoning everyone to confirm it was 'Set Fire To The Rain', but no one was answering. I even asked the waiter but he didn't know, the damn fool. The argument progressed to raised voices, and in the end, I was so annoyed I got up and stormed back home. When I got in, I grabbed 21 out of the drawer. IT IS 'Set Fire To The Rain'!

I hate it when Ethel thinks she knows it all. Remember that whole episode a few Christmases ago when she insisted that John Bon Jovi was called Long John Bovis? And when your Aunt Meryl had the 'Radioactive Thyroid'?

UGH!

Anyway, sorry to go on. Thank you again, love. And if you see your Nan, tell her it's 'Set Fire To The Rain'!

Mum xxx

JUNE

Monday 6th June 10.19
TO: submit@prisonlink.net

For Prisoner AG26754 - Adam Rickard

I went to Wilfred's christening on Saturday. It was every bit as hideous as I thought it would be. In fact, its hideousness exceeded expectations.

Rosencrantz wormed his way out of going. He was rehearsing for a new acting job, a TIE tour of London schools called *The Don't Drink Or Do Drugs Puppet Show*.

I travelled up to Milton Keynes with Ethel and Daniel. I haven't seen her since the 'Set Fire To The Rain/Lorraine' argument and I haven't seen Daniel since, well, I can't remember. We were all broke, so we took the SuperBus from Victoria Coach Station. It only cost a pound each way, but you could see every penny of it in the battered dirty seats. All the windows were painted shut so we sweltered in our synthetic fabric christening outfits. I wore a rose-coloured suit, Ethel was in some flowery creation, and a

Queen Mother-style hat with feathers, which shed everywhere and stuck to our sweaty skin. Daniel wore a brown suit.

"What yer doin' in that old thing?" said Ethel, looking at him in dismay as we took our seats on the coach. "There's gonna be posh people at this christening!"

"I paid a hundred and fifty quid for this suit," said Daniel.

"Iss bloody brown, and yer've got black shoes on!"

"What do you think, Coco?" he said.

"It looks nice," I said truthfully.

"Thanks Cokes," he said gratefully.

"An' what about yer bloody hair!" said Ethel.

Daniel has grown his hair out, and it now hangs past his shoulders in a good mix of salt and pepper. He also has a short beard; 'scruff' I think they call it. I sat there looking at him with a tinge of pity as Ethel told him he was "a shambles" and that he was "entering a house of God and not a betting shop".

"I blame Rosencrantz," she trilled as the coach pulled away from the station. "Ever since 'e bought yer that *True Blood* box set for yer birthday, you've fancied yerself as one of them werewolves!"

"I'm sorry, I completely forgot your birthday," I said to Daniel.

"It's all right, Cokes," he said kindly. "You've had a lot on your plate."

"An yer unemployed," went on Ethel. "Why don't you go the 'ole 'og and ave yer dole book poking out of yer top pocket"?

"Leave it, Mum!" he snapped.

The engine squealed loudly as we hit the ramp onto the M25. It didn't stop as we met the traffic and nudged into the slow lane.

"Gawd, what a racket," said Ethel. "'Scuse me! Driver? Can you put the radio on?"

The driver switched on the radio and Magic FM blared through the coach.

"Maybe they'll play 'Set Fire To Lorraine'," I said.

"Or that other Adele classic, 'Chasing Payments'," said Daniel. "Written about a debt collector who was sick of his job."

We both burst out laughing.

"Aren't you two meant to be divorced?" snapped Ethel, but we kept laughing.

She finally shut up and spent the rest of the journey scowling at the motorway as we rumbled towards Milton Keynes. I had a good chat with Daniel. He hasn't been able to find any work, and has been claiming Jobseeker's Allowance for four months.

"I never thought one of mine would end up down the labour exchange," interrupted Ethel. "You should be working! Yer not even fifty!"

Daniel said he is living in Croydon, in a one-bedroom flat with a "housemate", a female musician called Natalie who plays the bassoon.

"Course 'e ain't introduced me to 'er,' interrupted Ethel again.

"I don't want to scare her off!" said Daniel.

"Tha's not fair, Danny," said Ethel. "I made you very welcome when you were courting, didn't I Coco?"

Daniel and I burst out laughing again.

When we got to Milton Keynes, we took a taxi to the church, and it was nearly full when we got there. Tony and Meryl seem to have undergone a makeover. Gone are his shiny beige suits, slip-on shoes and string ties, and Meryl has dropped the frumpy floral dresses. I spied them in the

I was in the middle of my regular Adele listening party
th Adam when someone buzzed at the door.

"I've been calling you for ages," said Holly, Adam's
ughter. "I had to get the train from Heathrow."

"My mobile doesn't have a signal here," I said. "I thought
u were in America?"

"Well, I'm not," she said earnestly, in case I hadn't
rked it out. "My work visa ran out."

She came into the living room with a huge handbag
ked over her tiny wrist.

Have you met Holly? She is beautiful and willowy but
er thick.

"Is there really no signal?" she said getting out her
ne. "How do you ask Siri?"

"Siri?"

"You know on the iPhone... I ask her everything. Where to
what to do on my days off, where I can get my nails done."

"Well, you can ask her to get your luggage in," I said,
ating the front door and her pile of cases in the hall.

"What?"

"I'm not room service. I take it you're staying here?"

"Well, yeah. You're dad's... dad's..."

"I'm his fiancé," I said.

"Then yeah I'm staying, if that's okay?"

said it was fine. Rocco emerged from the garden and
d barking at her.

"Now, what's that?" she said.

"occo, my dog," I said.

barked louder and advanced on her. She jumped to
et.

"hat's he doing?" she said.

cco circled her, rounding her up like a herd of sheep
front door and her suitcases.

second row of pews, sporting sleek haircuts. Tony was
wearing an Armani suit and aviator shades, and Meryl a
powder blue Chanel suit topped off with a Philip Treacy hat.
If you squinted your eyes you could, almost, have mistaken
them for the Middletons. Wilfred was sat on Meryl's knee
wearing a long lace christening outfit.

"Did they save me a place?" said Ethel, pulling a disposable camera out of her handbag.

I saw that they hadn't.

"Oh," she said, her face crumpling.

We took a seat in a pew at the back just as the service
began. Meryl and Tony weren't too happy having to share
Wilfred's christening with a little Chinese boy called
Richard. She informed everyone in the congregation during
the photos that his parents "do a lovely Kung Pao chicken".

After the service, we walked back to Meryl and Tony's
for the buffet. They had paid for a huge marquee in the
garden and everything that wasn't nailed down was branded
with the *Funeral Pieces* logo, which consists of a coffin with a
cartoon hand emerging from under the lid giving the
thumbs up.

Meryl seemed rather embarrassed of me, Ethel and
Daniel, and we stood out a bit amongst the elite of Milton
Keynes. Lots of comfortable tanned local businessmen with
their sleek wives, and some distinguished older couples
from the tennis club.

They all seem to have been tipped off that you were in
jail, and their interest was bordering on the macabre. I was
grilled by several of them as the waiters circulated with trays
of Pimms. One thin-faced woman in an M&S twinset and
pearls was eager to know all about prison life. She asked
questions about shanking, razor wire, drugs, and murder.
She was desperate for even snippet of information — and
positively devoured the story about the Dairylea Stabber.

Why is it that the British middle class is so obsessed with scandal, sex, and murder?

I was telling Ethel to slow down on the Pimms (she'd had six glasses) when Tony tapped his glass and went to make a speech. Meryl stood beside him holding Wilfred.

"My lords, ladies and gentlemen, welcome," he said into a microphone.

"Who 'ere's a Lord?" asked Ethel loudly. "No one?"

There was an awkward silence. Meryl made eyes at me to shut Ethel up. Tony went on,

"I'd like to thank you all for coming to this the christening of Wilfred Ogilvy Thatcher Watson, our little miracle."

"Yeah, 'e is a miracle. Did yer know, they thought Meryl was barren!" said Ethel loudly.

Everyone turned round to look at her. Tony swallowed and went on.

"Please enjoy the food, it's lovely to see you all here."

Then Meryl grabbed the microphone and shifted Wilfred onto her other hip.

"If you get the chance, please log on to www.funeral-pieces.co.uk," she said. "We have everything you need to give a loved one the send-off they truly deserve... Now I have something very exciting. Wilfred has been learning a little poem and he'd like to share it with you all."

She put the microphone to Wilfred's mouth, and started to recite lines from 'The Lake Isle Of Innisfree', but Wilfred was having none of it and made barking noises.

"Now come on, Wilfred," said Meryl, getting angry at the poor boy. "Mummy will start again, *I will arise and go now, and go to Innisfree...*"

Wilfred batted the microphone away.

"Oh fer gawd's sake, give the little bugger a Ethel.

"I'm sorry, I don't know who that is," said M

"It's all right," said Ethel. "I'm only the fuc 'Ello Wilfred, iss me, Nanna!"

Wilfred saw her and clapped his hands in

"Mum! Really!" shrilled Meryl. "Not in fr I'd hate his first word to be..."

"Oh chill out, Meryl," said Ethel. "'E's everything... 'e'll be fine." She noticed every her in disgust. "You see how posh Meryl l garden with you poshos? Well, what you d she was very nearly a bastard!"

"Right we need to leave, NOW!" said Da

We grabbed Ethel, an arm each, and d from the marquee.

"She was!" shouted Ethel, as we passed 'ad to walk down the aisle in white with a h

I finally got home at eleven in t SuperBus had to keep stopping in lay-b Ethel could be sick.

I had a long bath and I thanked G Adam, and that waiting for us when you most wonderful life.

All my love, Coco xxxx

Saturday 11th June 22.47
TO: marikarolincova@hotmail.co.uk

second row of pews, sporting sleek haircuts. Tony was wearing an Armani suit and aviator shades, and Meryl a powder blue Chanel suit topped off with a Philip Treacy hat. If you squinted your eyes you could, almost, have mistaken them for the Middletons. Wilfred was sat on Meryl's knee wearing a long lace christening outfit.

"Did they save me a place?" said Ethel, pulling a disposable camera out of her handbag.

I saw that they hadn't.

"Oh," she said, her face crumpling.

We took a seat in a pew at the back just as the service began. Meryl and Tony weren't too happy having to share Wilfred's christening with a little Chinese boy called Richard. She informed everyone in the congregation during the photos that his parents "do a lovely Kung Pao chicken".

After the service, we walked back to Meryl and Tony's for the buffet. They had paid for a huge marquee in the garden and everything that wasn't nailed down was branded with the *Funeral Pieces* logo, which consists of a coffin with a cartoon hand emerging from under the lid giving the thumbs up.

Meryl seemed rather embarrassed of me, Ethel and Daniel, and we stood out a bit amongst the elite of Milton Keynes. Lots of comfortable tanned local businessmen with their sleek wives, and some distinguished older couples from the tennis club.

They all seem to have been tipped off that you were in jail, and their interest was bordering on the macabre. I was grilled by several of them as the waiters circulated with trays of Pimms. One thin-faced woman in an M&S twinset and pearls was eager to know all about prison life. She asked questions about shanking, razor wire, drugs, and murder. She was desperate for even snippet of information — and positively devoured the story about the Dairylea Stabber.

Why is it that the British middle class is so obsessed with scandal, sex, and murder?

I was telling Ethel to slow down on the Pimms (she'd had six glasses) when Tony tapped his glass and went to make a speech. Meryl stood beside him holding Wilfred.

"My lords, ladies and gentlemen, welcome," he said into a microphone.

"Who 'ere's a Lord?" asked Ethel loudly. "No one?"

There was an awkward silence. Meryl made eyes at me to shut Ethel up. Tony went on,

"I'd like to thank you all for coming to this the christening of Wilfred Ogilvy Thatcher Watson, our little miracle."

"Yeah, 'e is a miracle. Did yer know, they thought Meryl was barren!" said Ethel loudly.

Everyone turned round to look at her. Tony swallowed and went on.

"Please enjoy the food, it's lovely to see you all here."

Then Meryl grabbed the microphone and shifted Wilfred onto her other hip.

"If you get the chance, please log on to www.funeral-pieces.co.uk," she said. "We have everything you need to give a loved one the send-off they truly deserve... Now I have something very exciting. Wilfred has been learning a little poem and he'd like to share it with you all."

She put the microphone to Wilfred's mouth, and started to recite lines from 'The Lake Isle Of Innisfree', but Wilfred was having none of it and made barking noises.

"Now come on, Wilfred," said Meryl, getting angry at the poor boy. "Mummy will start again, *I will arise and go now, and go to Innisfree...*"

Wilfred batted the microphone away.

"Oh fer gawd's sake, give the little bugger a break!" said Ethel.

"I'm sorry, I don't know who that is," said Meryl.

"It's all right," said Ethel. "I'm only the fucking Nanna... 'Ello Wilfred, iss me, Nanna!"

Wilfred saw her and clapped his hands in delight.

"Mum! Really!" shrilled Meryl. "Not in front of Wilfred, I'd hate his first word to be..."

"Oh chill out, Meryl," said Ethel. "'E's got the best of everything... 'e'll be fine." She noticed everyone looking at her in disgust. "You see how posh Meryl looks in 'er posh garden with you poshos? Well, what you don't know is that she was very nearly a bastard!"

"Right we need to leave, NOW!" said Daniel.

We grabbed Ethel, an arm each, and dragged her away from the marquee.

"She was!" shouted Ethel, as we passed horrified faces, "I 'ad to walk down the aisle in white with a huge bump!"

I finally got home at eleven in the evening. The SuperBus had to keep stopping in lay-bys on the M25 so Ethel could be sick.

I had a long bath and I thanked God I am with you, Adam, and that waiting for us when you are released is the most wonderful life.

All my love, Coco xxxx

Saturday 11th June 22.47
TO: marikarolincova@hotmail.co.uk

I was in the middle of my regular Adele listening party with Adam when someone buzzed at the door.

"I've been calling you for ages," said Holly, Adam's daughter. "I had to get the train from Heathrow."

"My mobile doesn't have a signal here," I said. "I thought you were in America?"

"Well, I'm not," she said earnestly, in case I hadn't worked it out. "My work visa ran out."

She came into the living room with a huge handbag hooked over her tiny wrist.

Have you met Holly? She is beautiful and willowy but rather thick.

"Is there really no signal?" she said getting out her iPhone. "How do you ask Siri?"

"Siri?"

"You know on the iPhone... I ask her everything. Where to eat, what to do on my days off, where I can get my nails done."

"Well, you can ask her to get your luggage in," I said, indicating the front door and her pile of cases in the hall.

"What?"

"I'm not room service. I take it you're staying here?"

"Well, yeah. You're dad's... dad's..."

"I'm his fiancé," I said.

"Then yeah I'm staying, if that's okay?"

I said it was fine. Rocco emerged from the garden and started barking at her.

"Wow, what's that?" she said.

"Rocco, my dog," I said.

He barked louder and advanced on her. She jumped to her feet.

"What's he doing?" she said.

Rocco circled her, rounding her up like a herd of sheep to the front door and her suitcases.

He sat in the threshold of the door and barked at her.

"He wants you to bring your suitcases in," I said.

Holly looked at him uneasily and reached for her case. Satisfied, Rocco trotted off and let her haul her stuff inside. I was impressed. My little Maltese pup had achieved more than two parents with open cheque books have managed in a lifetime. To show I wasn't a complete cow, I ran Holly a bath, and whilst she was soaking, I rustled up some cheese on toast with a glass of wine.

I was sat outside in the garden when she emerged in a long LA Lakers football shirt, cut off denim shorts and her hair in a towel. She looked stunning. She came and sat on one of the Moët seats and started picking at her cheese on toast.

"I like your garden," she said. "It reminds me of the Polo Lounge, in LA..."

I looked at the astro turf, broken washing machine, and my old flip-flops on the floor and decided she was being polite.

"So what happened with your visa?" I said.

"Well, I got my American work visa and my Visa card mixed up... My Visa card expires in 2014, and that's when I thought I could stay in America until. I told the cop this, but they still had me deported."

"Why were you stopped by the police?" I said.

"I was jaywalking on Hollywood Boulevard."

"And what were you doing in LA?"

"I was working for a bit. I was kind of a cake decorator slash model. I stopped modelling because of all the chauvinistic men. Then I started working for this cake decorating company and the owner was just as bad; he called me a stupid girl!"

"Why?" I said.

"I mixed the wrong red for the icing on a Spiderman cake... I mean isn't red, red?"

"So what did you do after that? Mind you, I have a fairly good idea because that Visa card you were talking about is in your father's name and I'm paying the bill."

"Yeah, about that, I'm gonna get a job. I'll pay you back," she smiled.

It was a warm lovely smile and I almost envied her being on a different planet. The fact her life is all over the place doesn't seem to bother her.

She wanted to know when she could visit Adam and I told her we could arrange it for when I go next week. Unexpectedly, she got up and gave me a hug.

"Of all the women Dad has slept with, you're the nicest," she said.

Again, I think this was a compliment. She said she was jet lagged so I found some extra blankets and made up the sofa for her. Then I came back out here with my laptop. It is such a beautiful warm evening and apart from the noise of Holly snoring in the living room, it's idyllic.

I have no idea how long she is here for. As always, she is a bit vague...

Anyway, I'm off to bed.

Love you, Cokes xxx

Friday 18th June 09.41
TO: chris@christophercheshire.com,
marikarolincova@hotmail.co.uk

Holly surprised me this morning with a cup of coffee and a little plate of cupcakes with red icing and chocolate sauce drizzled over.

"Happy birthday," she said. "Look, I made you Spiderman cupcakes..."

"How appropriate for the birthday of a forty-four-year-old woman," I smiled, sitting up in bed.

"Who's forty-four?" she said innocently.

"Me," I said.

"Oh my God, that's so *old!*"

I stopped grinning.

"When did you make these?" I said. "And where did you find all the ingredients?"

"I went to that shop round the corner. I didn't have any money but the man was *so* nice... he told me I could pay him later."

"He gave you the stuff for free?"

"No, I have to pay for it eventually," she said, twisting a length of hair between her delicate fingers.

I couldn't believe it. Mr Gogi in the corner shop is as tight as a duck's arse. Once he wouldn't let me off when I was short 1p for a tomato!

"Isn't that the right colour red for Spiderman?" said Holly, holding up a cupcake.

"Yes," I lied.

She grinned happily. I took a bite and pronounced them rather tasty.

After breakfast we started the long journey to see Adam, and we arrived just after lunch. He was looking well, and was so excited to see Holly. He has a new job with responsibility, working in the hospital wing, and he now has his own room with an en-suite bathroom and shower.

"You've got a shower?" I said. "I have a jug in the bath."

I regretted it as soon as I said it.

Adam gave me his gift, a small envelope. I opened it and inside was a piece of black card. On one side, he had written in silver ink (borrowed from another inmate called Mick, seven years for GBH).

To my beautiful Coco, life is for the living...

"Turn it over," said Adam.

I did and taped to the back was a white feather.

"Wow..." said Holly. "What is it?"

"The other night after association I went back to my cell and I prayed, something I never do. I prayed that you would be safe. The next morning this white feather was on the floor of my cell."

It looked like a goose feather; it was pure white and perfectly formed.

"I don't know where it came from," he said. "My door was locked, we don't have feather beds or pillows in here, the windows were sealed and my cell is bare. When I told one of the guys who comes to the hospital wing, he said that a feather appearing is the sign of a guardian angel, and I want you to have it."

"Me?" I said.

"That's lovely, Dad," said Holly. "I smuggled a Taser through customs at Heathrow. That's my guardian angel."

I grinned at Adam and leant across the table and gave him a kiss.

"Ahhh. So when's the big day?" said Holly. "When are you two getting married?"

"Well, we have a wedding booked for August the nineteenth but..."

"Hang on," said Holly, pulling out her iPhone. "I think I'm free... Siri, when is London Fashion Week...?" she said, speaking into her phone.

"BUT," I said. "Your Dad is in jail for... well, it could be four years."

"Oh," she said. "I'm sorry. God I'm so stupid..."

Luckily, the bell rang for the end of visiting, and I didn't have to comment on that. Adam gave Holly a long hug and told her to stay safe and visit whenever she could. Then he asked if she could give us a minute.

"Coco," said Adam, as the other prisoners were filing out. "I want you to do something."

"What?"

"Start living your life again."

"What do you mean?" I said.

"You're just waiting around for me. Living in poverty in that scuzzy flat, not going out."

"I'm waiting for you," I said reaching out and touching his arm.

"You know you could be waiting until 2019."

"I thought you were being released early?"

"It's not guaranteed. Think about it. In 2019 we'll both be in our fifties. There's so much out there. You'll get your house back next year and..."

"What are you saying? You don't want to be with me anymore! Don't you *dare* dump me on my birthday, Adam Rickard. I'm not being dumped by someone who's in jail on my birthday!"

"No, I'm not..." Adam put his head in his hands, and then one of the prison guards came and told him he had to leave.

"I fucking hate this!" he shouted, and then he was pulled away.

"I'm waiting for you," I shouted after him. "Whether you like it or not!" but Adam was gone.

Holly had been standing a little way away, watching. She came over and hugged me.

"He's lucky to have you Coco," she said. "So am I."

I didn't say much on the long journey home, and neither did Holly. We got in very late, and after giving Rocco a walk, I found her already tucked up asleep on the sofa.

I spent a long time thinking in bed. It's strange how when so much is taken from you, you start to think about the otherworldly. Adam and myself would never have entertained thoughts of angels, or said prayers when we were riding high. I put the card with the feather on my bedside table and stared at it for a long time before I fell asleep.

I woke up at nine and when I tiptoed through to let Rocco out, Holly was already up and outside drinking coffee.

"You're up early, for you!" I grinned.

"Yeah, I think it's time I let you have your place back," she said. "I'm gonna get a train up and see Mum. It's about time, she's like rung me loads."

"Are you sure?" I said. "I was starting to enjoy having company."

I helped her pack and made her a sandwich for the journey and then around midday, she called a cab for the station.

"Thanks Coco," she said. "For giving me somewhere to stay."

"I hope you were comfy on the sofa," I said.

"I've slept better than I ever have here," she said. "But I have had this weird recurring dream, about this sweet old lady dusting the bookshelves... but it's probably just me being a ditzy brain!"

After she had gone I opened the door and the sun

streamed in. I made some toast as Rocco gobbled down his food. I didn't feel scared, but I've had the same dream again four times in the last week! Love you guys, thanks for your cards and presents, Coco xxx

Saturday 25th June 21.13
TO: marikarolincova@hotmail.co.uk

Adam has been locked away for 100 days now. There are 1,284 days left until he is released — IF he gets parole. I have stopped doing any more addition as it's killing me. I think we're going to have to listen to a different album soon. Adele, for all her gorgeousness, has sunk me into a deep, deep gloom.

JULY

Wednesday 13th July 20.47
TO: submit@prisonlink.net

For Prisoner AG26754 Adam Rickard

I started dog walking with Marika the other day, and in the heat it's harder than I thought. She walks up to six hours a day! Her dog walking business is booming. She has started to get queries from a couple of guys about overnight stays — for their dogs, that is, not for them!

She hasn't told her mother she is a dog walker. Blazena thinks she is temping at City Hall, and the only reason she is happy about this is that Marika has told her it's the perfect place to meet a rich husband.

On the way back from dog walking we've been stopping at a new café on Brockley Road that serves ice coffee in little glass jam jars, with a scoop of vanilla ice cream.

I have become addicted, and tried to replicate it at home, making a litre and a half of instant coffee with a little sugar in an old lemonade bottle that I keep in the fridge. I have also bought ice cream, and even splurged on a tin of coco powder for dusting. When you are released, I am going to make it for you.

I had three visitors the other day. I was expecting Rosencrantz, but shortly after he arrived, Meryl turned up with Wilfred.

"Oh Coco, it's... snug," she said, as I closed the door behind her.

"Hey Aunt Meryl," said Rosencrantz, coming in from the back door, "and Wilf!"

Wilfred was dressed in shorts, a little blazer, and tiny Trilby with a feather tucked in the brim. His plump little cheeks were very red.

"You look fucking cool, little man," said Rosencrantz.

"Please Rosencrantz, no toilet language. I live in fear of Wilfred's first word beginning with an 'f'."

"There are plenty of other nice f-words," said Rosencrantz, tickling Wilfred's tummy. "Fiddlesticks, fuddleflum, flibbedy flobbidy floo!"

Wilfred laughed in delight and shuffled his legs. Meryl took his Trilby off, and put him on the floor to crawl.

"I haven't hoovered, Meryl," I said as Wilfred started to turbo crawl and disappeared round the back of the sofa.

"It's okay," she said. "I want him to build up his resistance and be exposed to lots of germs. That's one of the reasons we popped over."

Rosencrantz and I looked at each other.

"Would you like an ice coffee?" I said. Meryl told us, over ice coffee in the garden, that she had been to give Ethel "a dressing down" over her antics at the christening.

"I don't understand my mother," said Meryl, in a rare candid moment. "I try to make the best of myself. I've fought my way up from nothing in a two-up two-down with an outside loo… I thought she'd be proud of me, of what we can give Wilfred."

"I think you should have included her more, in the christening," I said.

"Tony said the same," mused Meryl. "It's just… you never feel good enough…"

"What do you mean?" asked Rosencrantz, who was bouncing Wilfred on his lap.

"I could have the best christening and wear the most expensive clothes in the biggest marquee, but there will always be whispers: 'did you know she grew up in a slum, she failed the eleven-plus and went to her local comp…'"

"Why should you care what they say?" said Rosencrantz.

"Oh, the luxury of privilege," said Meryl. "And I don't mean that in a nasty way," she added. "That's why I so admire Carole Middleton, she came from nothing. And is now mother of a future Queen."

"That's what Wayne says about Mum!" grinned Rosencrantz.

Meryl looked confused.

"Rosencrantz," I said, shushing him.

This was fascinating; Meryl talking about how she felt. All I normally get out of her is recipes.

Meryl went to continue but Rosencrantz's phone ringtone blared out. He passed Wilfred to Meryl and answered.

"That reminds me, Coco," she said. "I've got a super recipe for cheese straws, it's as quick as a flash. I'll email it you."

Suddenly Rosencrantz started whooping.

"I got the job!" he cried, leaping up and down. "I got the flibbedy flobbedy job!"

Wilfred laughed and clapped his little hands and Rocco barked and ran round the table.

"What job?" I said.

"A television job! Well, it's one of those personal injury claims adverts. I'm a guy who breaks his leg ballroom dancing."

"Ballroom dancing?" I said. "I thought those adverts were for people who have accidents on forklift trucks."

"No, people have wised up to those. They're cornering the ballroom dancing market. You know how popular *Strictly* and *Dancing With The Stars* are? They figure there are millions of people out there who are joining dance classes and going arse over tit. What do they say? Where there's a blame, there's a claim."

We both gave him a hug.

"You'll have to give me your autograph!" said Meryl.

"Well, make sure it's a piece of paper you give me. Did you know, last week on my TIE tour one of the mums actually wanted me to sign one of her breasts!"

"No, it would only be on my jotter pad," said Meryl nervously.

"You know the best bit about this job?" said Rosencrantz. "It's five grand for a day's work."

He starts filming next week. It's an odd feeling, though, when your children start to earn more than you do!

That's all to report for now. It's baking hot and I'm sitting outside, even though it's ten in the evening. Can't wait to see you on Friday!

Coco xxx

Friday 15th July 20.14
TO: chris@christophercheshire.com

I got back late last night after a terrible journey to see Adam. Rail replacement buses and trains with no air conditioning. It ended up being a round trip of twelve hours. I collapsed into bed shortly after 11pm and didn't wake up until mid-morning. I had no food in the house, so I pulled on some clothes and went to the little corner shop. It was closed due a power cut so I walked the long way up to Honor Oak Park and went to the little shop near Marika's flat. I paid for my things at the till, and when I turned to leave, I came face to face with Xavier, the hot guy from Insomnia Café in Marylebone.

"Hey! Coco!" he grinned.

"Hello. What are you doing here?" I said, shocked to see him.

"I live here, what about you? Are you visiting someone?" he said.

He looked amazing. He had on a sleeveless white t-shirt, denim shorts, and flip-flops. His muscular arms were a warm caramel colour. His hair shone raven black and fell over his forehead in a sexy sweep. He smelt enticing, all wood and fresh soap, a smell which gave me goose bumps of the erotic variety.

"No, I live here too," I said.

"Really? Where?"

"Down the road in Brockley."

"I'm just up the road..." he said.

He had a black sausage dog on a lead with a red collar. It had long eyelashes and was standing there shyly whilst Rocco gave him the once over. I knew I had to make my excuses and go or I would be doing the same to Xavier. He was as melt in the mouth delicious as I remembered.

"Well, I'd better get going," I said.

I think I sounded a little blunt, but I had lust in my mind and I was alarmed it wasn't lust for Adam.

"Maybe I'll see you around, I walk my dog up on Hilly Fields," he said.

I smiled back at him then scuttled back home with Rocco. I had a long cold jug-wash in the bath, and I don't think it was entirely because of the hot weather.

I had just got dressed in a clean pair of shorts and a t-shirt, when the buzzer went for the door. I opened it and there was Xavier.

I looked at him. He looked at me. The low drone of a lawnmower working hard floated up from outside.

"You left this at the shop," he said, holding up my purse.

"Oh. Thank you," I said.

"I said I'd bring it to you, your address is inside... The guy in the shop wanted to send his father, Zoltan, but I didn't think he would make it in the heat in his mobility scooter."

I laughed. Xavier was sweating. We stood for a moment staring at each other.

"Would you like some ice coffee?" I said. "I'm just making one."

I *know* I shouldn't have asked him in, but nothing had to happen, I thought. There is no harm in looking, and the most pleasure I have had in months was leaning against the dryer at the launderette and waiting for my bed sheets to finish. Xavier came in with his little dog that was quirkily named Columbus. Rocco came running over and after a series of excited little barks and snorts, they ran off together into the garden. If I was fluent in dog, I'm sure it would have translated as:

Rocco: Hey, you want to come and play? I've got my own garden!

Columbus: Cool! Let's go!

"What are you grinning at?" said Xavier, following my gaze to the open door.

"I was imagining what they were talking about."

"Who?"

"The dogs..."

He looked at me oddly.

"I'll get that coffee," I said. I went to the kitchen and pulled some ice cream out of the freezer.

"So, why are you living in Brockley?" he said, looking around at the living room.

"Um... I'm renting out my house and writing. It's quieter here and it supplements my income..."

All of this was somewhat true, but I left out a big part of the truth: Adam. We carried on chatting but a voice in my head started to chant, *Adam, Adam, Adam, Adam, Adam...*

"Why don't you go outside and have a seat. I'll bring the coffees," I said.

Xavier went outside and I spooned ice cream into glasses, poured over the ice coffee then dusted both with cocoa powder. The chant of *Adam, Adam, Adam* kept up in my head.

"Will you be quiet," I hissed to myself. "I just want one piece of innocent excitement."

When I came out with the coffees on a tray, Xavier was sat in the sun.

"Who were you talking to?" he said, as I put them down.

"Um... My plants." I said. "They do really well if you talk to them, I do it all the time."

We spent the next minute or two in silence spooning ice cream out of our glasses.

"I like this garden," he said. "I'd like a space outdoors, for when I do my weights."

"Where do you do your weights now?" I said.

"I have to move all of the furniture in the living room. Still, it pays off. Look at this." He lifted up his t-shirt to show his six-pack.

I noticed the ripped curve of muscle from his hip which disappeared under the waistband of his shorts.

"How lovely," I said, sounding much like Meryl does when she's browsing colour charts in Homebase. I realised I would have to have another cold splash in the bath after he had gone.

"What are you going to do with that washing machine?" he said, pointing at it with his teaspoon.

"Oh that, it's a pain in the backside. It's broken but I can't get rid of it."

"I'll get rid of it for you," he said.

"You don't need to do that."

"My brother's hiring a skip next week. I pass by the end of your street all the time, so I can swing by and we can lift it over the fence."

He wouldn't let me say "no", so I asked him to call and gave my number. We watched the dogs playing for a while longer and then he said he should go.

"Maybe we could walk the dogs sometime?" he said eagerly.

"Maybe," I grinned, and waved him and Columbus goodbye.

I am in lust and I don't like it.

Wednesday 20th July 15.03
TO: marikarolincova@hotmail.co.uk

Rosencrantz phoned last night to say that he would be

filming his advert today and the location is literally round the corner from me, at The Rivoli Ballroom.

"The where?" I said.

"The Rivoli Ballroom, it's near the Co-op, on the way to Marika's place," he said. "Come and see me if you've time."

Ethel called round this morning. We left Rocco snoozing in the cool of the bathroom and walked up to the Rivoli, which was tucked away amongst the chip shops and junk shops on Brockley Road.

"Iss bin a long time since I came up to the Rivoli," said Ethel, stopping to catch her breath in the heat. "Me an' Wilf used to come dancing 'ere."

There were two lorries parked on the road outside, both with their back doors open showing endless coils of electrical cable and mysterious metal boxes. The front doors of the ballroom were open but I couldn't make out much else in the low squat building.

We went to go up the steps by the main entrance, but a girl eating a sandwich and wearing a headset blocked our path.

"You can't go in, it's a closed set," she said.

I tried to explain who we were, and that Rosencrantz was in there but she was having none off it. The girl pressed her radio and a big smelly ginger-haired guy in shorts and a filthy t-shirt came and told us to leave.

"Iss only a bloody accident insurance advert," said Ethel. "It ain't Carnegie bloody Hall."

"You can't go in," said the guy.

A fire exit opened and an old grey-haired woman of Ethel's age shuffled out with a mop.

"Ethel Dewberry?" she said.

"Bunty Brown?" said Ethel. "Well, I never! Iss bin years. Course I'm Ethel Pinchard now."

Bunty leant on her mop and squinted in the sun.

"This is Coco," said Ethel indicating me.

I said, "Hello."

"Are you in this telly ad?" said Ethel.

"Gawd no," said Bunty. "I'm the cleaner 'ere. You wanna come in?"

She opened the door for us and we marched inside, much to the annoyance of the security people.

I was expecting some old community centre with a bank of disco lights and a little plastic mirror ball. However, the inside was stunning.

"Iss the only surviving 1950s ballroom in the country," whispered Bunty, as we moved through an art déco foyer. She pushed open a large set of doors and we entered the ballroom. It was flamboyant and kitsch and like walking through a time portal. Three giant chandeliers hung from a long, shallow, barrel-vaulted ceiling, and in between were Chinese lanterns and delicate scallop-shaped lights. There were plump red velour padded walls and gilt picture-frame-style panels. The dance floor was a deep polished wood, the colour of maple syrup. It twinkled and shone and I felt I had seen it somewhere before.

"Tina Turner filmed 'er 'Private Dancer' video here," whispered Bunty. 'Iss used all the time for music videos and films."

A camera was set up to one side and a crew was milling about. The director, a handsome greying chap in a t-shirt and shorts, was sat in his customary chair in front of a small TV monitor with a set of headphones about his neck.

"Right, stand by," he said. The chandeliers roared up to their full twinkling brightness. "And action!"

A set of red velvet curtains parted on a raised dais at the back, and Rosencrantz emerged in tight black trousers and a skintight glittery shirt. His hair was combed up into a quiff and glitter speckled his face. His ballroom dancing partner was a tanned, almost leathery young lady in a green sequinned dress that shimmered as she strutted on his arm.

"And dance 2, 3, 4," said the director.

Rosencrantz and his partner did a short routine in silence, their glitter and sparkles catching in the light.

"And Rosencrantz... FALL!" he shouted.

Rosencrantz tripped and fell over.

"And cut! Let's re-set..."

Rosencrantz quickly came over to us.

"Hey," he said. "Isn't this cool?"

"Why aren't you dancing to music?" said Ethel.

"They're putting it on in post... post-production."

"And yer getting five grand just to fall over?" said Ethel.

"Yeah," said Rosencrantz excitedly.

Bunty and Ethel cooed over Rosencrantz a bit longer. Then he had to go back to work, so we said goodbye.

"How much is it to hire this place?" I asked Bunty when we were back on the steps outside. "I was thinking how wonderful it would be for a wedding reception."

"Ooh, they don't do them 'ere," she said. "It would get wrecked. All them young uns... Besides, you wouldn't see the likes of us three bein' able to afford a party 'ere," said Bunty.

As I got home I realised I had been included in Bunty's observation. The ease in which I was included in their little group of poverty-stricken pensioners scared me. I went to the bathroom and took stock. I have an inch of grey hair showing, I have run out of my fifty quid moisturiser. I look... well... old.

Thursday 28th July 21.14
TO: chris@christophercheshire.com

London has been unbearably hot. The last few days Rocco has been sleeping on the bathroom floor, which is the coolest place in the flat. I would have joined him this morning, had it not been for the grey pube I found behind the toilet (not mine). The pube seemed to herald the start of another very low day, feeling old and washed up. Thank you for the expensive face creams you gave me the other day. I know it sounds shallow but they made me feel a little like my old self again.

I ventured out to the shop in the afternoon and it seemed like so many bad things converged at once. There was a huge pile of vomit outside the gate, which really upset me, and then someone had smashed in the windshield of a car further down. Then just before the junction, a beautiful black cat I often stop to cuddle had been run over. Its burst corpse covered in flies. I turned round, came home, and spent the rest of the day attempting to write something, but I had no ideas at all.

At three o'clock there was a buzz at the door. I opened and Xavier was there with a younger, geekier version of himself.

"Hi Coco, this is my brother, Sam. We're here to get the washing machine," he said.

He was wearing a black vest and football shorts. His

brown muscular thighs bulged under the thin fabric. He looked all pouty and hot.

"Thank you," I said.

I took them through to the garden. They spent a moment inspecting the washing machine then picked it up and swiftly moved it up to the fence, which borders my garden and the road out front.

"We've got the van ready on the other side," said Xavier.

Sam went off, and when we heard a whistle, Xavier grabbed the washing machine and single-handedly hoisted it up, balancing it on top of the fence. I couldn't take my eyes off the back view of him, muscles straining. Sam's hands appeared and they steadied the machine on top of the fence panel. Xavier then darted off and round to the other side where there was a lot of grunting and swearing as they heaved it down. I heard a clank as I presumed it was put into their van, and then the engine started up and they drove off. I rushed through to the bathroom to see how I looked. My hair, now long and a little lank, was parted and tucked behind my ears. I had on no makeup.

I was in the middle of despairing into the mirror when Xavier appeared in the doorway. He was on his own and he had stripped off his vest to show an incredible torso. Sweat ran down between his smooth pectorals and he used the vest to dry himself off.

"My brother's gone to dump the machine," he said. "Can I wash my hands?"

"Sure," I said. "Help yourself."

I left him to it, but then popped my head back round the door to ask if he'd like a drink. He was now turned away from me, washing his hands. On his back was a stunning tattoo of an eagle. Inked across his muscular shoulders were the wings, beautifully etched in a blue-black ink, which complimented his smooth brown skin. The body of the eagle continued between his shoulder blades and its talons ended at the base of his slim back. As he washed his hands, his powerful shoulders flexed, and the eagle rippled and flexed along with him.

I must have been standing there for a while because he turned. I cleared my throat.

"Would you like something to drink?"

"Yeah. You got any more of that amazing ice coffee?" he said.

He grinned and ran his wet hands through his hair. I watched his arm as water ran from his wet hand, down his forearm and across his large bicep. I swallowed.

"Yes. I'll get you some... one... well, I'll make two, one for me and one for you. Oh look, I'm a poet."

"And you don't know it!" he grinned.

"Yeah," I said, going red and realising I was in the danger zone with this guy. Rocco rolled over on the bathroom floor and regarded me with a judgmental little eye.

I busied myself with making the ice coffee. He came out of the bathroom, still in only his shorts.

"Where do you want me?" he said.

"Um, I think outside is best," I said.

I didn't tell him where I really wanted him. The chant in my head started up again: *Adam, Adam, Adam, Adam...*

I put the coffee on a tray and made my way out to the garden. On the way out, I tripped on the edge of the fake grass and went flying. I hit the ground with an embarrassing thud. Xavier rushed over and helped me up. I hopped about a bit while he picked up the glasses and the tray. He shook the last of the coffee dregs off the glasses, and put them down on the table. I was leaning on the edge of the sofa, keeping the weight off my throbbing leg.

"Let me see," he said softly.

He crouched down and ran his hand over my knee.

"Does it hurt badly?"

"No, well, yes," I said.

He massaged my knee.

"I don't think anything is broken," he said.

Men always say that, but how do they really know? Unless they're a doctor? However, I just gritted my teeth gratefully. It hurt a lot.

"You need to keep rubbing, to get the blood going, and it won't hurt as much," he said, still crouched by my leg.

He carried on rubbing. His movements became slower and his fingers moved under the hem of my shorts and brushed my thigh. I felt a tingle of longing move up my leg. I looked down at him. A lock of his hair had fallen across his face. I pushed it back up over his forehead. I put my other hand on one of his powerful shoulders. He stood up to face me. I noticed he's a little taller than I am. He smelt intoxicating, a mixture of sweat and soap. He gazed at me intensely and slowly curled his hand around my waist and pulled me toward him. Pressed against him I could feel him getting hard. I averted my eyes and looked at his chest. He put his hand under my chin and tilted my face to his. He licked his lips and leant in to kiss me...

Suddenly there was a huge crash, followed instantly by a terrible sound from Rocco, a high-pitched squealing. I broke away and hobbled into the living room.

The giant bookcase by the sofa had toppled over. It hadn't fallen quite flat, and one corner was propped uneasily on the edge of the coffee table. The squealing was coming from under the bookcase.

"Oh my God!" I cried. "Rocco! He's underneath! Help me move it."

There was another clattering sound as someone tore downstairs from above. Then a quick knock on the front door as Shane burst in.

"Shit, Coco! Are you okay?"

"The bookcase, help, Rocco is underneath," I said.

He was still squealing like a banshee. It sounded like he was terribly hurt.

Shane and Xavier grabbed either end of the bookcase and tried to heave it back up against the wall. It wouldn't budge.

"Shit! Man, it weighs a ton," said Shane.

They strained and heaved, managing to lift it a foot or more. I crawled under, pulling away at books and papers which had slid off the shelves, trying to get to Rocco who was now howling so much I thought his back was broken. I finally saw his furry feet; he was caught inside one of the shelf partitions. Just then the guys managed to raise the bookcase a little more and the wooden partition between me and Rocco lifted. He darted out and jumped into my arms. I shuffled back and clear of the bookcase. The guys couldn't hold it any longer. They let go and it landed on the coffee table, which then collapsed and the whole lot crashed to the floor.

I stood there with Rocco in my arms, shaking.

"Jeez..." said Shane. "That could have been really nasty."

He noticed Xavier standing in just his shorts.

"This is, uh..."

"Hi mate, I'm Shane, I live upstairs..." he said.

"I'm Xavier."

They shook hands.

"Were you trying to move this?" asked Shane

"No. We were um... outside," I said. Xavier looked at me. "We suddenly heard it fall."

"How the hell did this thing fall?" said Shane.

"I don't know, we were ... We weren't in here and heard the crash."

"Had you moved it away from the wall?" Shane wanted to know.

"No," I said. "I haven't touched it."

"Shit, that's weird," said Shane circling the mess. "It's a bloody behemoth with a low centre of gravity, it shouldn't have just toppled... I study engineering," he said, by way of explanation for his interest.

"Come on Shane, we need to get this upright and help Coco clear up," said Xavier.

They both went to grab the bookcase.

"No. No, it's okay," I said. "Please can you ... I've had a shock and I want to calm down Rocco and I don't want to put it back up against the wall."

Rocco was still shivering in my arms and I was in shock in more ways than one.

"Is everything all right?" he said, looking between Xavier and me.

I said everything was fine. Shane said to let him know if I needed anything, and then went back upstairs, leaving me with Xavier.

"Can I do anything?" he asked.

"No, thank you," I said clutching Rocco.

He came to stand beside me and rubbed my arm.

"Xavier..."

"I really like you, Coco," he said. "You're..."

"I'm sorry. I think you should go," I said.

He regarded me for a minute.

"I have a fiancé," I said. "He's called Adam, he's in prison, and I'm waiting for him."

I thought of our wedding, still booked for the end of August. I tried to smile but tears came instead.

"I'm sorry, but you need to leave," I said.

Xavier nodded sadly. He shucked his vest top over his head and opened the door, and he was gone.

I took Rocco over to the kitchen, put him gently on the counter, and checked over every inch of him, gently squeezing his paws and running my hands along his back, stroking his head. He seemed fine, but very shaken. I gave him some treats and a little drink of water. I then went to the fridge and poured myself a huge ice-cold spritzer. I let him drink a little out of my glass and sat with him on the table beside me, trying to process everything.

What if that bookcase hadn't fallen? What if it had fallen a second earlier and crushed Rocco? I thought of the beautiful cat I had seen earlier. And Xavier, beautiful Xavier...

I suddenly noticed the patch of exposed carpet under the bookshelf. It was a lovely pale blue against the grey of the rest of the carpet. On it was an old photo album. I got up and went over to it. It was very thin, no doubt squashed by the weight of the huge bookshelves, and made of padded velvet. It was tied shut with a greasy old ribbon in a flattened bow.

I picked it up and came back to the kitchen counter. Rocco, who was still sitting there, sniffed it as I undid the ribbon. As I turned the thin cardboard pages they creaked with age. It was filled with a selection of 1950s photographs. Black and white pictures of ladies with dyed black hair and those Dame Edna glasses posing in front of their cars, back when cars where a luxury you took out on a Sunday afternoon for a drive. I found myself searching for the lady I saw in my dreams.

I finally found her in the last photo. A slim, younger version in a twinset perched on the bonnet of an old Daimler. She was smiling into the camera. The picture was taken outside this flat.

"Why am I dreaming about you?" I said.

I eased the photo out from its little cardboard corners

and turned it over, but all that was printed on the back was the Kodak Eastman symbol. I searched through the album a few more times, but there were only photos.

I put the album on the table and poured another big drink. For the rest of the evening I sat with Rocco out in the garden, him on my lap, thinking.

I'm not at all scared, but there is something very odd about this flat.

Friday 29th July 21.14
TO: submit@prisonlink.net

To Prisoner AG26754 Adam Rickard

We had a viewing party at Ethel's yesterday afternoon. It was the premiere of Rosencrantz's TV advert, during an episode of *Midsomer Murder's* on ITV3. It was me, Ethel, Chris, Marika, Wayne, Oscar, and of course, Rosencrantz.

Rosencrantz seems to be the matinee idol of The Aspidistra Sheltered Housing in Catford. The old ladies worship him. They attend all his performances. We all went to see him in *The Don't Drink Or Do Drugs Puppet Show* a few weeks ago, and those who still have good use of their knees gave him a standing ovation.

The episode itself caused a lot of excitement (it was the one where you see Orlando Bloom's bare bottom). Then, just after an archery arrow to the chest killed him, the episode went to an advert break, and there was Rosencrantz!

"Have you had an accident in the last five years?" came the voice-over and there he was, dancing away to some jazzy samba music before tragically slipping over. He also did a piece to camera where he said that Inter-claims helped him to sue his dance school for five thousand pounds on a no-win no-fee basis.

At the end of the advert, everyone cheered and clapped. I was so proud of him, and Ethel got one of the wardens to open a couple of bottles of Asti Spumante and we all gave him a toast.

"Speech!" yelled Ethel's friend Irene. "Give us a speech!"

Rosencrantz rose to his feet.

"Thank you for organising this, Nan, I love you, and thanks to all my biggest fans here."

The old ladies chorused him with a sedate "Woo-hoo."

"Most importantly I want to thank you, Mum," he said. I sat up in surprise. "You've always been there for me, always. When I was a kid and wanted to perform, you encouraged me. You paid for me to go to drama school. You even risked everything to rescue me from jail in America."

There was a collective gasp from Rosencrantz's elderly fan club.

"It was only class C drugs!" said Ethel chastising them all. "An' it was a set up!"

"Now you're having a rough time, Mum, especially when you have to go and visit Adam. So, I got you a present."

He handed me a little box. I opened it, a little miffed. Inside was a car key. I looked up. The whole room was on the edge of their seats/high backed armchairs.

"Look out of the window, Mum," said Rosencrantz.

I got up; the eyes of the television lounge followed.

Wayne had slipped out at some point and was standing at the kerb beside a midnight blue Smart Car. He leant in the driver's side, beeped the horn, and waved. I looked back at Rosencrantz with my mouth open.

"I bought you a car, Mum," he said. "It's second-hand, but it looks sweet."

The old ladies cooed like pigeons. I grabbed him in a bear hug.

"He looks like a young Tyrone Powell," I heard one of them say. We all went down in the lift, and out to the car.

"How much did this cost?" I said, stroking the deep blue paintwork.

"Not important," he said.

"How did you get it?" I said suspiciously

"Relax, it's kosher. I used some of my insurance advert money."

"It's true," said Wayne. "I went with him to choose it."

"And look, I got a doggy seat belt for Rocco so he can ride with you."

Chris, Marika, and Oscar all grinned as I eased myself into the black velvety driver's seat.

"They're cheap to run. The man in the garage said you could probably get to Norfolk and back for fifteen quid. You also don't pay any congestion charge," said Rosencrantz.

I looked at the shiny new car and I was so taken aback.

I drove Chris, Rosencrantz, and Marika back to my place, which was a big squash as there was only room for one passenger. I parked the car outside the flat and it felt so wonderful to be mobile again, so exciting to have a car.

They came inside and I made us all spritzers. The shelf was still looming large and toppled in the living room, so we came outside and sat on the champagne sofas.

I had told them all about the photo album and we'd chewed it over for a few hours, coming up with nothing. Chris had started talking about something else when Marika gave a yell.

"What is it?" I cried.

"Look! Someone's split the edge of the lining and made a compartment. There's something in here," she said.

She carefully pulled out a sheaf of old newspaper cuttings and put them on the table. We sifted through them.

"It's all crap," said Chris with disappointment in his voice. "Local newspaper crap."

Rosencrantz was sitting opposite, and started to look through them again. He unfolded one of them, a full-page article about a street fair, which was on in 2010. I noticed an article on the back and choked on my drink.

It was a photo of Sabrina Jones.

I screamed and grabbed it. The photo was taken outside the Magistrate's Court in Camberwell. Sabrina was reaching out to try to prevent a photographer from taking her photo. Underneath was written:

Suspended sentence for £40,000 benefit thief

A 27-year-old South London woman has been given a suspended jail sentence after pleading guilty to five charges of benefit fraud amounting to almost £40,000.

Sabrina Colter of Woolwich, London, was sentenced to six months in prison, suspended for two years, at Woolwich Magistrates' Court on Thursday, 14 May 2010.

Colter pleaded guilty to five offences of dishonesty, making false statements, and creating false documents to obtain benefits amounting to £39,568 at an earlier hearing on Wednesday 22 April. She was also ordered to return the money she took and pay £500 costs.

Colter had previously been given a conditional discharge in 2008 for not declaring that her mother was her landlady, but continued to falsely claim Housing and Council Tax benefit using four separate identities.

"This is her!" I said.

"I thought she was called Sabrina Jones?" said Chris. "This article says she's Sabrina Colter."

"She must have changed her surname!" I said.

I looked at the paper again. It *was* her, the fine wrists, and the long blonde hair. Her face was twisted into the same angry snarl I saw when she was on the phone by the Thames during the trial.

"Surely this means something?" said Rosencrantz.

"It means everything!" said Marika. "If they didn't know about her criminal record for fraud, it casts doubt on her reliability as a witness."

"And if they didn't know about it, it's new information to present in an appeal!" I shrilled.

I jumped up and phoned Natasha, but just when I need her, she has left for her two-week summer holiday in The Maldives. Her secretary said she's on a plane for the next twelve hours and unreachable.

I then grabbed my things and said I was going to go round and have it out with Sabrina.

"Mum, that's the stupidest thing I've heard," said Rosencrantz. "She doesn't know you know. Isn't that your trump card?"

"If you go round, she'll probably call the police," said Chris. "You look ready to kill her."

"And it wouldn't help Adam's appeal if you get arrested," added Marika.

I had to admit they had a point. I came and sat down and tried to stay calm.

Now that they have all left, I'm feeling increasingly frustrated. I'm also creeped out about all of these coincidences. The dream I kept having about the old woman pointing behind the bookshelf... it's her photo album... However, I am so excited. We have a crack at an appeal! Phone as soon as you can. I love you, and we are going to get you out of prison!

Coco xxx

Saturday 30th July 21.06
TO: marikarolincova@hotmail.co.uk

All the wind seems to have been taken out of my sails. I haven't heard back from Adam; he must have received my email letter by now. He didn't call before we listened to Adele, which he always does.

Natasha isn't answering her mobile and the offices of Spencer & Spencer are not open until Monday. Is the legal profession the only group of people who still have a two-day weekend?

I am so close to going over to Sabrina's flat and, I don't know, breaking in and looking for the cash, smacking her in the gob. Anything to make something happen!

AUGUST

Monday 1st August 13.12
TO: chris@christophercheshire.com

I haven't heard from Adam. It's been several days now. He normally phones before our listening party on a Saturday, and writes a letter, which he times to arrive on a Monday. When the post arrived this morning with nothing but junk mail, I phoned Cambria Sands Prison switchboard to ask if there was any way I could talk to him.

"You want me to 'put you through' to a serving prisoner?" said the gruff voice that answered.

"Why not?" I said. "He can go for walks; there are no bars on the windows. Can't you let him speak to me?"

"Well, I would let you, but Prisoner AG26754 is currently occupied on the croquet lawn before he takes tea in the conservatory," he said, without missing a beat.

"Okay. I get it..." I said. "Please could you at least tell me if Prisoner AG26754 is okay? You see I haven't heard from him in days. He *always* phones or writes to me."

"I can check if the prisoner is currently serving a sentence in the prison. But that is all."

"Thank you," I said.

The line went quiet and I held for several eternal minutes. The silence was deafening. There is no hold music in HM Prison Service. Finally, there was a click, a rustle, and the voice returned.

"The Prisoner is in solitary."

"What? Solitary... solitary confinement?"

"Yes."

"Why?" There was a sound of papers being sifted. "It seems Prisoner AG26754 was involved in a fight. Ah... yes... pulled up in front of the governor last Thursday."

"And by Prisoner AG26754 you mean Adam Rickard?"

"Yes."

"Was he badly hurt?"

"He wasn't admitted to the hospital wing, so we can assume not."

"When can I expect to hear from him?"

More pages turned.

"I see here Prisoner AG... Um, Mr Rickard, has lost all privileges for a month, and had fifty-six days added to his sentence."

"Fifty-six days?"

"Yes."

I put down the phone. Fifty-six days! That's another two months! To think how long two months is, especially during this terrible period. I was so angry. If I were at the prison, I'd put Adam in the hospital wing myself.

Later that afternoon the doorbell rang, and outside stood Wayne and Rosencrantz. I was in a t-shirt and shorts with a huge hammer and some clear goggles I had borrowed from Shane upstairs.

"Mum, what are you doing?" said Rosencrantz.

"I'm going to bash that bloody bookshelf to bits," I said. "It's all cracked across the back and I need something to take out my anger on."

I told them about Adam.

"You need to come down from your DIY cloud and the put the kettle on, Mrs P," said Wayne. "We've concocted a cunning plan."

"We have, Mum," grinned Rosencrantz.

I pulled off my goggles, went to the kitchen, and filled a pan with water.

"We've got the answer, Mum," said Rosencrantz. "And it's been staring us in the face."

"Social media," said Wayne, pulling out his iPad.

"What are you talking about?" I said, putting the pan on the stove and lighting the gas.

"We did some research on Sabrina Jones."

"Formerly Sabrina Colter," added Wayne.

"Sabrina is all over social media," said Rosencrantz. "She's very active on Facebook and Twitter."

"So?" I said, pulling out mugs and some chocolate biscuits.

"This Sabrina is stupid enough to share her whole life on the Internet," said Rosencrantz. "Just from looking at her Twitter feed we know a lot of the places she's been today. For example, she went to Nandos in the O2 at eleven this morning, and she's off to see a film..."

"*Harry Potter and The Deathly Hallows, Part Two*... With her friend Caitlin," said Wayne holding up his iPad.

"People don't realise, you can piece together their whole lives by silly updates they write. Her Facebook account goes back to 2007, her Twitter goes back to 2009," said Rosencrantz.

"You know how in old James Bond films, when they

wanted to follow the bad guy without him knowing, they'd stick a tracking device to his car and then watch a moving red dot on a map?" asked Wayne.

"Yes..." I said.

"This is our red dot!" grinned Rosencrantz. "The info flashes up on Facebook or Twitter."

"Does she say where she stashed the two hundred grand?" I asked sceptically, pouring milk into mugs.

"No Mum, but we're watching..."

We sat down for our tea and I told them about Adam not being in contact, about Natasha being on holiday, and how I felt desperate.

"This is going to work out, Mum, I know it," said Rosencrantz. I admired his positivity, but I didn't agree.

Tuesday 2nd August 19.15
TO: marikarolincova@hotmail.co.uk

Natasha phoned this morning! Her secretary had passed on my message. I told her about the newspaper cutting and Sabrina Jones having a criminal record for fraud as Sabrina Colter.

"This is very good, Coco!" she said. "It could be a mitigating factor in forcing an appeal... Can you fax me a copy of the newspaper article?" She gave me a number for her hotel. As soon as I came off the phone, I ran round to the little corner shop and paid £4 to fax the newspaper cutting to Natasha's luxury five-star hotel.

As I stood there in the stinking shop, watching the newspaper as it was sucked into the cracked old fax machine, I hoped that this would be our breakthrough moment.

I came home and waited. And waited. I've heard nothing all day. I hope that crappy fax machine was working.

Friday 5th August 16.47
TO: marikarolincova@hotmail.co.uk, chris@christophercheshire.com

There has been nothing from Natasha, or Adam. I took Rocco for a long walk and found myself up at the little church in Honor Oak Park. It was full of volunteers, old ladies bustling in and out with mops and buckets and bunches of fresh flowers. I wanted to go inside, but Rocco was with me and I didn't have a coat to hide him in.

I was convinced for so long we would get married there on the 19th August. A date now only two weeks away. I thought how unfair life is. I'm stuck. Frozen in time. Engaged to man who won't see the light of day until June 2015 — no, it's now August 2015! I'll be almost fifty! What's to say he won't be released and find some hot young thing?

Sorry to be such a misery. Love you both. C xx

Monday 8th August 17.11
TO: chris@christophercheshire.com, marikarolincova@hotmail.co.uk

I would love to come out for a drink with you both, but I have just had to transfer more money over to Spender &

Spencer law firm. Natasha still hasn't contacted me after I faxed the newspaper cutting, which is a major piece of evidence, but I do get a bill from her office for her time! It all feels so relentless.

I don't know if I will ever be able to move back into my house, or have a career... Sorry, am just very low. Have fun.

Love Coco xxx

PS Have you seen on the news, there are riots breaking out in North London.

Tuesday 9th August 16.54
TO: angie.langford@thebmxliteraryagency.biz

Are you okay, love? I saw the rioting is getting close to you in North London; they have spread to this side of the river too. People are going mad, smashing up shops and looting. Rosencrantz, Marika, and Chris came over last night for a drink and ended up staying the night. Chris had called for a taxi when it got late, but every cab company refused to drive through South London. The riots have broken out in Peckham (four miles away) Lewisham (three miles away) and just down the road, in Catford! We realised they were so close when the doorbell rang just before nine and there was Ethel in her best coat, shaking with nerves.

"Can I come in, love? I was on the bus 'ome and the driver just kicked us orf at the end of your road. Catford is closed orf by riot police!" she said.

I pulled her in and locked the door. We were all genuinely scared that the rioters would reach Brockley.

I made toast and tea and we watched a live feed from the BBC News Channel of the riots unfolding. One journalist was shown walking along the high street in Peckham filming people throwing bricks through shop windows and grabbing what they could. Just after they reported that people were taking to Twitter to organise riots, my Internet connection was cut.

"This is unbelievable," said Chris, stabbing at the screen of his iPhone. "I thought we lived in a democracy!"

"Democracy is an illusion at best," I said.

"We're all just pawns in the capitalist master plan," said Marika.

"You know woss worse?" said Ethel. "I left me smalls out on the rotary line! Do you think they'll get looted?"

"They want the latest gadgets, DVDs and flat screen televisions," I said. "Your knickers should be fine."

It was strange to be completely cut off from any television or radio. Every now and then one of us would go out into the street to see if anything was happening, but it was eerily quiet. In the distance there was an orange glow, but we couldn't tell if it was fire or light pollution. The uncertainty didn't do us any good.

Everyone stayed the night and bunked down where they could. I let Ethel have the bed. Marika and me shared the sofa. Rosencrantz and Chris pulled in a champagne chair each from outside, and curled up as best they could.

Around five, when it got light, we realised we were all awake, so I got up and made more tea and toast. Rosencrantz discovered the Internet was back on, so he switched on the laptop, and we watched the early morning news.

Rosencrantz suddenly stopped chewing his toast halfway to his mouth.

"Mum," he said. "That's Croydon... close to where Dad lives."

An aerial view of a street showed cars on fire, riot police charging groups of young men in face masks pelting them with sticks and bottles. A huge building in the centre of Croydon was on fire, flames leaping high into the air as people jumped from inside to safety. A look shot between us and I grabbed the phone and called Daniel.

"Hello," he said chirpily. "I haven't heard from you in a while, what's this? You've heard about my new relationship?"

"Have you seen the news?" I said. "Croydon is on fire!"

"Oh Lord, good job I moved then," he said gleefully.

"What do you mean?"

"I've met a lovely trombone player called Jennifer, and I've moved into her pied à terre in Hampstead. It's worth two million, are you jealous?" he teased.

"No. We were worried about you."

"Oh I'm fine, I don't need to mix with the poor anymore in South London... Oh, I er... I'm only joking."

"I'll tell everyone you're fine," I said, and put the phone down.

Ethel was happy Daniel was okay, and even happier he was now living in a posh area.

"I wonder if she's got big cheeks," said Ethel, when I told her about Jennifer.

"What, a fat arse?" said Rosencrantz.

"No, big cheeks from blowing on the trombone..." said Ethel. "Iss not the most flattering instrument, why couldn't 'e meet a nice girl who plays the violin?"

"People are rioting out there!" I reminded her.

"Iss 'orrible love, I know," said Ethel. "But life goes on. Believe me, I know. I lived through the Blitz."

Later in the morning, they opened the road. Ethel shared a cab home with Rosencrantz and Chris. I took Rocco for a walk with Marika.

We discovered what the glowing fire in the sky was last night. Rioters with petrol bombs had attacked several shops near Marika's flat. The fire brigade had managed to contain and extinguish most of the fire, but further up past the station one building didn't survive.

The church.

We stood at the bottom of the steps and watched as a fire engine slowly navigated the trees. It stopped beside us to pull out into the road. The passenger window was open and I leaned up and asked what had happened.

"The roof collapsed around four in the morning and took the spire with it... it crashed into the trees behind," said a young firefighter with soot on his face. "We've had to put a cordon round. The structure isn't safe. Watching a building burn is bad enough, but seeing all those stained glass windows, hundreds of years old, blowing out in the heat was depressing..."

The fire engine pulled out into the traffic.

"I need to go Marika, now," I said.

She grabbed my hand and we went back to her flat where we had a stiff drink, even though it was only nine in the morning.

Wednesday 10th August 20.14
TO: chris@christophercheshire.com,
marikarolincova@hotmail.co.uk

I still haven't heard from Adam. He lost all his privileges

including use of phone and postage stamps. I want to know what the fight was about. He isn't usually one for getting into scraps.

Rosencrantz and Wayne came over this afternoon. They've been doing more detective work, and printed off a series of Tweets and Facebook posts Sabrina Jones/Colter has been writing.

The riots came very close to her area of London (Woolwich) and she has had a few exchanges about being scared of looters and unable to leave her flat.

The tone suggests she has something of real value there. These are the Tweets and Facebook posts the boys have homed in on. I am now starting to take notice:

@SabrinaC really scared of #London2011Riots we have to sit tight and stay in d'flat to protect R future.

@SabrinaC a house is on fire at end of my road, does anyone no where I can get a Fireproof SAFE?

@SabrinaC I just bought a Fireproof Safe £29.99 @amazonUK

Then a day later she posted on Facebook:

Ugh! Waiting in 4 Parcel force. BORED!!!!

And later:

Parcelforce is still not here - mayb they're scared of the rioting????

Then on Twitter she tweeted:

@SabrinaC please retweet #parcelforceisshit lets TREND IT! I spent £20 on amazon next day delivery still not here! WTF?

Then about four hours later, the fireproof safe arrived. She posted a picture on Facebook of her cat sitting inside it, with the door open. Underneath she'd written; 'A CAT BURGLAR LOL LMAO!'

Then last night she posted:

@SabrinaC #London2011Riots OMG next door wuz on fire. Just helped to X-TiNG-Ish petrol bomb thrown thru front window.

@SabrinaC am gonna get online b4 the police cut the net again. Need 2do sum stuff 2 keep safe.

And on Facebook:

Packing my suitcase 4 2morrow! Big life changing trip ahead of us!

Finally she posted on Twitter:

@SabrinaC I just bought a single ferry ticket Portsmouth to Jersey @ExpediaUK

"Is she completely stupid?" I said, after reading them through.

"Well, we think the answer is 'yes'," said Rosencrantz. "What you can see is what we've weeded out of a glut of nonsense. She constantly posts on Twitter and Facebook."

"Okay," I said. "What can we read into this? If we didn't know her?"

"Well, she could have bought the safe for her iPod and her sovereign rings," said Wayne.

"That's true," said Rosencrantz. "But knowing her background with fraud, and what you heard her say by the Thames, I think she's going to move the money."

"To Jersey. Tomorrow," I said.

We looked at each other. Even though we were standing in my kitchen, and the sun was streaming through the door, a shiver went through me.

"I'm wondering if she knows someone in Jersey who can make the money vanish," said Rosencrantz. "And she might not be coming back. She only bought a one-way ticket."

We sat talking for another couple of hours, but kept coming back to the same thought: we have to follow her.

Thursday 11th August 03.13
TO: marikarolincova@hotmail.co.uk, chris@christophercheshire.com

We believe that Sabrina Jones could be moving £200,000 today. The problem is we have only vague details. We know she has booked a ferry ticket to Jersey, via Portsmouth tomorrow, well, today. We don't know what time the ferry leaves.

We hatched a plan yesterday to follow her. It seems rather far-fetched now Rosencrantz and myself are trundling along the A3 in my Smart Car, but we have nothing to lose. I'd rather go on a wild goose chase to free Adam than see him stuck in prison for something he didn't do.

The first ferry out of Portsmouth this morning is at 5.30 am. Therefore, we are planning to get there by 4.30. The roads are completely empty and we are making good time.

Wayne and Oscar are staying at my flat. They have access to the Internet, phone and they're looking after Rocco. Wayne is the one who is friends with Sabrina (online friend) so he will be keeping us up to date with anything she posts or tweets.

Thursday 11th August 04.28
TO: marikarolincova@hotmail.co.uk, chris@christo-phercheshire.com

We have arrived at Portsmouth Harbour. There is no sign of anyone or anything. It's also very cold. The seagulls are cawing in the pitch black, and we can see the sea rolling below the cliff in the moonlight. It feels ominous. We are counting down the minutes to 6am when we can get a McDonald's breakfast.

Thursday 11th August 06.40
TO: marikarolincova@hotmail.co.uk, chris@christo-phercheshire.com

We are a little sated; the sun is up and I'm on my second McDonald's breakfast. The world looks a little better. We are still sitting in the car and looking out at the sea twinkling in the morning sun. 'Price Tag' by Jessie J just came on the radio and we were singing as loud as we could. I love the song, but as we sang I started to listen to the words, and by the end, I was very scared.

Thursday 11th August 10.15
TO: marikarolincova@hotmail.co.uk, chris@christo-phercheshire.com

Wayne phoned. Sabrina has just posted something on her Facebook wall: Morning just woke up. Big life changing day!

The stupid cow is still at home in her pyjamas! We are going to go down to the beach for a bit.

Thursday 11th August 12.12
TO: marikarolincova@hotmail.co.uk, chris@christo-phercheshire.com

I smoked a whole pack of cigarettes whilst we stared out to sea. The beach isn't really much to write home about. It's not really a beach, just a strip of shingle in the shadow of the port, but it's calming to sit and be lulled by the waves.

I was suddenly seized with fear.

"Are you friends with Sabrina on Facebook and Twitter?" I asked. "Pinchard is quite an unusual name. She might twig something!"

"Relax Mum, Wayne's friends with her," he said. "And he's using our fake profile, Liam McCluskey."

"Who is Liam McCluskey?" I said.

"He the fake profile we use to check out stuff. He Likes pages we wouldn't dare admit liking. He's duped cheating boyfriends into admitting their infidelity, and he's spied on Sabrina. Liam McCluskey has been good to us..."

Just then, his phone rang. It was Wayne.

"She's on her way!" I heard him shrill excitedly. "I repeat, she's on her way! She just checked into a rest stop on the A3, and posted a picture of herself with a Starbucks Caramel Macchiato."

Wayne estimates she is thirty minutes away. She is travelling by car. We don't know if she's going to board the ferry on foot, or drive on.

I've made my way back up to the car. Rosencrantz has gone to get some refreshments. I'm terrified.

Thursday 11th August 21.51
TO: marikarolincova@hotmail.co.uk, chris@christophercheshire.com

I was in the car waiting for Rosencrantz to come back, when a Fiat pulled up beside. It was old and battered, and out climbed Sabrina! She was so close that when she got out, her arse clad in tracksuit bottoms actually pressed against my window. I ducked down pretending to search through my bag, but she didn't notice. She was with a rather mean-looking guy who had a buzz cut and was also wearing a tracksuit. They were arguing as he went to the boot and took out two huge suitcases, setting them down and slamming it shut. They pulled up the handles and trudged off across the car park dragging them behind.

As they got smaller in the rear view mirror, I quickly phoned Rosencrantz.

"She's just arrived! She's with a bloke. They're heading for the ferry terminal!" I said.

"It's okay, Mum. They must be on the two o'clock," he said. "I'll buy the tickets, you lock the car and bring our stuff."

I began to shake all over. I took a deep breath and flopped down the mirror. I applied some lipstick, which made me feel a tiny bit better. I straightened my hair and grabbed Rosencrantz's rucksack and my handbag. I locked the car and started to walk across the wide expanse of the car park toward the terminal.

Suddenly my phone rang.

"Mum! Watch out," said Rosencrantz. "They're coming back your way!"

"I thought they'd already bought tickets?" I said.

"I think they only came to collect them."

I spied them heading towards me pulling the suitcases.

"Act normal Mum, but don't let her see you!" said Rosencrantz, and he hung up.

I looked around. The section of the car park we were crossing was a wide empty expanse. It would look weirder if I *didn't* keep walking towards them. I fumbled with my bag to open it and put the phone inside.

I kept walking, pretending I was enjoying the sea view. The wind was helping, blowing my hair across my face. We moved closer together, closer. Then the wind ceased, leaving my face exposed! We were a few feet apart when Rosencrantz's rucksack slipped off my shoulder, pushing my handbag, hooked on the same shoulder, with it. My phone, wallet, make-up, and loose change clattered out and skidded across the tarmac. I bent down to pick it up, keeping my head down.

A pair of white trainers halted beside me.

"You need a hand?" said a smooth cockney voice.

"Oh, no it's fine," I said softly.

A pair of smaller pink trainers appeared too. I didn't look up. I carried on gathering up my things... seconds ticked by.

"Here, let me help," he said.

I saw him crouch down and begin gathering up the contents of my makeup bag that had skidded the furthest away.

"I'll be at the car, Simon," said Sabrina's bored voice.

Simon! I thought. *When I overheard her conversation all those months ago, she was talking to a Simon!*

My heart beat even faster. Out of the corner of my eye, I saw Sabrina's pink trainers shift as she struggled to get her suitcase going. She moved past and out of my field of vision. Only then I dared to look up (because I don't think Simon has seen me before). He had beautiful brown eyes. He smiled and handed me my nail polish and lipstick.

"You've got a whole makeup counter in there!" he joked.

I let out a squeaky little titter. He turned to pick up some loose change, and I noticed his suitcase. It was parked inches from my leg. It was dark blue and covered in padlocks, four or five in total. As the wind blew across the car park from the sea, they clinked and jingled.

"Here you go," he said, handing me my change. I saw his name written on the tag: Simon Milner.

"Thanks," I said taking it.

My brain was whirring *thinking... thinking...* what could I do? Grab it and wheel it away? Too heavy. Rip it open with my nail scissors? They were in the bottom of my handbag in one of those little cases with a popper fastener. Moreover, the car park was deserted. If I attempted anything, he'd probably hit me over the head and they'd speed off in the car.

Then the moment had gone. He was grinning, I was saying thanks in a breathy damsel-in-distress fashion, which he seemed to like. Then he tipped the suitcase back on its wheels and moved off under its weight back to his car. I walked quickly to the Ferry Terminal and didn't look back until I went through the automatic doors where Rosencrantz was waiting.

"What happened there?" he said. "Are you okay? What did he say to you?"

I told him about the encounter, then we saw their little Fiat move off toward the exit.

"Shit!" I said. "We've got to follow them."

"Hang on, Mum," he said. We watched as they left the car park. The toy-sized car in the distance joined a slip road, which ran beside the terminal. They passed us, then further down took a turn, and doubled back toward to the ferry.

"They're taking their car on the ferry!"

"Should I change our tickets? So we can drive?" said Rosencrantz.

"No," I said. "Whatever it is we do, we need to do it on the boat. It's an enclosed space."

We walked shakily towards the ferry. It was small, old, and grubby. Cars were lining up to board via a ramp and foot passengers were milling toward a little bridge.

We kept our heads down and walked up the ramp. Once on board we found ourselves in a little carpeted staircase which stunk of coffee, cigarettes, and fuel.

"Come on Mum, let's go up to the top deck," said Rosencrantz.

It was warm and sunny on deck and we went to the railing on the side looking out to sea. There was a view down onto the lower deck where cars were pulling up to park in rows. I spied the Fiat with Sabrina and Simon pulling into the second row of cars from the stern of the ferry.

"Crap," said Rosencrantz.

"What?"

"If we need to break into their car, then everyone up on this deck will see us."

"Whoa, hang on," I said. "What do you think we're going to do?"

"Grab the money!"

"It's in a locked bag. Well, we think it is. What if they haven't got the money?"

"They *have* to have the money," said Rosencrantz. "Everything that's happened in the last few months has led us to this moment."

We both jumped as ferry's horn blared. Slowly the side of the dock began to move away from us. We turned and the open sea beckoned. Rosencrantz flicked his cigarette into the choppy water below. We watched as Sabrina and Simon emerged from the Fiat and unloaded the suitcases. They dragged them slowly across the car deck.

"Man. Those are big suitcases," said Rosencrantz quietly.

"How much space do you think two hundred grand takes up?" I said.

Rosencrantz Googled it on his phone.

"Well, if it's in tens and twenties it could be twenty or thirty kilos... If it's in fifties it would be around five kilos. Of course they could be packing to emigrate too," he said.

"Who emigrates to Jersey?"

"Bergerac did..."

"This is stupid. We don't know *anything* for sure."

Sabrina and Simon disappeared through the doors and off the car deck.

"What if they come up here?" I realised, in a panic.

"I don't think they will with those cases. I'll go and

check." Rosencrantz went off and came back a few minutes later.

"They're sat with the bags on the bottom deck," he said. "It's closed in with rows of seating."

"You don't think they'll dump them overboard?" I said.

"And do what?"

"They could have someone waiting in a dinghy?"

"Don't be stupid, Mum. They're gonna risk it in their car. They hardly ever search cars on the Jersey border. They'll pretend to be holidaymakers. I bet they are going to bank the cash somewhere quiet. Jersey is the perfect place to make money vanish."

All this "I think" and "I bet" was making me nervous.

"I should call Natasha," I said. "Leave a message about what's going on here. If we're really going to do something stupid, we might need a lawyer."

I dialled her office at Spencer & Spencer and left a message with her secretary, who didn't seem too fazed with what I was telling her.

"I must remind you, Miss Hamilton is taking a holiday in the Maldives," she said.

"Please just tell her, it's important," I said.

The secretary reluctantly said she would.

Then my phone rang. It was Wayne.

"Which boat did you get on, Mrs P?"

I told him it was the 2pm to St. Helier.

"That's a ten-hour crossing!"

"I thought it was four hours?"

"No, we've made a mistake, that's the one from Poole," he said. "At least you have time to finalise your plans... What is your plan?"

"I have no idea," I said.

"Well, I can help as much as I can, but your phone signal

is probably about to run out at sea. If you need me to call the A-Team let me know soon," he joked.

We found a bench and spent the next few hours debating what to do. There were no police on board, only at the other end when we got to the Jersey border. If we left it too late Sabrina and Simon could zoom down the exit ramp and escape.

We debated stealing their car keys (tricky, illegal), or locking them in the toilet then calling the police (also tricky as there was only one toilet on the boat with a constant queue outside). We also thought about tipping off the Jersey police (but as the ferry chugged onwards we realised we didn't have a mobile phone signal).

We decided to have a break and went to get some food from the café; jacket potatoes with cheese and beans. We were looking out to sea when I told Rosencrantz about Wayne's comment, about calling the A-Team.

There was a clatter as Rosencrantz dropped his plastic fork.

"That's it!" he said.

"What?"

"The A-Team! When they were in a sticky situation, they used what they had, they used things lying around."

"Well, they had an awful lot of stuff in the back of their van," I said.

"It's the simplest things," said Rosencrantz. He grabbed his jacket potato. "What if we shoved this potato up their exhaust pipe?"

"Don't be silly."

"It's perfect! It means their car won't start... They won't know what the problem is. All the other cars will pull away. They'll be sitting ducks!"

Before I could say anything, he put the potato in the box and darted off. He vanished and re-appeared on the car deck. Quick as a flash he nipped across, weaving through the cars and stopped by the Fiat, pretending to do up his shoelace. He was back within minutes.

"Mischief managed," he grinned. "The car was also unlocked. I opened the boot a fraction and wedged a little piece of polystyrene in the lock, so it won't close properly..."

"What do we do now?" I said.

"We wait."

We had been awake for around twenty hours when we drew up in the port of St. Helier, Jersey. It was ten forty-five and dusk was falling. The engines droned as the ferry powered its way into a gap by the quay between a larger, more attractive ship. A rope was flung deftly out and caught by a young lad on the pier side. The engines cut out, and the ringing silence was filled with voices as they made their way toward the exit.

We stayed put in our spot and surveyed the people climbing back into their vehicles on the car deck. A clank signalled that the passenger ramp was down and foot passengers began to file off the ferry. This was followed by a deeper clang as the car ramp moved into place. A chorus of engines starting up roared into the summer night, and when the gates opened the first cars started to move off.

"What if their car starts?" I said anxiously.

"It won't," said Rosencrantz.

Although, he didn't sound too sure.

There was a lot of exhaust smoke to begin with, and all of the cars seemed to be moving. Then we heard it; the high-pitched *rih rih rih rih rihrihrihrih* of an engine failing to start. More cars moved off and now the Fiat was an obstruction. A chorus of horns and shouting began. Sabrina's window opened and her lethally manicured middle finger extended gracelessly into the air.

"Let's go NOW!" said Rosencrantz.

We darted across the deck and down the central staircase, emerging out onto the half-empty car deck. The beeping, shouting and exhaust smoke seemed to mask the madness of what we were doing long enough for us to reach the boot of the Fiat. Rosencrantz wrenched it open (the polystyrene had worked). Without a second thought, I grabbed at one of the suitcases and heaved it out onto the deck. Rosencrantz pulled out the second one. My nail scissors were ready in my hand. I dug them into a corner of the material and dragged them along, tearing the whole case open. I pulled at the contents, searching for cash, but all that tumbled out was clothes.

Sabrina and Simon flew out of the Fiat. I reached into the ragged tear of the suitcase desperately, but all I was pulling out was jeans and shoes.

"What the fuck are you doing?" shouted Simon.

I seemed to go deaf and cold all at the same time as panic swept through me. He raised his arm to hit me...

Then it began to rain down on us, like ticker tape at the end of a concert. Money. Fifty-pound notes were flying through the air. Slowly my hearing came back and I could hear screaming and shouting. People had stopped and were watching in amazement as money rained down around us. Simon was watching too, his arm frozen mid-air. Rosencrantz had got into the other suitcase! He was managing to hold Sabrina away from him, pull out handfuls of cash, and throw it into the air.

"POLICE!" he shouted. "THIS WOMAN HAS HUNDREDS OF THOUSANDS IN CASH! SHE'S A CRIMINAL!"

Sabrina broke free of his grip and clawed her nails down Rosencrantz's face. I lunged at her, grabbing a chunk of her blonde hair and yanked hard. It came away in my hand and I realised I'd pulled out her hair extensions.

Simon saw what was happening and ran for it, darting and weaving through the remaining cars and people who had got out and were trying to catch the money as it flew across the deck.

"STOP HIM!" I shouted.

Within minutes the police were on board and Sabrina, myself and Rosencrantz were taken away. It took a few minutes before we realised we were being arrested with her...

I'm in a police interview room, waiting. Rosencrantz is in another and I don't know where Sabrina is. I'd better go, someone is coming through the door.

Saturday 13th August 13.48
TO: marikarolincova@hotmail.co.uk, chris@christophercheshire.com

We arrived back in Portsmouth on Friday lunchtime. It was cold and misty and we hadn't slept for hours. We were lucky to be able to walk down the gangplank by ourselves. Sabrina was taken to a police car in handcuffs by two police officers. Simon hadn't been so lucky. He had tried to jump off the boat and swim away, only he had jumped off the wrong side, and landed on the concrete jetty. He's in police custody in a hospital in Jersey with two broken legs and a fractured pelvis.

We had initially been arrested and questioned by the police. Sabrina had alleged that we were involved with the fraud, citing Adam as our connection. There was a scary few hours when, tired and emotional, I thought they might buy her story. However, the phone call to Natasha had been worthwhile.

What I didn't know is that her team at chambers had been working with the Met Police on the information I had sent, and Sabrina's real name, Sabrina Colter, had flagged her police record, and the record of her boyfriend Simon. They had discovered that between April and August Simon had deposited forty thousand pounds cash into his bank account, at a rate of several hundred pounds a day, despite being unemployed and claiming benefits. The Jersey police managed to recover all the money from the deck of the ferry, which came to one hundred and forty thousand pounds.

We had just checked into a hotel in Portsmouth when the phone by my bed rang. It was Natasha.

"Hello Coco," she said. "I've just been to visit Adam."

"Is he okay? Is he hurt? How long is his sentence, can we get him off?" I sputtered.

"Calm down, please," she said. "I have an appeal hearing booked on Monday at The Royal Courts of Justice, the appeal court on The Strand. I will present our evidence and push for a re-trial."

"A re-trial?" I said in dismay. "Did you hear what happened?"

"I'm being conservative and cautious, Coco. I think we have enough evidence for an appeal. However, we have to tread carefully with a judge. I'll plead strongly for Adam to be released on bail."

"How does he look, Natasha? Was he hurt in the fight?"

"He punched another prisoner in the prison library. It seems they have a copy of one of your books and this prisoner had written a defamatory comment about you."

"Oh," I said. "What was the comment?"

I heard Natasha turning pages and consulting her notes.

"It's seems he wrote the word *slag*..."

It sounded so strange to hear the word "slag" in her upper class accent.

"That's what got him fifty-six days added to his sentence?" I said. "The idiot. You wait till I see him."

"Coco, he is fine, he's out of segregation, he's not hurt, but he still can't have visitors. Only his legal team can visit."

"What should I do?" I said.

"You should sleep, you sound exhausted. The hotel is taken care of. Rest and drive back to London tomorrow. We need you fresh for Monday."

I thanked her and hung up, then climbed into the soft warm bed and closed my eyes.

I woke up what felt like minutes later, but it was Saturday morning. I showered and met Rosencrantz in the breakfast room and we stuffed ourselves with everything we could from the buffet.

"I knew it was Sabrina," I kept saying. "I knew it!"

We got back to London around mid-afternoon. Wayne and Oscar were waiting excitedly for us, and we sat outside with drinks and told them everything.

"Ooh, how dramatic!" said Wayne, clutching at his imaginary décolletage.

"Tell us the bit again where you yanked out her hair extensions!" said Oscar.

As they were leaving a couple of hours later, I noticed the bookshelf was gone. There was a bright blue strip behind the sofa where it had been, and all the books and ornaments were neatly packed in a cardboard box.

"What happened to the bookshelf?" I said.

"We got ever so antsy waiting to hear about your fate on the ferry," said Wayne. "Oscar had his Allen key on his key ring so we took it to bits..."

"We snuck it out to a skip over the road during the night," grinned Oscar.

"I've left an Ikea catalogue out on the counter," said Wayne. "I thought a Littsjo, or a Liatorp, or maybe even a couple of Billy's would look nice in its place... You could also get a matching coffee table, maybe a Toffyterd, or a Klubklop..."

"Enough, let's leave Mum in peace," said Rosencrantz.

I said goodbye to them all, and prepared myself to wait. To wait for Monday morning.

I realised that the past four months have been all about waiting. Life has stopped. I haven't made plans, I haven't written anything new of note. I have plodded along fearfully, struggling to pay the bills, struggling to be good, but being scared. I have never felt so much fear as I have in the past few months.

At 8.30pm, I sat down and I listened to Adele, hopefully for the last time alone.

Sunday 14th August 14.56
TO: marikarolincova@hotmail.co.uk

Do anyone's dogs need walking? I'm going mad waiting.

Monday 15th August 22.00

TO: angie.langford@thebmxliteraryagency.biz

I don't know how to feel... I hardly slept last night. I woke up to the water pipes clanking upstairs and then a trickling sound inside the walls as it whooshed about the flat. It was a lovely hot day, then I realised that Adam would be transported all the way from Norfolk to court in the hotbox van. The radio said it could be 28 degrees, which was my first worry. The second was when I met Natasha at the Royal Courts of Justice on the Strand. She was tanned from her holiday and immaculate as ever.

"The same judge is hearing the appeal," she said, cutting straight to the chase.

"Judge Haute-Penguin?"

"Yes."

"What does it mean?"

"Everything, or nothing... I personally like a different judge to hear an appeal. Looks less like we are trying to pick holes in their original judgment."

"But it was a jury who decided?" I said.

"I know. But a judge is a proud creature." She looked at her watch. "I must dash, need to put my contact lenses in and get ready."

"Fingers crossed," I said, but Natasha had seen a judge she knew, a rather dashing seventy-year-old man in a black suit with a head of cobalt blue hair. His face lit up when she approached him.

I remember hearing somewhere that when you get old you lose the ability to see the colour blue, hence the many old ladies and gents you see with bright blue hair.

This old judge had very blue hair. If he ever strayed into South London he would no doubt attract scores of kids who would follow him down the road saying, "Look at that prat with the blue hair!" However, this was The Royal Courts of

Justice, his kingdom, and he was being deferred to by many of the lawyers who streamed past.

I read a chapter of *Chicken Soup For The Soul* last night about positive thinking, and I scrambled around for a way of spinning my despair. All I could come up with was at least I was still young enough to see the colour blue.

I had insisted on going to court alone. I find I am better on my own in a crisis; I can quietly panic and not have to keep saying how I feel to the other person.

I wished you and Chris were here with me though.

I was the only person in the public gallery at the hearing. A kind steward showed me in, and I made my way along the polished bench and sat. Below me was Adam! It was so wonderful to see him, but all I was getting was the back of his head. He was deep in conversation with Natasha, now in her lawyer's wig and without her glasses.

I cleared my throat loudly, but the sound was lost in the vast courtroom. I did it again and still nothing. So, I resorted to,

"PSSST! PSSSSSSSSSSST! Adam!"

Natasha, the court stenographer, several stewards, and Adam all turned. His eyes lit up when he saw me. I went to mouth something when we heard the somber, "All rise."

We stood and moments later Judge Ruby Haute-Penguin came in looking much the same as she did five months ago. She took her seat, told us to sit, and perched a small pair of half-moon specs on the end of her nose.

I couldn't read her face at first. She kept us waiting whilst she checked over several documents. The silence made me shiver. Then she looked up, surveying Adam and Natasha as if they were a pair of bugs squashed on the windscreen of her Range Rover.

"Proceed," was all she said.

Natasha did a brilliant job of presenting the information

and outlining the evidence that had come to light about Sabrina. Then she recounted what had happened on the ferry to Jersey.

"Ah, yes, Mrs Pinchard, our very own Jessica Fletcher..." said the judge, looking up.

Caught in her gaze, I rose to my feet and grinned.

"It wasn't a compliment, Mrs Pinchard, sit down."

I sat, chastened. She slid the half-moon glasses back up her nose and looked over the documents again. My hands were clammy with sweat and I was leaving huge wet patches on the polished wood.

We all waited. Every time she turned a page, the sound echoed in the silence. Even the court stenographer was still, her face motionless, her slim hands held like chicken feet above her little machine, waiting for the judge to speak.

Then she looked up.

"Ok," she said. "What are you angling for, Natasha?"

"Your Honor, I would like to request a re-trial..."

"What about asking Adam to be released on bail?" I shouted (inside my head). Bloody Natasha, she had chickened out!

"I'm calling a recess to consider all of this," said the judge.

She banged the gavel, a steward told us to rise, and Adam was handcuffed and carted away.

I went to the waiting room and I waited. After an hour, Natasha emerged saying she had been called to Judge Haute-Penguin's personal chambers, and that we would re-convene after lunch.

"Is there a problem?" I said.

"I don't know," said Natasha. "The judge is very thorough, she has asked for all of the case notes... Go and get something to eat, there's nothing you can do here."

I came out for some air, walked down to the embankment, and sat by the river.

A pleasure cruiser full of grinning tourists slowly churned past on the water. Scores of enthusiastic Japanese tourists had their video cameras out, the lenses winking back at me in the sunlight. As they swept past chattering like chickens in a coop, I gave them the middle finger. I know it was a horrible thing to do, but I felt so down at heel and defeated. My belly was hanging over my once smart suit. My hair was long and unkempt, I was more tired than I'd ever felt. Overall, I felt I had gone to seed. I didn't want to be Old Woman #1 in a bunch of Japanese home movies.

I squinted in the sun and looked over the rooftops to the courthouse. I wondered where Adam was. He could be only a few hundred yards away.

I came back at 1pm and we went straight into the courtroom. Adam was already sat with Natasha, he turned round to face me, and he just shook his head.

"What?" I mouthed.

He mouthed something back but I couldn't make it out, and then the melodious voice of the steward said, "All rise."

Judge Haute-Penguin came back in giving nothing away. She asked us to be seated.

"After reviewing the evidence I have come to a decision," she said.

Then she gave the longest X-Factor judge's pause...

"You are innocent, Mr Rickard," she said. "You should have never been charged with fraud or indeed sent to jail. Your conviction is hereby quashed. You can leave today a free man with no restrictions."

She banged the gavel. Adam was visibly shocked, as was Natasha.

"All rise," came the voice.

The judge left and I ran out and down to the public area. My legs were shaking with excitement; there were tears in my eyes. In the space of a minute, the world suddenly seemed golden again.

Natasha emerged triumphant and she gave me a big hug.

"Where is he? Where's Adam?" I said, looking behind her to the door.

"He has to sign a couple of forms, then he gets his belongings, and he's a free man."

"I can't believe this," I said. "What happens now? Is he on some kind of probation?"

"He's a free man, no record, no restrictions. I will be in touch to see if he wants to get compensation."

"I just want to take him home," I said.

"You two go and live your lives together, Coco," she smiled.

I thanked her, we hugged again, and she was gone.

I went to sit down then I noticed a vending machine. I really wanted to get Adam something, I hadn't thought about a gift. Is it an occasion? No doubt someone will come up with a *Getting out of jail* card soon, but for now I would just have to get him a Kit Kat and a bottle of water.

I was fumbling for some change when I felt hands encircle my waist.

"Hello," said Adam in my ear.

I turned to face him. I looked up into his eyes and he kissed me. He too looked a little ragged round the edges and down at heel (although he seemed thinner).

We held each other for a long, long time; I loved the feeling of him against me. His warm body, feeling his heart beating, being able to rest my head against his shoulder.

"I can't believe it," I said. "You're free."

"Oh man, you smell so good," he said. "I need to sit down."

He staggered over to the bench lining the wall.

"Aren't you excited to go outside?" I said.

"I just need a moment... I went from the thought of facing an appeal and being banged up in Belmarsh again for weeks on end, to suddenly being free."

I went and held his hand.

"I keep thinking someone is going to rush out and say they made a mistake," he said.

"No, you're free," I said and hugged him again. "What do you want to do?!" I said. "We can go on a boat trip or walk along the river or go and grab some food...?"

"Would you mind if we went home?" he said. "I am dying to just be at home, with you. I want to have a bath and eat a takeaway and drink a cold beer!"

I grabbed the giant plastic sack he was holding with HMP emblazoned across the front, and we left the court-house, emerging on a set of stone steps.

A journalist from *BBC London Tonight* was stood outside with a cameraman. I seized the chance, grabbed Adam's arm, and held it up triumphantly.

"Are you pleased with the verdict?" said the journalist, thrusting her microphone at us.

Adam looked between me and her, a little daunted.

"We're thrilled that Adam Rickard has been completely cleared of all charges," I said. "It's a wonderful Scooby-Doo ending."

"And what does Adam Rickard think of all this?" said the journalist, with a smile on her lips.

"I just want to live my life in peace after this terrible experience," he said.

"What's the first thing you're going to do?" she asked.

"I'm going to marry this woman, well, after I've had a bath, I've really missed baths," he grinned.

We thanked the journalist and moved off. A black cab

was waiting by the kerb. I asked if it was available and he said it was for us and that it had been paid for by the BMX Literary Agency. (Thank you.)

I am writing this to you from the garden. Adam is in the bath soaking; he has been in there for nearly two hours. I keep going in to check on him. He is fine but says he needs a bit of time to deal with everything. I'm so happy.

Tuesday 16th August 13.35
TO: angie.langford@thebmxliteraryagency.biz

Did you see the *BBC London Tonight* report yesterday? Adam being released was the third item on the bulletin. We were sitting inside the flat with the door open on a balmy night, watching on my laptop. They had made a real effort with the piece; they had mobile phone footage of the chaos on the boat when Rosencrantz was throwing the money in the air. Then they had images of Sabrina and Simon being taken in by the police. Then some archive footage; an interview with me on *Saturday Kitchen*. Then we were stood on the steps outside the court, Adam saying how pleased he is to be free, and then me saying, "our wonderful Scooby-Doo ending…" with mascara running down my face.

It has been incredible to be able to sit together and do *nothing*. Every conversation and meeting we have had for the last five months has been a race against the clock. Now we can just be.

My phone began ringing after the *BBC London* report with calls from Ethel, Meryl and Tony, Daniel, Adam's old work colleges, Holly, his ex-wife. I let him talk to everyone, loving the big smile on his face.

I opened the plastic bag he had with HMP Cambria Sands written on, and unpacked the things he had kept in his cell: a picture of me, a toothbrush, the famous CD/Radio player from the Dairylea Stabber, Adele's *21*, six pairs of underwear, two t-shirts, a pair of trousers, four pairs of socks and a big pot of moisturiser. At the bottom of the bag was a piece of paper. It was the receipt we had signed when we booked our wedding at the church. I saw the date of the wedding: the nineteenth of August, this Friday. *We almost did it,* I thought. *We almost made it …*

I went and took a long shower, shaved my legs and attempted to make myself look as good as I could. When I came out of the bathroom Adam was asleep on the sofa with Rocco laid out beside him. I took my cigarettes and a big glass of wine and I went to sit outside. At ten in the evening, it was still warm. I lit up a cigarette and sat back. It was the first time I felt completely relaxed in months, maybe even a year.

Wednesday 17th August 11.12
TO: angie.langford@thebmxliteraryagency.biz

We were eating breakfast this morning when the door buzzer went. Adam jumped off the sofa, spilling his coffee.

"Are you okay?" I said.

"Sorry Cokes," he said. "I'm not used to a buzzer just meaning someone is at the door. In prison it usually meant a cell search."

"Let's leave it," I said.

The buzzer went again, stridently. Then again.

"Bloody hell," I said, getting up and opening the door.

It was Ethel, all out of breath with her shopping trolley on wheels.

She leant on the doorjamb to catch her breath. I saw she had her mobile in her hand.

"I'd love to come to yer wedding!" she squealed. "I was just passin' an' thought I'd RSVP in the flesh!"

She bustled past to give Adam a big hug. He looked at me over her shoulder.

"What?" he mouthed.

"Iss lovely to see you out of the slammer," she said, pulling away to look at him.

"Thank you," said Adam. "And thank you for all the letters you sent,"

Then Ethel did something strange, and hugged me.

"I'm so pleased you both want me at yer wedding," she said, welling up. "I know we've 'ad our differences."

I opened my mouth, Adam and I looked at each other. A text message came through and Ethel peered at her screen.

"Ooh, tha's Meryl... she wants to know if you two want the bride and groom on top of the wedding cake?"

"Um..." I said.

"She needs to know sharpish, coz she'll 'ave to buy some black food colouring for the little marzipan Adam to go next to the little marzipan Coco."

Ethel mistook our shock for something else.

"Oh I'm sorry love, is that racist?"

"No. No, a little marzipan Adam would need to be black," gulped Adam.

Suddenly Marika crashed through the communal entrance and came to the front door out of breath. She must have been running fast.

"Why aren't you answering your phone?" she said

"You know I haven't got a signal," I said.

I went to the landline; it had been cut off.

"Oh, I can't have paid the bill in time," I said, embarrassed.

"It's okay," said Marika still catching her breath. "Coco, Adam, I've wanted to apologise to you for everything that went down — me not believing you were innocent and for all the horrible stuff. I thought, to show how much I love you guys, that I could arrange a last-minute wedding so you can get married on Friday, the nineteenth!"

"Oh Marika," I said taking her hand. "The thing is, we haven't got much cash..."

Everyone looked at the phone for a moment.

"Coco, don't worry about a thing. We've arranged to have the wedding in the ruins of that little church on the hill. It's going to be exquisitely simple... You do want to get married, don't you?"

"Yes," I said, dazed.

"Adam?"

"Yes," he grinned, "yeah, I want to be with Coco."

Ethel grabbed Adam again.

"You're so thin love! Isn't he thin, Coco? 'E needs feeding up,"

"I've been feeding him, Ethel," I said.

She let out a laugh.

"You'll be crying out for the prison slop after you've 'ad 'er cooking!" she said. "Right Marika, we'd best be orf, I am at your disposables, and I can help with whatever you need."

"So we're cool with this?" said Marika.

We both nodded.

"Right, let's get cracking," she said.

When they'd gone and I'd closed the door, I looked at Adam. He was grinning from ear to ear.

"It looks like we're going to have that wedding after all!" he said.

Thursday 18th August 19.29
TO: angie.langford@thebmxliteraryagency.biz

I am gutted you won't be able to come to the wedding. I had no idea you are in Los Angeles. Preparations are well underway, but it's all being kept a secret from me. All I have been allowed to do is choose my dress and the flowers, and I have found the most wonderful wedding dress!

I had refused to let Chris or Marika pay for an expensive wedding dress, so this afternoon I found myself with Wayne, Rosencrantz, and Marika in a vintage/thrift shop in Camden. We had split up and were rummaging through racks.

"Are we going with white? Or ironical white?" said Wayne quizzically, pulling out a dress much like the one Madonna wore in the *Like A Virgin* video.

"My days of wearing white are long gone," I said. "Let's stick to champagne."

"I think you should be bold and wear red!" said Rosencrantz, pulling out a crazy red see-through lacy number.

"You know what my mother would say about that dress?" said Marika. "Whore of Babylon!"

Just as we were about to give up, I found, tucked away at the back of a rail, a beautiful and simple ivory wedding dress. I beckoned them over. We all cooed in agreement.

"Try it on, Mrs P!" said Wayne.

I went to the cramped changing room and took a deep

breath, praying it would fit. It did. It fit perfectly. I opened the changing room doors and went out.

"Mum, you look beautiful," said Rosencrantz.

Wayne fanned his hand in front of his face, unable to express his delight.

"Oh my God, Coco," said Marika, being uncharacteristically girly. "It's perfect." She looked at the tag in the back.

"Jesus," she said, shoving me back into the little changing room. They all followed and Marika shut the door.

"What?" I said.

There wasn't any place to move. Marika mouthed something.

"What?" I repeated.

She showed Wayne and Rosencrantz the label in the back of the dress.

"Oh no, is it crazy expensive?" I said.

"No, it's ten quid!" said Rosencrantz.

"Then what?"

"It's a Vera Wang," Marika whispered.

"No!" I hissed, craning my neck around to see.

It was indeed a Vera Wang.

"We mustn't let them suspect we have it, it must be a mistake," whispered Marika.

"Well, we should all get out of the bloody changing room," I said.

I took the dress off and we approached the till, terrified the mistake would be rumbled. However, the tattooed youth couldn't be less interested and we got a genuine Vera Wang for ten pounds!

Saturday 20th August 13.46

TO: angie.langford@thebmxliteraryagency.biz

On the morning of our wedding I was up at five, I was too excited to sleep. I left the snoozing Adam in our single bed and came outside to the garden. Rocco ate his breakfast, then snuffled about in the early dawn light. I drank coffee and sat, content and happy.

After a while, Adam came padding out in just a pair of shorts rubbing the sleep from his eyes. I still have to pinch myself when I see him in this flat. After all the long nights of despair when I was alone.

"Ah, it's my beautiful girlfriend," he smiled, sitting down beside me. He leant over and gave me a long sweet kiss.

"Not for much longer," I said. "By three this afternoon I'll be the old ball and chain."

'You're very lucky Coco, because I find single women just as attractive as married women..."

"What are you saying?"

"I'm saying I only have a few hours left to sow my wild oats and sleep with single women, so I'll expect you in the bedroom in five minutes!"

We got ready together for our wedding. Adam looked stunning in a sharp black suit and tie. The look on his face when I emerged in the Vera Wang dress made me feel like the most beautiful bride on earth.

We arrived at the church a little before three, but as our car pulled into the trees leading up to the church, I could see a commotion up ahead.

The entrance to the church was blocked by a huge lorry. Our wedding guests were crowded round watching something. Adam helped me out of the car, and we walked up the crowd. Wayne was on the edge and turned as I approached. He clutched his chest.

"Beautiful Mrs P, and Mr R."

"What's going on?" I said.

"This lorry won't move," he said. "And it's got a very shirty driver."

I pushed my way forward, saying "hello" to all our guests, and saw that Meryl was elevated five feet off the ground standing on the giant lorry's front bumper. On the bonnet, she had rested our three-tier wedding cake.

"You must move, now!" she shrilled.

"I'm from the council," said the driver, leaning his head out of the cab. "I've told you, you all need to leave. This church is a designated health and safety risk."

I turned and caught sight of the church, or ruins of the church. A few pillars were all that remained now but the debris had been cleared. Chairs had been laid out and hundreds of candles were lit, dotted around the ground and on some of the remaining pillars. It looked breathtaking.

"Can you wait for at least a couple of hours?" shouted Adam. "This is my girl and you're ruining her wedding."

"I've got my orders, no one goes in," he said.

"No, NO, NO!" said Meryl hammering on the bonnet with her free hand. "I refuse to let you ruin this wedding, and this cake is *royal icing*, do you know how much work it is to make royal icing from scratch?"

"It's a three-hour job," yelled Tony supportively.

He was standing to one side with Wilfred in his arms.

Meryl turned to Tony,

"Tony! Cover Wilfred's ears!" she shrilled.

He quickly put his hands over Wilfred's little ears. Meryl turned and pointed her finger at the driver.

"Now you listen here. I'll give you one last chance. Move now, or face the consequences. You really don't want to fuck with me!"

We all clapped and cheered.

"Yeah! Bugger off, this is my mum's big day!" shouted Rosencrantz, who was standing with Oscar and wearing his black suit.

"Let Mrs P have her big day, she deserves it!" shouted Oscar.

Rocco, who was being held in his arms, barked in agreement.

"This health and safety bullshit is killing this country! Be gone, you capitalist bastard!" shouted Marika.

I think she'd had a few drinks in her capacity as wedding planner.

"Do you know how long it took to light four hundred bloody candles with one box of matches?" protested Chris in his white suit, banging on the driver's door.

"And see 'ow nice the bride looks," shouted Ethel, from under the brim of a huge hat. "'Er dress! Iss a genuine Vera Wank!"

"It's Vera *Wang*," I added.

Our guests all took a step toward the lorry. The driver went pale.

"You've got until the ceremony is over," he said.

"You chose wisely," said Meryl.

She lifted the cake, and Adam helped her down. The driver quickly put the lorry in reverse, the crowd parted, and he drove off.

The ceremony was one of the best moments of my life, looking into Adam's eyes as we said our vows, and then, when the vicar pronounced us man and wife, Adam leant in and gave me a deep knee-buckling kiss and everyone clapped and cheered.

After the ceremony I realised I had no clue what was happening next.

"It's a surprise," said Marika.

We walked down the steps to the road and a line of taxis was waiting when we emerged from the church grounds. We all piled in excitedly, however, the journey was short. We pulled up outside The Rivoli Ballroom. I looked at Adam.

"I'm just as clueless as you!" he grinned.

"I 'ad a word in Bunty's ear," said Ethel with a wink as we climbed the steps to the front entrance.

It was the most stunning wedding reception. In the red velvet splendour and bedazzle of the ballroom, we ate proper fish and chips washed down with champagne. We cut Meryl's beautiful cake to a round of applause and then we danced: we danced until we could drop. Chris had arranged a free bar and it was one of those fabulous nights which passed in a whirl of happiness. I didn't want it to end.

Meryl got completely slaughtered and switched back to her cockney accent of birth.

"I'm pissed out of me brains!" she trilled, as she flew past as the head of a conga line.

I don't remember a lot about the reception, much of the wedding is a happy blur. I just remember being with Adam, seeing his face, holding him in the knowledge he's not going to be snatched away from me.

We emerged from the Rivoli early next morning as it was getting light. It was a perfect summer morning. Crisp and bright with dew on the grass. We spent a long time on the steps saying our goodbyes before everyone dispersed happily into taxis and cars, wishing us luck and happiness.

We staggered home, me with my dress hitched up and bare feet, Rocco asleep in Adam's arms. I have never enjoyed the walk home to my little flat as much as I did. When we got back in, we found on our pillow an envelope. Inside was a note from Ethel.

Ello love. I suppose now you really aint my daughter in law no more... I ope we get to stay friends, or should I say I ope we can be friends now!

Anyhow, we ad a little whip round, for yer honeymoon.

Now, its not nothing huge, Rosencrantz and me found this lovely little cottage in Tuscany on the Internet, jus for a week mind. Its in the middle of nowhere but I think you mite like it. Rosencrantz ad the idea, said e'd seen a film called Under A Tuscan's Son... sounds a bit blue if you ask me, but 'es promised its a very romantic location.

Have fun, you two deserve it!

Ethel x

We're on our way to the airport now. A week ago I never imagined we would be together, let alone married and off on our honeymoon to Italy. Thank you for all your love and support, Angie. See you in a week!

Love Coco xxx

Saturday 20th August 14.50
TO: rosencrantzpinchard@gmail.com

Hello love, we are about to board the plane and I forgot

to tell you that Rocco is going through a bit of a chewing phase.

So if Chris comes over, make sure you put his Dolce and Gabbana shoes somewhere he can't reach them (Rocco, I mean).

Also, Angie is in Los Angeles and she just phoned me terribly excited and breathless.

"Jeez girl," she said. "Things have gone ape shit here in Hollywood!"

"What do you mean?" I said.

"I think I'm gonna sell the film rights for *Chasing Diana Spencer* and *Agent Fergie*!" she said. "Two of the big studios suddenly got interested, and there's gonna be an auction later this week! Also, now that Adam has been released, your publishing house is planning to publish *Agent Fergie*!"

She's told me to keep my phone on whilst I'm in Italy.

See you in a week!

Love, Mum xx

A NOTE FROM ROBERT

First of all, I want to say a huge thank you for choosing to read *Coco Pinchard's Big Fat Tipsy Wedding.* If you did enjoy it, I would be very grateful if you could write a review. I'd love to hear what you think, and reviews really help new readers to discover one of my books for the first time. If you want to drop me a line, you can get in touch on my Facebook page, through Twitter, Instagram or my website www. robertbryndza.com. I love to hear from readers, and it blows me away every time I hear how much you've taken my books into your hearts. There are lots more to come including, yes, more adventures from Coco Pinchard, so I hope you stay with me for the ride!

Robert Bryndza

ABOUT THE AUTHOR

Robert Bryndza is the author of the international #1 best-seller *The Girl in the Ice*, which is the first in his Detective Erika Foster series. Robert's books have sold over 3 million copies and have been translated into 28 languages. In addition to writing crime fiction, Robert has published a best-selling series of romantic comedy novels. He is British and lives in Slovakia.

www.robertbryndza.com

 facebook.com/bryndzarobert

 twitter.com/robertbryndza

 instagram.com/robertbryndza